CW00584696

When it all goes wrong...

Ron Bush

2019

Ron Bush asserts the right to be identified as the author of this work. All rights reserved.

All characters are fictitious. Any resemblance to real persons, either living or dead, is coincidental.

This book is sold subject to the condition that it shall not, by way of trade or otherwise, be lent, resold, hired out, or otherwise circulated without the author's prior consent in any form of binding or cover other than that in which it here published and without a similar condition, including this condition, being imposed on the subsequent purchaser.

Chapter 1

5th November 1986

Two plain-clothes police officers struggle to remove a body wrapped in polythene from a Ford Escort Estate car.

Laboured breath hangs in the cold night air as they carry it into the woods. Frost-encrusted leaves crunch underfoot. Every twig that snaps jolts Woman Detective Constable Mary Wells back to the gunshot which brought about this situation.

Far above the trees a sky-rocket explodes, sending balls of colour screaming across the winter sky, lighting up the shallow grave and Mary's tear-stained face.

Tipping the corpse into its final resting place, Detective Sergeant Joseph Fargough picks up his spade and shovels excavated soil into the hole.

Mary watches in silence. Adjusting her gloves, she steps forward to help lift heavy logs onto the mound of earth.

Satisfied, Joseph nods towards the car.

Chapter 2

23rd July 1986

Sitting in his bedroom, with both hands beneath a bath towel, Joseph assembled metal parts. As the magazine holding seven cartridges slid into place, he lifted the towel and smiled. *Pity these aren't standard issue*, he thought as he re-wrapped the gun in greaseproof paper. Hearing the doorbell, he placed the gun on his bed and rushed downstairs.

He opened the front door of his two-bed semi and smiled. 'Hello Mary, you're early. Help yourself to tea, you know where everything is.' Pointing up the stairs he added, 'Just putting my shirts away, won't be long.'

He put the gun into a recess in his wardrobe and replaced the false shelf. In the bathroom he washed gun oil off his hands, dried them and sniffed his fingers. Satisfied, he went back down to join Mary.

She sat engrossed in the televised broadcast of the Royal Wedding.

Bright sunlight spilled across the room as Joseph pulled the curtains aside. 'Sorry to spoil your fun, but our shift starts soon and this will go on for ages. Don't worry, I've got a three-hour tape in the recorder, just need to set it to long-play. You can watch it later.'

She brushed biscuit crumbs from her grey skirt. 'Okay, but I wish now I'd put in for one of my days off. Fergie looks so lovely . . . and doesn't Prince Andrew look handsome in uniform?'

Mark glanced at the screen. 'I have to admit he's nearly as good looking as me. And I'll say one thing, he's got guts. We could have used him on some of our ops, although marriage would have barred him from our group.' He ducked to avoid a flying cushion.

'There you go again,' Mary said. 'You know you're not going to elaborate, why keep dropping hints?'

Turning the television off, he ran a finger across his throat. 'Sorry, I'm bound by the Official Secrets Act.' Pulling her towards him he whispered, 'But talking about marriage, any news from your husband?'

'Not much, apart from changing his mind about a divorce. He keeps telling me it was only a fling, and he's sorry. But it's over as far as I'm concerned, I'll never be able to trust him again.'

'Like I've said before, army life and marriage doesn't always work. You two aren't the first, or the last.'

'The trouble is without his money coming in, I don't see how I'll be able to pay the rent for the flat.'

'That's a bummer.' Joseph scratched the side of his head. 'If it wasn't for our jobs you could move in here.'

'I know. Thanks.'

'Don't worry, we'll think of something. Come on, let's get to the station. See what the day has in store for us.'

*

The heels of Joseph's shoes came down heavily as he marched down the corridor. Reaching the far end, he took out his handkerchief, breathed onto the gleaming nameplate and polished it. DETECTIVE CHIEF INSPECTOR. With a sarcastic grin, he saluted.

Checking his tie in the reflection, he knocked.

'Come in.'

'Good morning, sir. You wanted to see me.'

'Yes, Fargough. A woman has been murdered in Jubilee Park. I want you and WDC Wells to attend. Forensics are on site. *Try* not to upset them again.'

'I only tried to point out the obvious. If they –'

'Yes, yes. Save your petty squabbles for the canteen. Report back as soon as possible.'

*

Joseph handed coveralls to Mary. 'Get this lot on,' he said, 'then we'll see what they've found.'

She pushed wayward strands of brown hair under the protective hood. 'Not the best way to start a day,' she said.

A constable held up the tape as they ducked beneath.

Walking towards the canvas enclosure, Joseph looked around the park. At night it was a popular spot for lovers. Now it would provide a front-page story for local news reporters.

'What do we know?' Joseph pointed at the young woman sprawled on the grass.

'The park keeper found her. Been dead approximately ten hours,' the pathologist said, checking his watch, 'judging by the Livor Mortis.'

'Somebody's inflicted a lot of pain,' Joseph grunted. 'This is not your usual frustrated would-be-lover scenario.'

'I couldn't agree more. Her lower jaw's broken, the gag's soaked in blood.'

'Bastard. Has she been raped?'

'You'll have to wait for my autopsy report.'

'Okay, have it on my desk as soon as poss.' Turning to Mary, he said, 'That's two in a week. I bet my balls it's the same killer.'

Mary turned her head away. 'She's not much more than a kid.'

Joseph glared at the body. 'The bloody newspapers will have a field day with this. When we catch the psycho, I'll make sure he wishes he'd never been born.'

'I won't argue.' She managed a weak smile. 'I know you too well.'

'And when we get back, I'll recommend surveillance in case our friend returns.'

'I doubt he will.'

'Why?'

'Because there are tyre marks over there.' She pointed. 'In my opinion she was killed elsewhere then dumped where they found her.'

'Well spotted.' He sighed. 'Oh well, there's not much we can do until we get the report, may as well get back.'

*

Mary handed Joseph a slim folder. 'Here's the latest on the girl in the park.' She looked back over her shoulder. 'Misery Guts, as you so fondly call him, was his usual charming self.'

'No change there then.' Opening the folder, he studied the report. 'I see Forensics now estimate she'd been dead for eight hours.'

'Yes, I read it. She kept me awake last night. I don't know why? I've seen my share.'

'You should have phoned, or come over. It's not bedtime reading, that's for sure.' He passed the folder back.

Mary frowned as she read aloud. 'Punched by somebody wearing a large ring. All fingers broken. Nipples severed from both breasts.'

'The last time I saw anything like this was when …' He shook his head. 'Oh, never mind.'

Opening the filing cabinet, she placed the folder inside. 'They should never have abolished hanging if you ask me. Why don't politicians listen to the voters?'

'Beats me. But to be fair, Duncan Sandys did try to get the decision reversed, bless him. Pity we can't get this pervert for treason, or piracy with violence.' He put a hand to his throat and jerked his head back. 'They can still hang you for both.'

'There's our answer then.' Her eyes twinkled. 'All we have to do is plant a plan of Buck House on our man, make him wear an eye-patch and shove a pistol in his pocket.'

'He's got to live long enough to get to trial before we need worry about that.'

Chapter 3

August 1986

The evening sun caressed the golf course. Long shadows from marker flags encroached onto grass mown to within an inch of its life. Sand pits yawned an invitation to the unwary. The sound of clubs striking balls punctuated conversations in the privacy only a round on the green can supply. People's futures hung in the balance as small white balls arced through the air against a golden sky. The benefits of not having notes taken, which could come back to haunt them, was a lure many found attractive.

Mark Payne glanced back towards the course as he lowered his clubs into the boot of the Jaguar XJ12. 'Are you sure you won't change your mind? It's a good offer.'

The scar on his cheek, olive skin and greasy black hair gave him the appearance of a Hollywood gangster. Mark's physique bore testament to the use he made of a gymnasium installed alongside the Grade II listed house he called home. In addition to the gym a triple garage and covered swimming pool had set in motion a vociferous campaign by local protestors. Bribes, given to those who gave planning consent, made sure the angry voices were ignored.

James Newton, his golfing opponent, was *Mr Average*. Nothing set him apart from the ordinary man in the street. 'It's not a good enough offer,' he said. 'When my plans for Nero's Palace are passed, the place will be a real money spinner. In comparison it'll make Hornigold's look like the spit-and-sawdust pub it was before that bloke poured money into it.'

'But first you need to convince the council,' Mark said, 'and I don't think you will.'

James frowned. 'Why? Hornigold's crappy pirate theme set a precedent. I don't see how they can turn me down.'

'Don't you? Always remember, it's not *what* you know, it's *who* you know. If you want my advice, take the money while it's on the table.'

'No thanks. I'm sure the planning department will give it the thumbs up.'

'Don't chance your arm too often, Jimmy, my friend.' Mark wagged a finger.

'Meaning?'

'Nothing. But if I were you, I'd make sure my insurance cover was up to date. Be a shame if your place was to go up in flames.'

'Are you threatening me?' James glared.

'I don't make threats, only promises. But if your pub *was* to burn down . . .'

'It's not likely lightning will strike twice. The fire at Bob's fish restaurant was down to dodgy wiring they said.'

Mark opened the car door. 'Of course, it was, Jimmy. Get in, I'll run you back to your place.'

'This coast road's the long way round,' James said. 'Its quicker to drive through town.'

'I know,' Mark agreed. 'But I told my driver to take this route. Who knows? We may see something of interest.'

Glancing at the rear-view mirror, the chauffeur suppressed a grin.

'Here we are, *Bob's Seafood Restaurant,* or what's left of it.' Mark's diamond ring clicked against the window as he waved a hand towards skeletal remains overlooking the sea.

James glared at the letters stencilled on the bulldozer completing the demolition. '*Ocean Developers*? They bought Bob's place? They're one of your companies, aren't they?'

'Yes.'

'What are you planning to do? Re-build?'

'Why not, Jimmy? Plenty of visitors come to the Wash. Would have been better to buy it as a going concern, but life's a crock of shit as they say. Shame about Bob, suicide's never the answer.'

'It's his wife I feel sorry for,' James said.

'Me too. I'll give it a bit of time, then offer her a job. Typist or something. I feel it's the least I can do for the poor cow.' He reached forward and put his hand on the chauffeur's shoulder. 'Let's get Jimmy back to his pub, safe and sound.'

Mark sank back into the seat as the Jaguar pulled away.

*

The car purred to a stop outside the Mariner's Arms, a mock Tudor building.

'Here we are, Jimmy. How about offering me a drink?'

James ran a finger around his shirt collar and swallowed. 'Why not?'

'Top man. We can settle our business over a pint.' Stepping from the car, Mark gazed at weeds breaking through a large expanse of tarmac alongside the building. 'Nice. Plenty of space for a nightclub and still leave room for parking.'

'Yes,' James said. 'The youngsters are the ones with money these days, and they want to drink somewhere with a bit of atmosphere.'

'Which is why Hornigold's attracts them. The theme idea was a brilliant bit of thinking.'

James frowned. 'Makes you wonder why he sold up. I mean, no sooner does he start coining it in, then bingo, he sells the lease and disappears.'

'Probably got his feet up, enjoying the sun and cheap booze. Talking of which, let's get inside and drink some of your profits.'

'Try this,' James said. 'It's a new one.'

Mark raised the glass and sipped. 'It's different.' He took a mouthful and swallowed. 'What is it?'

'*Lowenbrau*. It sells better than the cheap froggy lager ever did.'

'It should. That bloke turned you over, he brewed it in his garage. It was no more French than you are.'

'Are you're joking?' James banged a fist on the table. 'If not, I'll have a word next time I see him.'

'I don't think so. He tried the same stunt on me.'

James swallowed. 'Did he?'

'Yes. Now, got a copy of your plans? I'd like to see this new venture of yours.'

'Okay, come on through to my office.'

With a theatrical flourish, James removed the cloth and lifted the roof off his model. 'What do you think?'

'Did you make this?' Mark bent down. 'It's good . . . very good. But I see why the council are dragging their heels, it looks like a cheap film set from the Fifties.'

'No, it don't.' James puffed out his chest. 'It's real upmarket.'

Touching an oblong piece of clear Perspex on the ground floor, Mark asked, 'What's this?'

'It's my trump card. A glass tiled dance area, lit from underneath. The lights are going to pulse in time to the music.'

'Do they? I have to give it to you. It's something different all right.'

James took a deep breath and blew it out through his nose. 'It should be. I've put a lot of thought into this.'

Mark touched the scale model. 'The entrance is a bit much. All those blood-red banners and gold eagles. Looks like a far-right meeting place. The council won't stand for it.'

'I think they will. It's so it looks Roman, and you got to admit, it's classy. Once this is up and running, I can sit back and take things easy. I'll get car like yours, foreign holidays, all that sort of thing.'

'Dream on, Jimmy.' He put his arm around him and pulled him close. 'Why don't you be sensible for once in your life and take the money? I'll go as far as another ten grand but it's my final offer.'

'The answer's still no. I'll take my chances.'

On the way back from the Mariner's Arms, Mark reached forward. 'Stop. Pull over. I want a word with her.'

Lowering the car window, he waited as the young girl hurried across the road. Make-up did nothing to hide the lines her short life had awarded her. Her skirt could have served as a lamp shade.

'Wotcha, boss,' she said, throwing a half-smoked cigarette to the ground.

Mark glared at her. 'What are you doing on this street? This isn't yours.'

'I got frush. I been to the clinic.'

'Have you, well I need you earning, get back to work.'

The girl pouted. 'But I'm sore. I oughta have some time off.'

'In your dreams. Get your arse into gear and keep the punters happy.'

'If you say so. I ain't got much choice. But why you putting a new bitch on my patch? There ain't enough work for two of us.'

Mark's eyes narrowed. 'That's been taken care of, I told you, you're under my protection.'

'She a druggie? I reckon she was high as a bleedin' kite when I had a go at her.'

'Good for you. Let me know if anyone else tries to muscle in.'

Chapter 4

August 1986

Perched on the handrail separating the promenade from the beach, seagulls waited for a soggy chip to be thrown in their direction.

Getting up from the bench, Joseph shook the damp paper, screwed it up and looked for a bin. Scraps of battered fish hit the pavement and were pounced on by a raucous mob of scavengers.

'Have you finished?' he asked. 'The salt and vinegar's given me a thirst. Let's go for a cuppa.'

'Now look what you've done,' Mary protested, clutching her lunch to her chest. Standing up, she turned her back to the sea. With a wary glance towards the voracious birds eyeing her every move, she scrunched the wrapping around what was left of her meal and headed towards Joseph's Rover.

Gazing out to sea from the safety of the car, she wiped greasy fingers onto the paper, transforming it from white to transparent. 'What shall I do with this?'

'It's tempting to leave it in here. Make a better air freshener than this cardboard pine tree thing.'

Taking the paper from her, he opened the car door and walked back to the bin.

'Where now? Sheila's café?' Mary checked her watch. 'We've got time, we're not on duty for an hour.'

'Good idea. Drive on Macduff, and don't spare the horses. I'm gagging for a drink.'

She turned the ignition key. 'You could have chosen your words better after the poor girl we saw in the park. And apart from the fact the horses belonged to King Duncan, Macbeth said *lay on*, not *drive on*. Your Shakespeare's a little rusty, me thinks.'

'Smart arse.'

'Hmm, I'll take that as a compliment.' She turned to face him. 'I've noticed you've stopped calling me Bill. Why?'

'I only started because of all those Joseph and Mary jokes . . . and the star they hung on my office door.'

She grinned. 'I keep waiting for them to pick up on Wells and Fargough. Can you imagine? They'll have a field day. I can see it now, cops in cowboy hats and horse shit all over the car park.'

'There's a way around it.' He placed his hand over hers.

'Meaning?'

'Nothing. Not while you're still a married woman. Come on, let's get a drink.'

*

Inside the café, Joseph sat back and waited.

'Sheila had a lot to say, what's the problem?' Joseph nodded towards the woman busying herself making drinks.

'It was about the prostitute in the park. She said she may have been in here, said the artist's impression in the newspaper looked a lot like one of her customers.'

'Does she know her name?'

'No. She did –' Mary turned to face the street. 'What the hell!'

Joseph jumped to his feet. 'That sounded like a gunshot!'

Opposite the café a man stood in the shadows of the betting shop doorway. Another shot echoed inside the building, seconds later a man ran out brandishing a handgun.

'Stop! Police!' Joseph yelled, running towards the men. The larger of the two jumped onto a motorbike and kicked it into life. His accomplice leapt on the back and clung on as the bike roared away.

'Shit!' Joseph punched the air.

Back in the Rover he grabbed the car-phone. Tyres squealed in protest as the car sped off in pursuit.

The man on the pillion seat of the motorbike turned and aimed. Mary ducked and jerked the wheel to one side.

Joseph swayed in his seat. 'Put your foot down.' He jabbed at the windscreen. 'They've made a mistake. That's a cul-de-sac.'

'Stop!' Springing from the car Joseph ran along the pavement. An alleyway divided the houses. Glaring into this urban canyon he shook his head. Rusty bed frames, bicycle wheels and all manner of household detritus cluttered the footpath. 'Very clever, we'll never get a car down there.'

He ran back. 'They've gone through the alley. Turn this thing around. Try to catch them at the other end.'

Staring down the escape route Joseph's eyes narrowed. 'Now what? Either we've missed them, or they've gone to ground in one of these houses.'

'You're right. We could get a search warrant for a couple of these properties, but a whole street? I think we should get back to the betting shop. Somebody may need our help.'

*

Joseph sniffed. The air was tainted by gun smoke. 'Anyone injured?' He held out his warrant card. 'Are you the manager?'

'Yes, I am. He got away with the day's takings, but Donna wasn't hurt.' The balding man pointed upwards. 'He told her they were warning shots.'

'Can you describe the gunman?' Joseph said, looking at holes in the ceiling.

'You'd do better asking Donna,' he said, beckoning her. 'I was in my office.'

'Didn't he tell her to open the safe?'

'No.' Tugging on a chain he produced a bunch of keys from his trouser pocket. He wiped his brow with the back of one hand. 'I must sit down. My legs won't stop shaking. I'll be in my office if you need me.'

'This doesn't make sense,' Mary said. 'Why would armed robbers settle for the contents of the till?' She spread her hands. 'And why fire the gun? The sight of one's more than enough for most people.'

'I agree. None of it adds up.'

Turning his attention to Donna he said, 'You did the right thing, giving him the money. Now, what can you tell us?'

Donna clenched her hands, knuckles turning white. She took a deep breath. 'It was weird. Everything seemed to be in slow motion. He tried to use an accent, but I could tell he wasn't Irish.'

'Anything else?'

'Not much. Most of his face was covered, but I could see his eyes. They didn't match.' She shivered. 'One was brown. Well, more like hazel I'd call it. But the other was green. I've never seen anyone with two different colour eyes before.'

'Would you be able to recognise him?' Mary asked.

'Only by those eyes again, sorry. He was wearing a workman's overall and a knitted mask sort of thing, there was not much else to see.' The colour drained from her face. 'Can I go now? I keep needing the toilet. I want to go home.'

A siren wailed in the distance.

'Here comes the cavalry,' Joseph said. 'Let's have another word with the manager before they arrive.'

'How can I help? I've told you everything I can remember.' The manager gave Joseph an apologetic look as he opened a drawer to put the half bottle of whisky away. 'I gave Donna a drop in her coffee,' he said, 'to steady her nerves. Poor girl, she's quite shaken. To tell the truth, so am I. You don't expect to have a gun pointed at you and be robbed in broad daylight.'

'I quite understand,' Mary said. 'Perhaps you should close for a week. Give both of you time to get over it.'

'No. I can't. I'll be out of pocket enough as it is, having to close tomorrow while the ceiling's being repaired.'

'What about insurance?' Joseph asked. 'I assume you're covered?'

'Yes, I am for what it's worth. It's a safe bet they come up with all manner of reasons not to pay out.' He shook his head. 'Same as they did when the front window was smashed Thursday before last. Maybe I should have taken out cover with the chap who called in two or three weeks ago.'

'Did he have an appointment?'

'No. He walked in off the street.'

'Which company was he from?'

'I don't recall. In fact, I don't think he told me. But he did say my business would be covered against everything. Accidental damage, fire, robbery, all sorts of things.'

'And how was the policy to be paid?'

'He said if I paid monthly in cash he could get me preferential rates. Said someone would call in to collect the money.'

Joseph glanced at Mary. 'Did he? What more can you tell us about him?'

'Not a lot I'm afraid. I remember it was busy, which is why I was helping out behind the counter. I tried to get rid of him as quickly as possible.'

'There must be something, hair colour, height … anything.'

'He was average build. Nothing really, apart from his eyes.' The manager hesitated. 'A cousin of mine had a dog with different colour eyes, lovely animal. But I've never seen a person with eyes which don't match.'

'It's known as heterochromia,' Joseph said. 'And you're right, it is unusual in people.'

Chapter 5

August 1986

The tropical fish in the warehouses gave boxes imported from South America legitimacy, but the accompanying bags of white powder were not a suitable replacement for their diverse diets.

Mark Payne crossed his office, lifted the lid of the aquarium and sprinkled a pinch of flake. 'Right, that's you lot fed,' he said. 'Let's give my brother a call. Time to scuttle Jimmy Newton's plans.'

'Yes, Donald Payne, planning department.' Mark put a hand over the mouthpiece. 'Dozy bitch.' Taking his hand away from the phone he drummed his fingers on his desk. 'Hello, Don. What took you so long? Never mind. How's things?'

'Fine, but I've asked you not to call me here. What are you after now?'

'I hear you're dealing with consent for a new nightclub. Right?'

'Nero's Palace? Yes. We held preliminary discussions last week. There were no major objections. Why are you asking?'

Mark's grip tightened on the phone. 'Because I want it rejected.'

'I can't. It's up to the committee. I'm only head of department.'

'Okay, instruct them to turn it down. Simple.'

'It's not that easy.'

'Don't talk bollocks. You got my building plans through.'

'Yes, and remember all the trouble it caused?'

'For you? Or for your precious committee? Money *always* gets things done.'

'All I'm saying is there isn't a good reason to refuse the application.'

'Then let me give you one. How about a certain visit to a certain flat? If I was to let the police know –'

'You wouldn't. Besides, I would have heard from the interested parties.'

'Interested parties? You're talking out of your arse. Is there someone with you? Get rid of them. *Now.*'

Mark flicked his lighter and lit a cigar. As he exhaled, smoke drifted lazily across the room. 'Have they gone? Good. Now listen. I can prove it was you who killed her. I've got photos.'

'Of what?'

'Of you having sex and punching her.'

'Don't talk shit.'

'Trust me, I'm not. Vickie took a lot of money for me from idiots like you, then I raked in more by threatening her clients with photos. Am I still talking shit?'

'Yes. There was nobody else there. How could anyone take pictures?'

'By using a hidden camera. The extension cable worked a treat.'

'You bastard. I'm your own brother.'

'But Vickie didn't know, did she? Her instructions were to take photos of men who bragged about how much they earned. She used her charms to find out where they worked. The rest was easy.'

'I don't believe you.'

'You should. My man called in as usual to collect the takings and change the film. When he saw she was dead, he removed the camera.' Mark paused. 'The coppers dragged the landlord down the nick, but his alibi was easy to prove. The only thing they've charged him with is, allowing a property to be used for prostitution.'

Mark heard Donald take a deep breath before replying. 'You're bluffing. If you've got photos, send them to the police. Even then it will be your word against mine. Mum was the only one who could tell us apart for certain. Prove it wasn't you with that slut.'

'Idiot. Okay, I will, but remember your fingerprints must be all over the flat. Mine aren't, I never go there. Now, do you want me to send these to your other half?'

'If you've got pictures, why haven't you asked for money?'

Mark stubbed out his cigar. 'They're worth more than you could stump up. Now, stop pissing me about or I'll put them in the post.'

'No. Don't. You win. I'll block the application, but I want the negatives first.'

'You must think I'm stupid. They stay with me. No more greasing your sweaty little palm to get things done in future.'

'What about my committee members? Have you got pictures of any of them?'

'No, so I'll pay them cash when you push this through.'

'If I can. It was one hell of a game persuading them about your garage and swimming pool. It'll cost a lot more this time.'

'Okay, fine. I'll use what would have been your share to pay the others, share it around. There you are, job done. Now, one last thing, why did you kill Vickie? I know you enjoy roughing women up, but why kill her?'

'I didn't mean to. And you can talk. I remember the blonde –'

Mark slammed the phone down.

*

The stale smell of spilt beer and tobacco smoke pervaded the saloon of the Mariner's Arms.

James Newton finished polishing a glass and placed it on the shelf next to others. Running a wet cloth along the bar he removed sticky circles and cigarette ash.

The morning post clattered through the entrance door. Gathering up a scattering of envelopes from the mat, he sighed. 'Bills, bills, bills and more bills. They must think I'm made of bloody money. Huh, still nothing from the council. What's taking them so long?'

James held the phone in one hand. Pushing a glass up against an optic dispenser he waited to be put through to the planning department.

'What? What do you mean it's not approved? Last time we spoke you said my plans were some of the best you'd seen. I've put a lot . . . sorry, could you say that again? You had a vote and it was turned down? Why? Can I appeal? Hello? Hello? Are you still there? Sod it, I've been cut off!' Tipping his head back, he swallowed the rum.

His wife appeared, rubbing her eyes, hair concealed beneath a knotted headscarf. A cigarette bobbed up and down in her mouth as she spoke. 'Who was it? The brewery? Tell them they're supposed to deliver on a Wednesday, not whenever it suits them.'

'It wasn't the brewery. I sorted them out yesterday. I was on the phone to the council. About Nero's Palace. The sods have chucked out my application. I can't believe it, all that money getting plans drawn up and they've turned it down.'

'Do what? I'll phone them myself. Give me the number.'

'It's worth a try I suppose, but I don't think you'll get them to change their minds. They're stuck in the past. They don't want anything new.' He handed her the phone.

A minute later she glared at the phone then put it back to her ear. 'I don't understand. Who raised the objections? You're not allowed to say. I see.' She tapped her cigarette into an ashtray. 'And there's no appeal. What? Oh, so we can alter the plans and re-submit them, good. Pardon? Well, if they'll be refused again, what's the point?' Slamming the phone down she turned toward James. 'It's not fair, the club idea of yours would have turned things around for us. Now what?' She blew smoke up at the ceiling. 'Can you take up your friend's offer?'

'He's not a friend, only someone I play golf with.'

'Don't split hairs. I think we should sell this place, find another pub and start again. Ask him.'

'I don't mind giving it a go, but don't hold your breath. Who knows what he'll say if I go back with cap in hand?'

*

Mark Payne ignored the phone as he slipped an elastic band around banknotes. The fifth time it rang he picked it up. 'Mark Payne Enterprises. Jimmy? You sound dreadful. What's the problem?' His lip curled. 'Sorry to hear that. But I did warn you. What? Is my offer still on the table? Yes, but not the extra ten grand. You should have taken it when you had the chance. And don't wait too long, property prices can always drop.'

Mark smiled as he listened to his brother capitulate. 'Good. Here's the number of my solicitor, call him.' Putting the phone down, he doodled on his desk jotter. 'Hmm, I believe you've got something, Jimmy. Girls in togas, I like it.'

Julie used her backside to open the door. 'I guessed you'd be wanting another coffee.'

'You must be psychic.' He smiled. 'The young designer you were shagging, the one who came up with the idea for

Hornigold's, get him on the phone. I want him to draw up some plans for me.'

'Not a problem. Be nice to see him again.' She ran a hand over her breasts. 'He was very imaginative.'

'Tell him to call into the office. I want to show him my next project.'

'Okay, I'll phone him right away.'

'Good. But don't get carried away and forget why you're calling. I expect to see him in here before the end of the week. Got it?'

'Yes.' She swallowed and put a hand to the side of her face. 'It's as good as done.'

Chapter 6

August 1986

Mary lifted the bicycle and carried into her flat. Leaning it against the hall wall, she headed for the kitchen. A quick search of the fridge produced a bowl of salad and two slices of beef.

Resting the plate on her lap she settled back to watch the television news. The item concerning mad-cow disease stopped a forkful in mid-air. Pushing the slices of meat to one side she played with the salad.

Back in the kitchen she tipped her meal into the pedal-bin. Taking a clean plate from the rack she cut slices of cheddar and tipped crackers from the air-tight barrel.

Clutching a cup of tea in one hand and the plate in the other, Mary pressed an ear against the bathroom door. 'Blast. Sounds like the shower's running. If I've left it on all day, there won't be any hot water. My fault for rushing this morning.'

She pushed the door with a foot.

The room was full of steam. A hand pulled back the shower curtain. 'Hello, love. I wondered what time you'd get home.'

Mary gasped and dropped the plate. 'Graham? What on earth are you doing here?'

He bent down and turned off the taps. 'Taking a shower. What's it look like?'

'But you should be in the Falklands.'

He swung a leg out of the bath, grabbed a towel off the pile and dried his face. 'I thought I'd surprise you.'

She raised her gaze to meet his eyes.

'All good soldiers stand to attention when being inspected.' He grinned. 'Good to be home.'

'Home? This isn't your home any more. You had it off with some tart, remember?'

'Haven't I explained? How many more times? It wasn't serious. I was in the stores one day and she –'

'Spare me the sordid details.' Mary spat the words. 'You're a married man, or doesn't that mean anything.'

'Sweetheart, you know it does. It was over ages ago, I told you in my last letter.'

'The same letter in which you said you'd changed your mind about a divorce? And cover that thing up, get your clothes on. It's disgusting.'

'Not what you used to say. Come here, give me a kiss.'

'No chance.' She slammed the bathroom door.

'Better?' He looked down at his corduroy trousers as he finished buttoning his shirt. 'I don't remember you being so fussy.'

'Well, I am now. I should have changed the locks, but I didn't expect you to have the nerve to come back.'

'Why? We're married. I'll make it up to you, you'll see.'

'You must be joking. Go back to your slag.'

He reached out. 'You don't mean it. We were good together, in bed and out. We could be again, give it a chance.'

Mary shuddered. 'Thinking of you with your whore makes me cringe. I'd rather join a convent.'

'Bullshit.'

'Is it?'

'You'll change your mind. Why don't we snuggle up on the sofa? I'll soon get you in the mood.'

'Forget it.' Mary sneered. 'I want you gone.'

'Listen. This place is in my name and I pay the rent. If anyone's leaving, it's you.'

*

'Close the office door,' Joseph said. 'Now, start again. You said he was in the bathroom when you got home last night.'

Mary took a deep breath. 'Yes, in the shower.'

'Why didn't he tell you he was coming home? Was it a spur of the moment decision?'

'No. He tried to surprise me … and he did. Then he had the arrogance to think I'd welcome him with open arms.' She wriggled in the chair. 'I had to use the put-you-up, which isn't comfortable. There wasn't any alternative, apart from sleeping with him.'

'What are your plans? I said before, you can always move in with me.'

'No, it won't solve anything. I'm staying put.'

'Does he know about us?'

'Not yet. I didn't see it was any of his business.'

'Maybe you should tell him. Might help him change his mind.'

'I don't think so. He's convinced he's God's gift to women. Said I should be grateful he still wants me. Tosser.'

'If you get any problems, call me.'

'I should be okay. I'll string him along until it's time for him to go back. Probably only be a couple of nights. As soon as he goes, I'll get the lock changed.'

Joseph frowned. 'I don't like it, but I suppose there's not a lot I can do. After all, you are married to him.'

'Thanks a lot, why remind me?'

'Sorry. Right, let's get back to what we're meant to be doing. Has there been any response to our appeal on Crimewatch UK regarding the murder in the park? I missed it last night, forgot it was on.'

'Yes. There were a lot of calls, including one from her parents.'

Joseph straightened up. 'Go on.'

'We've got a name, Jeanette, Jeanette Walters. It seems she had a drug problem and ran away from home.'

'And?'

'She grew up around here, we pulled her in a few times. Then the family moved to London, but Jeanette never settled. A man phoned to say she was a prostitute. He wouldn't give his name but described her as the new girl on the block, only he didn't put it quite as delicately. We should question the women who work the streets, they tend not to report things.'

'Good thinking. I don't suppose you're in a hurry to go home, so we may as well get started. Before we do let's check your notes on the robbery at the bookmakers. We can do without idiots waving guns.'

'And trying to kill us, don't forget,' Mary said.

'Trust me, I won't.'

*

'You're late, where have you been?' Graham gripped Mary's arm. 'I had to get fish and chips. I couldn't wait any longer for you to cook dinner.'

'Shame. Where's mine? In the oven?'

'I didn't get you any. Now, I asked where you've been. Your shift finished hours ago.'

'If you must know, I've been talking to the class of women you seem to favour. The only difference is they want cash.'

'Very funny. What did you ask?'

'If any of them had been attacked. A prostitute was murdered and left in the park.'

'Any luck?'

'No. I got the impression someone warned them not to speak to us.'

'Who?'

'Good question. We've got our ideas.'

'Shame you lot don't carry guns.' Grasping his hands together he mimed holding a weapon. 'American cops don't take any crap. Shoot first and ask questions later is their motto.'

'You ever shoot anyone?'

'Not yet, but I would if I need to. It's what I trained for.'

'Stop talking about killing people.' She yawned. 'Time for bed.'

'Good idea. I'm off to get my head down, are you coming? Could be what you need to relax you after a long day.'

'Hot chocolate will do far better than wrestling a hairy gorilla.'

'Don't be so negative, sweetheart. How do you expect us to get back together if you don't try?'

'We're not, so I don't need to.'

'You'll see sense. You need to realize how lucky you are.'

'Huh. All I know is how lucky I'll be when I get a divorce. Move your arse, I need to get some pillows.'

Chapter 7

August 1986

'Not much progress.' DCI Hughes looked up. 'Two women murdered in the space of weeks and you're getting nowhere. What's the problem?'

'Motive. The only two things our victims have in common are prostitution and the level of violence used against them.'

'I know, I read your report. Do you think it could be the same person responsible for both?'

'Hard to say, sir.'

Hughes raised his eyebrows.

'It's possible,' Joseph said.

'And you have no ideas?' He scratched the back of his neck. 'A reporter phoned the front desk for information.'

'If he calls back, I suggest we tell him we're acting on information received and an arrest is imminent.'

'You know full well I expect to be kept informed at all times.' Hughes interlaced his fingers. 'If you've had an update, why isn't it in your report?'

'Because we haven't had anything, but nobody knows do they.' Joseph tapped the side of his nose. 'Why not use the newspapers for our own ends?'

'Lie to the public? I can't sanction it, not ethical.'

'Look on it as slight exaggeration. The papers do it all the time. Take the other day –'

Hughes waved a hand towards his office door. 'I can't go along with your methods.'

'I understand, sir.' Joseph turned to leave.

'One more thing, Fargough. The Vantyghem case last year, Anna Vantyghem won't be standing trial. She was –'

'Not being tried? After she admitted killing Charles Bradshaw? What's the matter with –'

'If you'd let me finish. She was found hanging in her cell. There's going to be an official inquiry.'

'Why? It's saved the taxpayer providing board and lodging for life.'

'The report also said she miscarried. They put her on suicide watch, but she still managed to take her own life. Her brother is threatening legal action.'

'Is he? The man's responsible for wrecking lives and probably a few deaths too. I don't imagine *any* judge will have much time for him.'

'Off the record, I agree with you.'

*

Mary looked into the driving mirror and touched her hair. 'What did Hughes want?'

'He's concerned we're not getting anywhere with our murder enquiries.'

'Perhaps he should come out from behind his desk and give us a hand. Did he have anything else to moan about?'

'No, but he told me Anna Vantyghem is dead. She hung herself.'

'No! What about her baby?'

'She lost it.'

'Poor woman, I feel sorry for her.'

'Why? She killed her lover. Why not save your sympathy for his wife?'

'We're skating on thin ice here. I am married don't forget. Where's the difference between what he was doing and us? I'm cheating on my husband, or don't you see it that way?'

'No. He found someone else and asked for a divorce. And…and I love you. You know I do. As soon as you're free –'

She stared out the car window before turning to kiss him on the cheek. 'Enough, we've work to do.' She slipped the car into gear. 'I was speaking to the desk sergeant while you were in with Hughes. He said there'd been a phone call. Someone saw a van entering Jubilee Park. The caller said he didn't pay much attention at the time, assumed it was council workers, but when he heard about the murder, he called us.'

'Did he give an address or phone number?'

'Both. I returned the call. He's agreed to meet us this evening, around seven.'

*

Mary drove down the street at a leisurely pace while Joseph peered at the house numbers. 'Are you sure he said seventeen, not seventy?' he said.

'Yes, it can't be far now.'

'I hope this mystery caller gets the ball rolling.' He pointed ahead. 'Look, there it is. The one with the Mini on the drive.' He leaned forward and pointed ahead. Settling back in his seat, he said, 'Getting back to what I was saying, I suggested we let the papers know we've had reliable information. All bullshit of course, but worth a try.'

'Maybe we should offer a reward.' She smiled. 'There's always someone willing to sell their granny.'

'Let's go over this once more, sir,' Mary said, placing her cup back onto the saucer. 'You say you saw this van, which could have been dark blue or green, enter the park through the side gates. You think it was an Austin Maestro, but you can't be sure. Is that correct?'

'Yes. It was getting dark.' The man wiggled a finger in his ear. 'Even so, I'm ninety percent sure it was an Austin, like British Telecom use. But it wasn't yellow.'

'Was anyone else in the van, apart from the driver?'

'Can't say, it was over in a flash. One minute it was coming towards me, next the bugger swung across the road and shot into the park.' The man clenched the fingers of one hand, leaving the index one extended. 'I shouted, "Swivel on this!" Good job the brakes on my car work.'

'Did you get his registration, sir?' Joseph said. 'Would you recognise the driver?'

The man shrugged. 'Afraid not, sorry. I said on the phone I didn't get a good look. It was only when I read about the poor girl getting murdered, I decided to call you lot.'

'We're grateful you did, sir. It's possible we may receive other sightings of this vehicle.'

'Yes,' Mary said. 'Thank you. And please thank your wife for the tea.'

'Where now?' Mary asked. 'Back to the station?'

'No. It's getting late, drive to your place then I'll drive myself home.'

'But my bike's at the station. I need it to get to work.'

Joseph put his arm around her. 'Don't worry, I'll pick you up in the morning.'

'And my husband? Have you forgotten he's there too?'

'No, I haven't. He can catch the bus.'

'Don't be daft. You know what I meant. It could be misconstrued, you coming to collect me.'

'Misconstrued? What a big word.' He grinned. 'Have you swallowed a dictionary?'

She took one hand off the wheel and dug him in the ribs. 'Cheek. It was in my crossword if you must know.'

'Fair enough but what's so strange about picking you up? He knows you work with me, or are you keeping it a secret?'

'No, why would I?'

'I tell you what, why don't you sleep at my place tonight? Save all the hassle?'

'I must admit it's tempting.' She turned and smiled. 'Okay, your place it is.'

*

'How do you want your eggs, Joe?' Mary asked, cracking a second one into the pan.

'Runny. I like to dip my bread in.'

'There's an answer to that, but I'm a lady.'

Joseph laughed. 'Now, now, leave the barrack room humour to your husband.'

'Did you have to mention him? I've had a lovely night, don't ruin it.'

He nuzzled her neck. 'Sorry. Let's get back under the covers.'

'Get off. I'm trying to cook breakfast.'

'I know, and I'd like it in bed.'

'Don't mess about. There isn't time, we're on duty in an hour, don't forget.'

'Spoil-sport. I wish you'd move in, lock, stock and barrel.'

'And lose both of us our jobs? You know what they're like about other ranks fraternising.'

'Pity your other half doesn't realize he's fighting a losing battle. Things could be so much simpler.'

'Meaning?'

He put his arms around her from behind and pulled her close. 'Wait and see. And watch those eggs, you can have those, they've gone hard.'

Mary smiled. 'They're in good company then.'

He patted her backside. 'Sorry about that.'

'Don't be.' She said, turning the gas off. 'You win. I didn't fancy breakfast, anyway.'

Scooping her into his arms he carried her back to the bedroom.

*

'Good morning,' Joseph said, 'anything new?'

The desk sergeant closed his newspaper. 'Morning, sir. No…oh, yes, there was one thing. There was a call last night, a burnt-out vehicle on the beach.'

'Where?'

Turning to the map on the wall the sergeant tapped it with a pencil. 'Somewhere about there. My guess is yobs joy-riding again. And it isn't a car, it's a small van. The council are arranging to remove it sometime this week.'

'Sounds interesting,' Mary said to Joseph. 'Let's drive out there.'

'This is the place,' Mary said. 'If it was joy-riders, they may have run out of petrol.'

Joseph took a deep breath. 'Ah, sea air, you can't beat it. Come on, let's take a look.'

Seaweed hung from glassless windows; silt covered the interior. The acrid smell of burnt rubber was doing its best to overpower the tang of sea water left behind after holding the vehicle in its embrace. Rust was doing its best to add a touch of colour to the blackened metal shell.

Mary turned her coat collar up as light rain fell. 'Who on earth would drive all this way? And why the beach of all places?'

'Good questions, now all we need is good answers,' he said. 'It's an Austin Maestro, or to be precise, it was. When we get back to the car, I'll call in, tell them to have this picked up. I want Forensics to go over it with a fine-tooth comb.'

'Even if it is the right van, there's not much left.'

'Very true, but they may find something.'

Mary shivered. 'Sorry, Joe, I'm cold. Pneumonia rain my mother use to call it. Gets right into your bones.'

'I know what she meant. Let's get to the nearest café and have a hot drink.' He rubbed his stomach. 'And I fancy a cheese sandwich or a sticky bun.'

'Why choose? You always end up with both. Come on, it's my treat this time.'

Chapter 8

August 1986

Her shift over, Mary cycled home. The ticking of a clock was her only greeting as she entered the kitchen. Dirty dishes lay in washing-up water which had lost its sparkle.

'Huh, I might have known, some things never change,' she muttered, running the hot tap.

Drying her red hands, she moved into the lounge.

Flicking between channels on the television, Mary sighed and turned it off. 'I was right, some things never change. Especially finding anything interesting to watch.'

Two hours later she woke to find the room in darkness. Pulling the sleeve of her cardigan back, she held her wrist towards the street light shining through the window. 'Almost midnight? It can't be? It is, it's ten to twelve. If he's staying out, I'll sleep in my own bed tonight.'

Switching on the bedroom light, she dropped her underwear into the laundry basket.

Graham pushed back the covers, shielding his eyes against the sudden brightness. 'Changed your mind, love?' He patted the bed. 'Come on, climb in.'

'Get lost. I thought you were out.'

'No, I decided to have an early night. Come on, get your gorgeous body between these sheets.'

'You must be joking.'

He leapt out and grabbed her wrists. 'I told you to get into bed. Now, do it.'

'Get off. You're hurting me.' She kicked out and winced as her toes bent against his shin. Her knee found its target. He grasped his crotch. 'Bitch!'

She glared at the marks on her arm. 'I could arrest you for assault. And attempted rape.'

He held out a hand. 'Don't be daft. I only want to make love to you. We are married for Christ's sake.'

'Not for long. You made your choice. Now live with it.' She slammed the bedroom door.

Next morning Mary took the slices from the toaster and smothered them with butter. 'This'll do for now. Joe's bound to find an excuse to go to a café.'

Graham sniffed as he entered the kitchen. 'Hmmm, smells good,' he said. 'I think I'll have some.'

'Help yourself.'

'About last night,' he said, leaning against the door frame. 'Am I being charged?'

'Not this time. But try anything else and your feet won't touch the ground.'

'Thanks, sweetheart.'

'Don't sweetheart me.'

Using a knife, he picked burnt crumbs from the butter. 'How's it going with the murder in the park?'

'Why?'

'Just taking an interest in what you're doing.'

'Well don't.'

'No harm in trying,' he said, sucking the knuckles of his right hand.

'Have you been fighting?' She frowned.

'It wasn't a fight, one of the drinkers in the Admiral Nelson said something I didn't like, so I hit him. I expect I'm banned but who gives a toss, it was worth it. I didn't like his eyes. One brown and one green.' He grinned. 'And a black one by now I should think.'

'What are you on about?'

'The man I hit. He had funny eyes.'

'Did he? Are you sure? His eyes I mean, were they really different colours?'

'Yes.'

'At last you've come up with something useful.'

'Have I? Does it mean I'm forgiven?'

'No. If you think you can get round me that easily, you've got another think coming.'

'Okay, you win.' Graham held up his hands. 'What time do you finish today? I'll have a meal ready.'

'Not for me. I don't fancy fish and chips.'

'No, I mean I'll cook. My roast dinners are to die for.'

'As bad as that?' She suppressed a smile. 'I think I'll settle for indigestion at the greasy spoon.'

*

Joseph scrawled his name across the bottom of the page and tossed it onto the growing pile. Picking up the next one he folded it time and again then launched the paper aeroplane across his office. Its flight came to an abrupt stop as it struck the wall.

A knock at the door interrupted further research into flight.

'Come in.'

Mary entered, bent down and retrieved his toy. 'Is this to be filed?' She smiled. 'I take it you're diligently checking the paperwork so close to your heart.'

'Cobblers. If I had a pound note for every bit of bumph I've had to deal with, I'd be a millionaire.'

'Cheer up. I've got news for you. The waste of space who calls himself my husband got into a fight the other night.'

'And? Has anybody made a complaint?'

'No.'

Joseph blinked. 'So?'

'The man he fought, had eyes which didn't match.'

'Where was this?'

'The Admiral Nelson.'

Pushing his chair back, Joseph reached up and took his jacket off the hook. 'Let's go. Any excuse to get out of the office.'

Timber beams gave a hint to the age of the Admiral Nelson. Local legend attributed them to a ship lured onto rocks by wreckers. Cutlasses took pride of place above the inglenook fireplace. A witch's cauldron, filled with flowering plants, stood in the hearth. Two old men looked up from a game of dominoes as Joseph and Mary entered.

Mary coughed and waved a hand up and down in front of her face. 'If we were at sea, the foghorns would be busy,' she spluttered. 'One deep breath in here could be fatal.'

Joseph approached the bar. 'Afternoon,' he said, glancing up at the clock on the wall. 'A lemonade…and half of best, please.'

The barman placed a glass under a pump. Joseph leaned closer. 'I hear you had a fight in here the other night.'

Putting the glass of beer on the counter, he poured Mary's drink. 'It was nothing. All over before it started. What's it to you?'

Joseph produced his warrant card. 'One of them is a suspect. Were they regulars?'

The man turned his back and punched the keys of the till. 'I know Graham from before he joined up, but I've never seen the other one. What's he wanted for?'

'I can't tell you.' Joseph sipped his beer. 'Do you know what the fight was about?'

'Something and nothing. An insurance agent kept on at me to take out cover for the pub. Graham asked for a drink and the man accused him of pushing in. Graham hit him, and down he went.'

Joseph glanced down at the floorboards. 'And then what?'

'Nothing. He got up and left and I asked Graham to leave.'

'What car was the man driving?'

'He wasn't, he was riding a motorbike.'

Joseph passed Mary her drink. 'The barman said our man objected to your husband interrupting his sales patter. It's why he hit him.'

'He does tend to lose his temper a lot lately,' Mary said. 'Before we married, he was all sweetness and light.'

'Well anyway, the interesting thing is the man was trying to sell insurance.'

Mary looked over to the bar. 'The bookmaker said he was pestered about insurance before his window was smashed. Sounds like someone's running a protection racket.'

'I agree.' He touched her glass with his. 'Cheers.'

'Anything else?'

'Yes. He was on a motorbike. I'm sure he's our man.'

Chapter 9

August 1986

Joseph sat with legs crossed, feet resting on his desk. 'Think of all the hours this must have taken,' he said, turning a page. 'Sieving through all those ashes. Not the job for me.'

'Nor me. The stench on the beach was enough.' Mary pinched her nose. 'But you've got to hand it to Forensics, finding a human tooth is impressive.'

'Yes, it is.' Switching his attention from the report to the stapled photocopy, he said, 'And this. How on earth did it survive the fire? Well, almost. But half a business card is better than none.'

Turning her copy in different directions to catch the light she said, 'Not much to go on, is it? Pity it's not the other half. I mean, *ne Enterprises*, something *Road* and a few numbers.'

'Get the Yellow Pages and meet me in the car. We'll adjourn to the café for breakfast while we sort out who this card belonged to.'

'Breakfast?' Mary checked her watch. 'It's gone ten o'clock.'

'If you're going to be picky, make it elevenses. Or early lunch.'

'Or we could work here,' she said.

'We could, but I find the ambience of a café more conducive to contemplation.'

'Listen to you. What you mean is, it's a good excuse for a fry-up.' She patted her stomach. 'I don't know how you eat like you do and not put on weight.'

Mary turned a page in the business directory and pretended not to see Joseph stab a rasher of bacon from her plate. She ran her finger down the long list. Joseph's fork darted out, this time spearing a fried tomato.

'Aren't you eating any of your breakfast,' he said, 'if not, why order it?'

'I didn't. I asked you for poached egg on toast.'

'So, you did. Sorry, I must have forgotten. Shall I send it back?'

'How can you? You've eaten most of it.'

He licked his lips. 'Any luck with the name?'

'I've found two possibilities so far. If you've finished eating, take over while I get myself another drink. Do you want one?'

'Yes, please. I'll have a coffee.'

Joseph scanned the entries in the Yellow Pages. He scratched the side of his head. 'I agree, this would have been easier with the left-hand side of the card.'

Joseph sniffed as Mary put her plate onto the table.

'Don't even think about it,' she said, 'this is mine.' She shook the salt pot before slicing into the egg. 'How many more did you find?'

'Only one. Enjoy your snack while I finish looking.'

Joseph closed the directory. 'All done. there's only three. When you're ready, we'll make a start on these addresses.'

*

'The word enterprise doesn't spring to mind, looking at this place.' Joseph stared at the boarded-up shop. '*Sterne Enterprises* was bad enough, but at least they're still trading. More than can be said for this place.'

'Shall I drive on?' Mary said, running a pencil through the address.

'No, I still want to check. Won't be long.'

Mary sat with a newspaper resting on the steering wheel. She scrunched up her eyes, trying to conjure up the answer to five across in the crossword. 'Got it. Lepidoptera. Okay, that helps. Now . . . what can two down be?

Joseph opened the car door, got in and rapped on the dashboard. 'Move on,' he said, fastening his seat belt. 'There's no vehicle access at the rear. Add double yellow lines and it's no wonder a lot of these places have gone under.'

She folded her paper and tucked it into the door pocket beside her. 'Upwards and onwards then. Let's hope we have more luck with the last one on our list.'

'Here we are,' Mary said, pulling into the kerb. '*Mark Payne Enterprises.*'

'Good, now let's go and –' Joseph put a restraining hand on her arm. 'No, wait a minute, look, there's a van. It's either delivering, or picking something up.'

A pair of wrought iron gates, topped with barbed wire, allowed access to a large courtyard. Oil stains on the tarmac glistened after an early morning shower of rain. Two men, carrying a heavy aquarium, appeared from one of the buildings forming a horseshoe around the yard. One of them walked backwards, turning his head from side to side. Reaching the van, they manoeuvred their load into the back. After shaking hands one of the pair got into the vehicle and drove from the premises.

'Are we going in now?' Mary pointed across the road.

'Yes.'

Inside the door marked RECEPTION, a young girl slid open a glass partition.

'Good morning. How can I help?'

Joseph showed his warrant card. 'We'd like to speak to Mr Payne.'

She turned away, spoke on the phone then said, 'He's gone out to meet a client. Would you like to make an appointment?'

'No.'

'Can I tell him what it's about?'

'Say we've found something we believe belongs to him.'

'Strange? He hasn't mentioned losing anything. What is it?'

Joseph tapped the side of his nose. 'When will he be back?'

The girl made a show of looking through a desk diary. 'Not sure. He's very busy. And there's no appointments free until next week. How about Monday or Thursday?'

'Have you got one of his business cards?'

'Of course.' She passed it under the partition. 'There you are.'

Joseph showed it to Mary. She nodded.

The sound of a motorcycle ricocheted back from the buildings in the yard. Rushing to the door Joseph flung it open. As the bike sped past, the rider glared at him. For a moment Joseph stood rooted to the spot.

He spun around. 'Does he work here?' he shouted.

'Who?' The receptionist leaned back and inspected her nails.

'The man on the bike.'

'Couldn't see. You were in the way.'

'I could arrest you for hampering police officers in the course of their duty,' he said. 'Open the door and let us through to Payne's office.'

'No, I've been told not to allow anyone past this partition. I'll report you to my boss.'

Moving towards the end of the cubicle, Joseph tried the handle. Turning his back, he lashed out with one foot. The door smashed against the wall.

The girl screamed. 'Mark! Help!'

Joseph barged past.

'You can't go in there, it's private,' she yelled.

He ignored her.

A door opened and a man confronted Joseph. 'Who do you think you are?' he demanded. 'What's going on? Who smashed the door?'

'Police,' Joseph said, holding out his warrant card. 'Sorry about the damage. I tripped and fell.'

'He kicked it,' the girl protested. 'You saw him,' she said to Mary.

'Did I? You must have been in the way. I didn't see a thing.'

'Why don't we use your office?' Joseph said. 'There are questions which need answers.'

'Suppose I refuse?'

'Then I'll arrest you.'

'You're making a big mistake.' Mark Payne's top lip curled. 'I know people. You could find yourself back on the beat.'

'It's a chance I'll take. Now, shall we do this here, or would you prefer the station?'

'Come in. Let's get this over with. I've got a business to run.'

Mark Payne glared at Joseph across his desk. 'Get on with it. I haven't got all day.' Striking a match, he attempted to light a cigar.

'Who was the man who just rode out? The one on the motorbike?'

'No idea. Next question.'

'So, he doesn't work for you?' Joseph said.

'No. What's this all about?'

Joseph handed him the photocopy and business card. 'Yours I believe?'

Mark studied them. 'What of it? Someone's burnt one of my cards. What's the big deal? I'll make a few phone calls, you'll –'

'Be asking more questions, such as, how did the card come to be inside an abandoned vehicle? Did it belong to you?'

'What van?'

'I didn't say it was a van.' He looked across at Mary.

'It was a guess. I had one stolen recently.'

'Did you report it?'

'I told Julie to call you.' He pointed to the door leading through to the reception area. 'Didn't she phone?'

'Not to my knowledge. Why would anyone set it alight?'

'My guess is kids. They're always nicking cars and burning them.'

'I think there's more to it. When we find the motorbike rider, we'll be back.'

'If you still have your jobs.' Mark sneered. 'You're messing with the wrong man. I run a respectable business, and I've got friends in high places.'

'Good for you. When you speak to them, mention the fact you're under investigation.'

Mark laughed. 'Are you accusing me?'

'Not yet. But I suspect you of being involved in murder and attempting to pervert the course of justice by destroying evidence.'

'On your bike. Come to think of it, it's probably where you'll end up. You can't go to court with what you've got. I give out those cards all the time.'

Joseph clenched his fists. 'I expect you do. But do you always include body parts with them?'

Mark's face drained. 'Don't talk shit.'

'I won't. I'll leave that to you. Some bastard mutilated and killed a young prostitute. It's my job to find him.'

'Good luck. Now, if you've finished, I've got work to do,' he said, trying again to light his Havana.

'So have we.' Joseph pointed to the door. 'Let's go.'

'Here,' Mark said, opening a side door. 'Use this, you've upset Julie enough for one day.'

Chapter 10

August 1986

'Hello, sweetheart,' Graham said. 'Glad you're home early, I've got a surprise for you. How does that sound?'

'Like one of my worst nightmares.' She removed her coat, took clips from her hair and shook it. 'I need a shower. Is the water hot?'

'Yes. And I've done the washing-up. Put one of your posh frocks on, I'm taking you out to dinner.'

'You're not. I've got my meal in the fridge.'

'Correction. You had a meal in the fridge. I ate it for my lunch.'

'Then I'll settle for beans on toast.'

Putting his arm around her waist, he said. 'You deserve better. It's our favourite restaurant. We can have one last meal together before we go our separate ways.'

She pulled away from his embrace. 'You're leaving? What changed your mind?'

'You did.'

'What about the divorce?'

'You can have it. We'll put everything behind us and enjoy the evening.'

'Let me make sure I've got this right. You're going back to the Falklands and the divorce goes through. Promise?'

'Promise.'

Mary's stomach rumbled. 'Okay. But no hanky-panky, do I make myself clear?'

'Yes. I get the message, loud and clear.'

*

'Not bad,' she said, pushing the glass dish away.

'I knew you'd enjoy it. More wine?' Graham held the bottle towards her. 'Did you notice? Blue Nun. See, I don't forget.'

'Huh. Apart from forgetting you're married when it suits you.'

'Don't spoil the evening, sweetheart. We agreed, remember?' He filled his glass.

'No more,' she said, placing a hand on the bottle. 'I don't want to get sloshed.'

The waiter hovered. 'Are you ready for your next course, sir?'

'Yes. Thank you. And another bottle, please.'

'I told you no more wine. You know why.'

'Yes.' Graham grinned.

'Look, I may as well tell you. I'm seeing someone else.'

'Which makes us quits. Let's both admit we've made mistakes and give it another go.'

'I only said I was seeing someone. Don't jump to conclusions.'

'Are you saying you're not sleeping with this other man? Surely you don't expect me to believe that?' He unfolded his napkin. 'Here come our meals.'

*

'There, now tell me you didn't enjoy it,' Graham said, falling back onto his side of the bed.

'You shouldn't have got me drunk,' she slurred. 'You know what it does to me.'

'Of course, but all's fair in love and war. Now you've got something to tell lover boy.'

'Don't. I shouldn't . . . Oh no, I'm going to be sick.' Falling off the bed she crawled to the bathroom.

Rain pattering against the window roused Mary. Sitting up, she waited for the room to stop spinning before swinging her legs off the put-you-up bed and stumbling towards the bathroom.

Graham met her in the hall. 'Good morning, sweetheart. Why didn't you come back to bed?'

'You bastard. I didn't, did I?'

He grinned. 'Twice. Don't you remember? You were all over me.'

'I don't believe you. Thank God you're going soon.'

'You can forget about me going anywhere. I've kissed the army goodbye.'

'Why?'

Graham put a hand on the back of his neck. 'The woman was my commanding officer's wife. He –'

'Spare me the sordid details. You aren't leaving, you've been chucked out.'

'Something like that. Anyway, it's all behind us now. Tell your boyfriend he's yesterday's news, and we'll start again.'

'No. You made your bed, now you can lay in it.'

'But, sweetheart, can't you see it's you I love?'

'All I see is a cheating bastard who'd have it off with any woman given half a chance.'

'I won't give up. You'll come round.'

'What about your promise? Apart from going back to the Islands you said we'd get a divorce.'

'And it got me what I wanted.' He grinned. 'You fell for it, hook, line and sinker.'

*

'I can't drive today,' Mary said, 'I had too much to drink last night.'

'Strange. You don't usually drink at home.' Joseph frowned.

'It wasn't at home. My rat of a husband told me a pack of lies to get me to go out for a meal.'

'It's okay, do me good to drive for a change.'

Lowering her gaze she said, 'There's more to it, he –'

'Don't tell me. He got you into bed.'

'How did you guess?'

'When a man takes a woman out for a meal and a drink there's often a price to be paid. And he *is* your husband, what did you expect?'

'Him to keep his promises.'

'Life's full of disappointments.'

'You're not upset about the sex?'

'I am, but what can I say? You're married to him.'

'It won't happen again, I promise. It's you I want.'

*

Mary unscrewed the top of a bottle, tipped her head back and drank. 'I can't seem to drink enough water,' she said. 'Now I know how a camel must feel in the desert.' She fidgeted. 'How much longer do we have to sit in the car? I'm getting cramp.'

'Give it a few more minutes. I know Payne denies knowing our motorcycling friend but I've got other ideas. He'll turn up, I'm sure.'

'Then we'll arrest him?'

'Yes, but only if he's with Payne. We need to prove a connection.'

Mary looked at her watch. 'We've been here two hours. I don't think he's coming today.' She fidgeted. 'I need the loo, sorry.'

'Drive to the café at the end of the road. But hurry, I don't want to miss him.'

Joseph sounded the horn. Mary rushed out. 'What's up?'

'A motorbike went into Payne's yard. I saw it in the wing mirror. Hang on while I turn this thing around.'

Chapter 11

August 1986

The man leaned back in the chair and held up an arm to ward off the attack. The veins on Mark Payne's brow stood out, his cheeks red with rage. 'You – stupid – bloody – prick.' He punctuated each word with a blow. 'I told you to take her in the van, then torch it. Why did you leave her in the park?'

'She wasn't dead,' the man protested. 'You said she was, but she wasn't.'

'You should still have burned the bitch. Why didn't you follow orders?'

'She groaned, so I thought I'd take her to the park and have some fun. It was okay getting her out, but I couldn't get her back in.' Rubbing his mouth with the back of a hand he stared at the blood. 'I panicked. The sun was coming up. I didn't want to get caught with her, so I drove off. I did burn the van though, like you said.'

Mark reached underneath his desk and located a button. 'Okay, you've got nothing to worry about then, have you.'

A man sporting a cauliflower ear filled the door frame. Mark pointed. 'Our friend here needs a change of scenery. Show him what grass looks like from six feet under.'

*

Joseph and Mary crept across the yard, keeping close to the side of the buildings. The clicking of hot metal cooling down enticed Mary toward the Kawasaki lurking in the shadows,

'This is the bike we saw,' she said. 'He must be in there.' She opened the warehouse door.

Heat from the rows of aquariums kept the room very warm, air bubbles providing stimulation for fish to dance aquatic ballets. Condensation dripped from steel girders supporting the warehouse roof.

Joseph touched her sleeve. 'Keep watch by the door while I search,' he said.

'I knew this wasn't a good idea. If you find him, remember he had a gun.'

'If he's still got it, I'll shove it where the sun don't shine.'

'I bet you would.'

Five minutes later Joseph appeared from between the rows of fish tanks. 'Nobody,' he said. 'He's either in the other warehouse, or with Payne. I'll go and have another word with Mr High and Mighty.

'Okay, I'll wait here. Be careful.'

After a few minutes Joseph came back. 'He denies knowing the man,' Joseph said. 'And he's adamant the bike doesn't belong to any of his staff.'

'I don't believe it. We've seen the motorbike here on two occasions.' Mary dodged as a vehicle came close to hitting her. 'Prat!' she shouted. 'Did you see that, Joe? It was one of Payne's, I'm sure.'

'Add dangerous driving to the list of charges. Speaking of lists, remind me to get the bike's registration traced.'

'Huh. Now we've started asking questions it'll go the same way as the van.' She looked at her watch. 'There's two hours before our shift ends, what do you want to do?'

'Sit in the car and watch in case our friend comes back for his bike.'

A man wielding a spade was making sure Joseph and Mary were doomed to disappointment.

Chapter 12

August 1986

Lights from the hotel appeared to intensify the darkness enveloping the fields and lanes around it.

In the eating area, Donald Payne dabbed the corner of his mouth with a napkin. 'If you'll excuse me, my dear, I need to pay my respects to the porcelain.'

The blonde woman at his table opened her clutch bag and produced a mirror. She rummaged around for her bright red lipstick.

Mark pulled at his zip as he turned away from the urinal. 'Hello, Don,' he said. 'Didn't expect to see you.'

Donald's cheeks reddened. 'What are you doing here? This is the first time I've tried this restaurant. I thought it would be a quiet place to eat.'

'Aha.' Mark turned the tap on and washed his hands. 'I guess you mean the wife isn't with you. Right?'

'Yes. Edna doesn't like eating in public. It's another one of her funny ways. I'm with my secretary, it's her birthday, I thought I'd treat her.'

'Pull the other one, it's got bells on. Your secretary, her birthday? It's your brother you're talking to, not one of the thick planks you work with.' He tugged at the towel in the roller machine. 'Anyway, it's no skin off my nose who you're shagging. Now listen, I've got something I want to discuss.'

'What is it?'

'Business. Shall I join you and your *secretary* at your table?'

'No, I'd rather talk in here. I know you're always up for *ménage à trois* but this one's with me. Apart from women, what are you after this time?'

'Nothing much. I just wanted to tell you I bought the Mariner's Arms.'

'Oh? I didn't know it was up for sale.'

'It wasn't, but it's mine now. Time to get the nightclub built.'

'What? After me getting the plans rejected? What am I supposed to say to the committee?'

'Whatever you like. Just make sure they get passed.'

'I can't guarantee anything. You know how difficult these things can be.'

Mark took out his wallet and stuffed notes into the top pocket of Donald's tweed jacket. 'As I said on the phone, I don't have to bung you anything, but I'm feeling generous. Treat your secretary, it's her birthday I believe.'

Donald put a hand over the bulge in his coat. 'You don't mess about, do you. That club must be important.'

'It is.' Taking hold of his brother's arm, he squeezed. 'You make sure the plans go through or there'll be hell to pay.'

'Where have you been? I thought you'd run out on me.' The blonde swirled the last of the wine in her glass.

The Mateus Rosé bottle in Donald's hand trembled above her glass as he looked back toward the toilets. 'Shall I top you up?'

She giggled. 'Yes, please. What took you so long? It was embarrassing sitting here on my own. People were staring.'

'I met a man in the toilet.' Donald scowled at the look on her face. 'No, it was nothing like that. He's someone I know in business.'

Reaching across the table she plucked at the banknotes. 'Funny place to keep money,' she said. 'Most of my men friends use –'

He pushed her hand away. 'It's something the man owed me.'

Her mouth opened wide. 'That's a lot of cash. What did you have to do?'

'That's for me to know. Eat your profiteroles.'

'They don't look as nice as your pancakes. I wish I'd ordered them instead.'

'Crêpes Suzette actually, with brandy and double cream.' Cutting a small piece, he offered it on the end of a fork. 'Try some. Open wide, you'll enjoy it.'

Closing her eyes, she murmured, 'I always do.'

Using one slip-on shoe to dislodge the other, he hooked his foot around the back of her leg. She responded by arching her back against the upholstered chair. He ran his tongue over his top lip.

*

Windscreen wipers squeaked across the windscreen. Donald
stared out at the dismal blocks of flats. Dark stains, from
corroding iron framework put in place to support balconies, broke
the grey monotony of concrete. Light summer rain, drifting
aimlessly, did nothing to soften the gloom.

He grimaced. 'Unbelievable. How could some toffee-nose
architect dream this up in the comfort of his office and condemn
people to live in these places?'

His blonde companion placed a hand on his knee. 'It's not that
bad. Are you coming in?' Her fingers tightened their grip. 'My
place is nice and cosy and I put clean sheets on the day before
yesterday.'

'No. Even the wife knows council meetings don't go on all
night.'

'But I thought you wanted to … you know … have your wicked
way with me as usual.'

'You're right, I did, but I've changed my mind. Next time, eh?'

Her face took on the look of a sulking child. 'You told me you
loved me. I even had a bath before I came out tonight. I wouldn't
have bothered if I'd known you weren't coming in.'

Reaching across, he opened the door. 'Off you go. I'll phone
you sometime.'

She kissed his cheek, leaving a bright red smudge. 'Promise?
Are you sure you don't want a nightcap?'

'Yes. I've got to be going. See you soon.'

She danced a few steps on the pavement to regain her balance.
'Don't forget to tell her you want a divorce, Bunnykins.'
Touching her lips to the palm of her hand she blew him a kiss.

He checked his face in the rear-view mirror. Rubbing his cheek,
he spread the evidence. Spitting on his handkerchief he tried
again.

Winding the driver's window down a fraction he drove off at
speed. The cold air seeping in helped expel the cheap scent of his
dinner companion.

The force of the impact threw Donald against his seat belt. Looking back over his shoulder he saw a dog dragging its back legs, head lifted, howls bouncing back from the buildings. A woman with her hair in curlers clutched a nightdress to her body as she ran towards the animal.

Braking hard, Donald pulled into the kerb.

Throwing open the door he leapt out and ran around to the front of his car. 'Shit!' A single beam lanced through the drizzle, the other headlight an eyeless socket.

Donald walked back to the where the dog lay cuddled in the woman's arms. 'That bloody dog smashed one of my headlights,' he shouted.

The woman looked up at him, rain and tears combining to soak her flimsy nightdress. Her eyes vacant, her face a twisted caricature. 'It's Winston,' she said between sobs. 'It's his legs.' She cuddled the distraught dog closer. She glared at Donald. 'Why did you do it?'

'I never saw the sodding thing, that's why. What's it doing roaming the streets? And who's going to pay for the damage to my car?'

She spat at Donald then kissed the top of the dog's head. 'It's okay, Winston. You'll be okay.'

'Can't you shut the damn thing up?' Donald said. 'Stick a bag over its head or something. It's waking the neighbourhood.'

He looked up at the sound of footsteps. A baseball bat dangled from a teenager's hand. Donald left the distraught woman slumped over her dying pet and ran to his car.

*

Unlocking the front door, he turned and glared back at his car. 'Bloody woman, sodding dog.'

A voice called from upstairs. 'Is that you?'

'Who were you expecting, Father Christmas?' He loosened his tie. 'Why aren't you asleep? It's late.'

'I waited up for you,' she said.

'Well, you needn't have bothered. I've had a bad day. I'm off to bed. Good night.' At the top of the stairs, he opened a door and turned on the light. Crossing to the single divan in the spare bedroom he picked up his spare pyjamas.

Chapter 13

September 1986

DCI Hughes removed a sheaf of papers from a folder. 'These are the latest results from the vehicle examination,' he said.

'Thank you, sir.' Joseph took them, handed a set to Mary and read his copy. 'So . . . Jeanette Walters *was* in the van. It's her tooth.'

Hughes held up a page. 'Yes, now read the rest. It seems your suspicion regarding Mark Payne Enterprises is well founded. The Vehicle Identification Number was easy to find as no attempt had been made to grind it from the vehicle.'

Mary looked up. 'And it proves the vehicle is registered to him. No wonder he claimed it was stolen.'

Joseph scratched the side of his head. 'Yes, but we can't prove it wasn't.'

'And if it was, it removes him from your enquiries. These results confirm the van was used to convey the woman's body, but not who drove it,' Hughes said.

'I have a suspect in mind, sir. In my report on the robbery at the bookmaker's I mentioned a man with unusual eyes. I'm certain I saw him at Payne's yard.'

'Then bring him in for questioning.'

'Yes, sir.'

Hughes picked up a second folder. 'Anything on this other case? The prostitute killed in her flat?'

'Not yet. They may be connected, but …'

'They may not. What do you propose to do next?'

'Apply for a search warrant under Section 8, sir. I'd like to see what Mark Payne Enterprises has to hide.'

'What reason will you give?'

'His vehicle was involved in murder, with or without his consent.'

Hughes paused. 'Oh, one other thing, Forensics have updated their results on the woman in the flat. Although cocaine was not found on the premises, she was an addict.'

'Right, I'll add suspicion of handling drugs to my application. I thought once the Dutchman and his sister were banged away our drug problem was over.'

'It seems not. Don't forget to include any safes on the premises in your request.'

*

The last notes of *Barwick Green* brought another episode of the radio programme to an end. Mary changed the station and sang along to, *I just called to say I love you.*

'I didn't know you could sing,' Joseph said. 'You should do it more often.' He put a tray onto the coffee table. 'Tea and biscuits. See, I told you I can cook.' Slumping into the settee he put his arm around her. 'Shame you can't stay the night, but I understand.'

'I wish he'd see our marriage is finished. I'm beginning to see another side of him.'

'What do you mean? Is he tight with money?'

'No, he's not mean, but he can be aggressive.'

'Why don't I show you a few things? Nothing lethal, just a few techniques to boost your confidence.'

Mary smiled and cuddled closer. 'Thanks.'

'Well, it makes sense,' he said. 'I can't be there all the time.'

'I know. And self-defence may come in handy tomorrow.'

'At Payne's place, you mean?' Joseph frowned.

'Yes. If he's connected to these murders, he could be a handful.'

'Don't worry, I'll be taking a friend with us.'

'Oh? Since when have we taken civilians to execute warrants? Who is he?'

Joseph grinned. 'I can't tell you. What you don't know can't be taken down and used as evidence. Hmm, now I've mentioned taking things down, why don't we –'

'You're unbelievable. At least Graham bought me dinner.' She unbuttoned her blouse. 'But you're right, why don't we?'

*

A milkman drove down the road, pausing at intervals to collect empty bottles and deliver full ones. His electric float did little to disturb the silence of early morning.

Opposite Joseph's car a young boy struggled to deliver the morning papers. The heavy satchel full of doom and gloom threatened to pull him over at any moment.

Joseph eased himself from the Rover and joined Mary on the pavement. 'Nice to see we're not the only ones up at this time of day,' he said, pointing. 'By the way, what did your husband say when you got home last night?'

'Nothing. He was asleep. He was still snoring when I left, I could hear him through the wall. The neighbours are bound to complain if he keeps it up.'

'And Payne will be complaining too when the Section 8 warrant comes through. Violating his right to privacy and all that shit. But first things first, let's see if Forensics missed anything in the prostitute's flat.'

Mary pinched her nose as she followed Joseph up to the second floor. People and dogs had left their marks. Concrete steps exuded the stench of urine. 'Not exactly high class,' she said. 'Easy to see why we have problems with kids from around here.'

Joseph took a key from his pocket. 'This is our last chance. I don't think the court will allow us to deny the landlord access to his property much longer.' Opening the door of the flat he picked up letters littering the narrow hallway and shuffled them. 'Can't see anything interesting,' he said, handing them to Mary. 'Double check, then drop them back where they were.'

Objects in the bedroom bore traces of powder. Numbered pieces of paper marked areas which had justified photographs being taken.

'All looks pretty thorough,' Mary said.

Joseph used a handkerchief to open the bedside cupboard drawer and the door beneath. 'I want to check,' he said in response to the look she was giving him. 'You never know. There could be the odd fiver tucked away, the forensic boys did find cash in here.' His fingernails rasped on wood as his hand delved deeper. 'Aha, there is something jammed between this shelf and the back.' Dropping to his knees, he put both hands in. 'I give up. I can't get a grip. You try, you've got longer nails.'

'Oh, they're okay now are they, after you moaning about them last night?' She bent her fingers and held them towards him. 'Anyone would think I drew blood. Come out of the way. Let me see what you've found.' Bending down she felt inside the cupboard. 'You're right. There is something.'

Joseph smoothed the creases from the remains of a delivery note. 'Are you sure the rest of it's not there?'

'Positive. Anyway, what's it got to do with our murder enquiry?'

'Not sure it has. But how did an invoice for aquarium filters and heaters, dated eight months ago, end up in here?'

Mary shook her head. 'This is becoming a paper chase,' she said. 'First a piece of a business card, and now this. Do you think they're connected?'

'They could be. After all, the only person in this area who would buy items like this in these quantities is Mark Payne. Let's go talk to him and search his premises.'

'With all due respect, Joe, we can't prove we found this here. If Scene of Crime had discovered it –'

'I expect they did, probably forgot to log it in. I'll have a word with them when we get back to the station.'

'You can't do that.'

'Why? I've told you before, actions get results.' Staring across the room at a picture on the wall, he shook his head. 'Look at that, it's pissed. I never understood why they called it the *Green Lady*. In my book her face is blue.' Grasping the sides of the frame he straightened it. 'Sorry. Army training. Can't bear things looking cock-eyed. What the hell?' He removed the print and pushed the tip of a finger through it. 'Somebody's given her a proper nostril.'

Mary frowned. 'And there's a hole in the wall. Do you think the victim hid her money in there?'

Joseph put the picture to his face and looked through the orifice. 'No. My guess is, it was to hold a camera. And, no pun intended, it faces the bed.'

'Pornographic movies? Can't be, they always have someone to do the filming.'

'I hope you're not speaking from experience.' He moved aside to avoid the jab from her extended fingers. 'Now, now. I'm only kidding.'

'It's you who seems to know about hidden cameras. Perhaps –'

'You're right, but not always to film heterosexuals doing push-ups.' Joseph grinned. 'Best not to ask.'

Chapter 14

September 1986

Mary peered through the wrought iron gates. 'No sign of any motorbike. But look at the Jag parked at the end of the yard. I don't think a car like that belongs to a member of staff.'

'Good. That must mean Payne's in his office.' Joseph put a hand beneath his jacket. 'Time to spoil his day.'

Julie put her magazine down. 'Back again? You're wasting your time, he's not here.'

'Are you sure? His car's out there.' Joseph looked towards the yard.

Picking up the phone she turned her head away. The door behind her opened.

'Come through.'

'Good morning, sir.' Joseph held out the warrant. 'We're here to carry out a search of these premises.'

Mark Payne lit a cigar and blew smoke towards Mary. 'Why?'

'There are things I'd like answers to.'

'Such as?'

'Murder. Drug dealing. Running prostitutes.'

Mark slapped a hand to his forehead. 'You had me worried for a minute. I thought you'd called about my parking tickets.'

'Very funny. Now, open your safe.'

'Wish I could oblige.' He held his hands out, palms up.

'Are you are refusing to allow me to check your safe?'

'No. But unless you two detectives can find my keys, we're both out of luck. I've been looking everywhere for them. Anything else I can help you with?'

'Your Austin Maestro van, tell me –'

'Stolen. I've already told you. Some thieving sod nicked it from the yard.'

'So you say. A stolen vehicle, lost keys, all very convenient.'

'Are you calling me a liar?' Mark stubbed out his cigar.

'Not yet. If you'd step aside, my colleague will check your filing cabinet while I search your desk.'

'You can't.'

'We can. I've got a search warrant.'

'You can't, because the keys to the cabinet and my desk are on the same ring as the one to the safe. Understand?'

'Yes, I understand and I'm not taking any more of your crap. I can arrest you for –'

'Go ahead. My solicitor will make mincemeat of you.'

Mary placed a restraining hand on Joseph's arm. 'Leave it, sir. I'm sure this gentleman's keys will turn up.' She glared at Mark.

Joseph eased Mary's fingers from his sleeve.

'Fine. Let's take a look at the out buildings. They can't all be locked.'

Mark waved a hand towards the racks of aquariums. 'There you are. Search away.' He grinned. 'I expect you'll be calling in the underwater search team next.'

Joseph ignored him. 'Start at the far side,' he said to Mary. 'Meet me in the middle.'

Mark turned and motioned to a man leaning against a wall across the yard.

As Joseph lifted lids off of some of the tanks, the grating sound of the sliding door attracted his attention. Racing towards the warehouse entrance he glimpsed a van driving past as Mark Payne slid the door along its track.

'Stop that van!' Joseph yelled.

The two men collided as Joseph lunged for the handle.

'Nobody's to leave these premises until we've completed our search,' he yelled.

'You didn't say that.' Mark sneered. 'Besides, my man will be back soon.'

'I don't know what you're up to, but trust me, I'll find out.'

'Am I stopping you? Where would you like to look next? How about where I stash the drugs? Or perhaps you'd like to speak to the prossies in my brothel?'

'You think you're smart, don't you? Well, let me tell you, I've had men who thought they were cleverer than you banged away. Your turn will come.'

'If you say so. Have you finished in here? There's another building at the end of the yard.'

Mary's cough echoed in the vast warehouse. Mark Payne pointed to polystyrene boxes stacked around the walls. 'Empty. Waiting for collection,' he said. 'You're welcome to check. If you find any dead fish, you can take them home for your cat.'

'Check over there,' Joseph said. 'Open a few at random. Take some from the bottom of the stacks. I'll do the same this side.'

Mark's eyes narrowed. 'Good luck. I'll be in my office when you've finished.'

Joseph ran a hand across his brow. 'Anything?' he asked. 'We must have been at it for half an hour.'

'Nothing. It all looks legitimate.'

'There's more going on than meets the eye, I'm sure of that,' he said, offering her his handkerchief. 'Here, dry your hands. We're done in here.'

His diamond ring sparkled as Mark Payne swung the key-ring round his finger. 'Look what I found,' he said. 'They were in my other coat.'

'What a surprise,' Joseph said, turning to Mary. 'While I check the safe, search the filing cabinet.'

'Yes, then get off these premises. You've wasted enough of my time.'

'One more thing. Last time we were here there was a man on a motorbike. Who was he?'

'How am I expected to remember everyone who comes in here?' He pointed to the bow-fronted aquarium on an ornate stand. 'This tank and the fish are mine. Everything else is for sale to the trade. He may have been a customer.'

'What do you think?' Mary said, starting the Rover. 'The whole place was as clean as a whistle.'

'You're telling me. His safe was as empty as my wallet.'

'Could we be wrong?'

'We could, but while we were searching the first warehouse a van drove off. It's possible it took anything incriminating. And it's my bet those keys weren't missing.'

'I agree.' Mary put the car into gear. 'Now what?'

'When we get back, I'll talk to Hughes. See if I can arrange for a constable to keep an eye on this place, make notes of vehicles coming and going.'

'Exactly what I was about to suggest. Shall we go back to the station?'

'Yes, but stop off at my place on the way.'

As the Rover pulled up, Joseph opened the door and got out. 'I won't be long.'

'Okay. I'll have another go at my crossword.'

In his bedroom, Joseph took off his jacket and removed the canvas shoulder holster. Opening the wardrobe door, he pushed down on the bottom shelf. With an audible click the catch released its grip. Removing the false floor, he placed the holstered gun back into the recess.

Mary smiled as Joseph climbed into the car. 'I meant to ask, your friend who was supposed to be coming with us today,' she said. 'Did he change his mind?'

'Something like that. Do you fancy going for a drink tonight?'

Mary turned away. 'I can't. Graham talked me into watching a Rambo video he's hired. I only agreed to keep the peace, it's not my type of film.'

'Fair enough.'

'He still believes he can make things right between us.'

'And can he?'

'No.'

'Good. Enjoy your film, I'll see you in the morning.'

'You won't. I'm not on duty tomorrow, remember?'

'I do now. Officially I'm off as well, but I decided to put in a few extra hours. I want to go over our case files. Not sure if it'll do any good, but you never know.'

Chapter 15

September 1986

Mary peered into the mirror. Pushing her hair up, she used a clip to fasten it into place. 'I know you prefer my hair down, so . . .' Using a wipe, she removed the last of her make-up. 'There . . . Nothing to encourage you tonight.'

'Come on,' Graham called from the lounge. 'What are you doing in there? It's only a video, you don't have to get all dolled up.'

Closing the bathroom door behind her she moved across to the lounge. He smiled. 'You look nice. I like the perfume.'

'It's soap. Imperial Leather.'

'Smells nice anyway. Oh, and by the way, I bought chocolates, they're your favourites.'

'I'm surprised you still remember.'

'But I always got you chocolates when we were courting.'

'Start the film, let's get this over.'

He reached down beside the settee and produced a bottle. 'Asti,' he said. 'It's as good as champagne. The corner shop doesn't stock much in the way of booze.'

'Hmm, you're full of surprises tonight.'

'And there's more to come, sweetheart.' He crossed to the recorder and pushed a switch, then sat beside her. 'You'll enjoy this.'

She edged away, tense at this uninvited invasion of her personal space.

He fast-forwarded the trailers. 'I don't know why they put all this rubbish on,' he said. 'I only want to watch the film.'

Mary gave up wrestling with the cellophane and gave the chocolates back him. The opening music jerked her attention towards the television. 'This isn't Rambo,' she said, pointing. 'It's Out of Africa.'

He grinned and raised his glass. 'I know. I thought I'd surprise you. Cheers.'

Watching the steam train crossing the African veldt she said, 'I love Meryl Streep. But I'm not keen on Robert Redford, although I've heard he's good in this.'

He placed the open box of chocolates on her lap. 'I reckon Stallone would have played it better.'

She turned and glared.

'Forget it.' He grinned. 'It was a joke.'

Mary gathered up the wine bottle and chocolate box and put them in the swing-bin.

Graham lit the gas cooker. 'What would you like for breakfast, sweetheart? Toast and jam, or the full monty?'

'Toast. And we're not sweethearts.'

'We could be,' he said, sliding a frying-pan onto the flames.

'I told you, I'm seeing somebody else.'

'Tell him to sod off. You're my wife don't forget.'

'It wasn't me who forgot. One flash of some tart's knickers and you developed amnesia.'

'It was a mistake. I've said I'm sorry and –'

'What good's sorry?'

He put his arm around her and pulled her close. 'Give me a chance,' he whispered into her ear. 'We can make it work, trust me.'

'I did. That's where I went wrong.' She pushed him away. 'Your bacon's burning.'

'Shit. Never mind, I like it like this.' Tipping the contents of the pan onto a plate he carried it to the table. 'I was thinking, why –'

'Thinking? Bit early, isn't it?'

'I was about to say, why don't we spend the day together? I'll take you somewhere nice, have a pub lunch perhaps, show you the old magic is still there.'

She dropped two slices into the toaster. 'You don't give up. I give you that.'

'So . . . will you come?'

'If it will settle this once and for all, yes. But you're wasting your time.'

He grinned. 'Want to bet? It was a nice evening, wasn't it? I chose a film I knew you'd enjoy, bought your favourite chocolates, what else –'

'Tried to get me drunk.'

'Which didn't work, but it was worth a try.'

'Maybe, but once bitten, twice shy.'

*

Mary shielded her eyes against the glare as she stared up into the cloudless sky. High above, an invisible bird taunted her with its melodic song.

Graham's arm wrapping around her waist spoilt the moment. 'Lovely, isn't it, I've always been keen on skylarks.'

She freed herself from his grasp. 'And lots of other larks too. It's why you're in this mess.'

A swan swooped low, wings extended, legs thrust forward. Mary turned to watch as it ploughed a furrow through the surface of the water. Ducks scattered towards the safety of the river bank.

Graham kicked a stone from the footpath towards the swan. 'I thought the idea was to enjoy ourselves, not keep harping on about the past. How many more times do I have to say I'm sorry?'

'Sorry is just a word. And so is bullshit.' She walked ahead of him, along the path by the river. The reflections of moored motor cruisers distorted as other craft passed. Sunlight danced and sparkled, adding daytime stars to the surface of the water. Thatched cottages, their gardens kissing the water's edge, provided inspiration to artists dotted along the river bank.

'This isn't working, is it,' he said, catching up with her. 'I thought this would be what you wanted. It's why I borrowed my mate's car. Look, there's supposed to be a nice pub near here. How about at least having lunch?'

Mary looked at her watch. 'Okay, but I'll pay my for my own.'

Mary pushed her plate aside. 'I enjoyed that . . . and the cider's nice.'

Graham tilted his head back and drained his pint. 'We should do this again.'

'I don't think so.'

'Why? We could have lots of days like this.'

Mary placed her glass on the table. 'How many more times do I have to say this? I'm seeing someone.'

'Tell him you're going to give our marriage another chance.'

She frowned. 'But I'm not. I want a divorce.'

'What's he like, this knight in shining armour? What's he got I haven't?'

'A steady job for a start. You'd get on well with him. He served in the army and –'

'Where does he work? What does he do?'

'Let's say if Batman wanted to retire, Joe would put in for the job.'

'Joe, is it? At least I'm getting somewhere.'

'Let's leave it, shall we? Why don't we change the subject?'

Laying in the shade of a tree, Mary turned towards Graham. 'I hate saying it, but this has been a nice day.'

'Pity it wasn't nice enough to get you to change your mind. I love you. I'll find myself a job. Prove I'm as good as lover boy.' He gripped her arm. 'I won't give up without a fight.'

'Ouch. Let go, you're hurting me.'

'Sorry, sweetheart.'

Mary followed Graham as they walked back to the car, the silence between them contrasting with laughter from passengers of boats on the river.

Chapter 16

September 1986

DCI Hughes ran a pencil down the sheet of paper.

Exploring his teeth with the tip of his tongue, Joseph waited.

Hughes pushed the file across the desk. 'I thought you'd like to see this,' he said. 'A van exceeding the speed limit in a built-up area.'

Joseph frowned as he reached out. 'A traffic offence, sir? That's not my department.'

'I appreciate that, but I want you to speak to the driver.'

Joseph's eyes widened as he read. 'I knew it. The bastard pulled a fast one. Bags of money. Traces of cocaine? Now we've got him.' He jabbed at the page. 'And to top it all, a garden spade.'

The female officer greeted Joseph. 'Good morning, sir. I've been assigned to you for the interview.'

'Morning, Joan. Yes, I know, I asked for you.'

The colour rose in the young officer's cheeks. 'Thank you, sir.'

'Do you know who the solicitor is?'

'No, sir.'

'Okay, let's find out.'

Joseph held the door open for Joan to enter the interview room. A man wearing a dark grey suit got to his feet. 'Good morning,' he said, extending a hand.

Joseph ignored the gesture. 'Has he admitted his guilt? Can we wrap this up?'

'I am here to listen to your disclosure. My client is innocent of all charges brought against him.'

Joseph checked Joan was taking shorthand notes before continuing. 'Is he? Police officers don't make a habit of charging people without good reason.'

'Surely you are not proceeding against him for travelling a fraction too fast?'

'Sixty miles an hour in a residential area?'

'Do you have witnesses to this incident?'

'Yes.'

'In which case I may be prepared to advise my client to offer a guilty plea. I take it he is free to go?'

'No, he isn't. You have spoken to him, I presume.'

'Naturally.'

'Then let's move on to the other charges. How does he explain evidence of a controlled substance? And a quantity of cash?'

'He would deny all knowledge of any items being in the vehicle at the time of his arrest.'

Joseph got up from the table. 'I suggest you speak with your client in private, as is your right. Then I shall proceed with the charges.'

Joseph switched on the tape recorder. 'September the fifteenth, 1986, eleven a.m. Interview with Mr Samuel Beckworth in the presence of his solicitor, Mr Twyford, and WPC Miller.' He cleared his throat. 'Mr Samuel Beckworth, I am obliged to issue this caution. You have a right to remain silent. Whatever you say may be used against you in a criminal case in court. If you don't mention something now, which you mention later, a court may ask why you didn't mention it at the first opportunity. Do you understand?'

'I don't have to say anything.'

Twyford nudged his client.

'I mean, no comment.' Beckworth shifted position in his chair.

Joseph looked surprised. 'I haven't asked you anything yet.'

'No comment.'

'Do you deny driving in excess of the speed limit and in a reckless manner on the fourteenth of September?'

'No comment.'

'How do you explain traces of a controlled substance along with a large envelope containing banknotes, both of which were found in the van you were driving at the time of your arrest?'

'I don't know.'

Twyford leaned towards Beckworth and whispered into his ear.

Beckworth mumbled. 'I mean, no comment.'

'Do you deny the charges?'

'No comment.'

'Why don't you help yourself? Tell us who put the drugs in the van.'

'No.'

Twyford glared at him.

'I mean, no comment.'

'Where did the money come from?'

'No comment.'

Ten minutes later Joseph turned off the tape recorder.

Twyford put his hands together as if offering up a prayer. 'As you are not charging my client, I presume he is free to leave.'

'He hasn't been in custody for twenty-four hours yet. I intend to hold him while further enquiries are made.'

'Then I shall return when the statutory time has elapsed.'

Joseph approached at the officer behind the desk. 'Morning, George, I'd like to speak to the prisoner.'

'Certainly.' He winked. 'After I open his cell, I'll pop down the canteen for a cuppa.'

The cell door slammed. A key turned in the lock.

Beckworth looked up from the bed. 'What do you want?'

Joseph thrust both hands into his trouser pockets. 'Sam, listen to me. Somebody's setting you up. Give me a name and you'll be back on the streets in no time.'

Beckworth stood up, crossed to the toilet bowl in the corner, cleared his throat and spat. 'I don't have to tell you anything. Twyford told me.'

'And he also left you in here. Give me a name.'

'Why? You lot can't prove a thing, otherwise you'd have charged me.'

'You will be, all in good time.'

'Piss off.'

Joseph grasped Beckworth's shirt. 'Watch yourself. The walls in these cells are harder than your head.'

'Let go or you'll be sorry. I used to box for a living.'

'Then let's see how good you are,' Joseph said through clenched teeth.

Beckworth gasped and folded at the waist as Joseph's punch to the solar plexus caught him off guard. He took a punch to the chin and his head snapped back striking the wall with a sickening thud. Raising his fists in line with Marquess of Queensberry rules did little to ward off the attack.

Joseph pounded his fists against Beckworth's ribs. 'Tell me who you are protecting.'

His opponent pushed him away and sucked air. 'Piss . . . Stop, I've had enough.'

Joseph stood back. 'Give me a name.'

'I can't. He'll kill me.'

'Who? Mark Payne?'

Beckworth turned as he heard the sound of the cell door being opened.

'Never heard of him,' Beckworth sneered.

The desk sergeant entered. 'Sorry, Hughes came into the canteen.' He held up both hands. 'It's okay, he didn't see me. But I'd better get back.'

'Okay. By the way, you didn't tell me our friend here had a fall.'

George grinned. 'I'll make sure it's in the book. I've said before, these wet floors are an accident just waiting to happen.'

Hughes looked up. 'Come in.' Opening a drawer, he secreted a glossy magazine.

'Good afternoon, sir. Following my interview with Samuel Beckworth I'd like to –'

'Let me stop you there. His solicitor has arranged bail. I know it's frustrating, but Beckworth denies all knowledge. Without proof to the contrary, you can't charge him.'

'He's protecting somebody. I know he is. Can't we act with what we've got?'

'His solicitor doesn't think so. And I agree. I doubt we would get a conviction.'

Joseph gritted his teeth. 'So, he goes free. It makes me sick.'

'It's the law. Every man is innocent until proved guilty.'

'But sometimes –'

'That's all. Go back to your duties.'

As he turned towards the door, Joseph paused. 'The spade in his car, sir, did Forensics find anything?'

'Yes, Beckworth's prints are on it, why?'

'I would like to request a further examination. For soil.'

'You think he may have cached drugs somewhere?'

'Could be. May I proceed with this line of enquiry, sir?'

'Yes. But you're clutching at straws.'

*

Joseph pushed his chair back as Mary entered his office. 'Good morning. Did you enjoy your day off?' He waved towards another chair. 'I missed you.'

'It was okay. He took me for a pub lunch. Oh, and I'm sorry, I let your name slip.'

'Does it matter? He was bound to find out sooner or later.'

'I suppose so. Anyway, anything else exciting?'

'Yes. You remember the van in Payne's yard? It was stopped for speeding.'

'Wow. How exciting. I bet –'

'Don't be sarcastic. The vehicle contained a large amount of money in an envelope behind the driver's seat and traces of cocaine.'

'So, you were right. When do we arrest Payne?'

'We can't. Not yet. The driver's out on bail. We couldn't prove a thing.'

'But you said he had the stuff in his car.'

'He did. And a spade. But he denies all knowledge. We need to prove a connection between him and Payne.'

*

Beckworth lifted a pint glass. 'Cheers. What did you say?'

Mark Payne glanced around the bar. 'Keep your voice down. I said, I take it you're okay to move to Spain?'

'I don't mind, but what about all my stuff?'

'No problem. I'll have it sent out. Anything you think you won't want, burn.'

'And I still get my wages?'

'Yes. I'll arrange a bank account.'

'Sounds good. A place in the sun with nothing to do all day.'

'Got it in one. But when I'm ready you'll be working for me again.'

Chapter 17

September 1986

'Come in.' Joseph looked at the door.

'Excuse me, sir, Forensics asked me to bring you this.' The desk sergeant held out an envelope. 'They caught me as I was passing.'

'Thanks, George.'

'What have they come up with?' Mary asked.

'Hmmm. There's a bit about the soil found on the spade, acidity and such, but it seems *Ophrys Apifera* is the main point of interest.'

'And it may well be, if I knew what it was.' Mary held out a hand. 'Have you finished reading?'

'Yes. I think we need to speak to Kimberley, it's her signature.'

The fresh-faced laboratory technician, teasing the flame of a Bunsen burner with a test tube, ignored Joseph and Mary. The end of the tube glowed red; the contents changed colour. 'Sorry,' she said. 'But once I start, I have to finish.'

'Hello, Kimberley,' Mary said, handing her the report. 'Nice to see someone enjoys their work.'

The technician glanced at the typewritten sheet. 'Yes, I love it. Sir Bernard Spilsbury has always been my hero. He was a brilliant pathologist, shame he killed himself.'

'Napoleon was one of mine,' Joseph said. 'Now, about this *Apifera* at the bottom of the page. What is it, and why underline it?'

Her eyes widened. 'The Bee Orchid. You don't know?'

'It may come as a complete surprise to you, but we don't.' Joseph frowned. 'What's so special about an orchid?'

'Our Bee Orchid in Norfolk is unique. I found a crushed sepal in the soil on the spade.' Her cheeks flushed. 'I get so angry when people destroy flowers. This one's becoming rare, which should help establish where the sepal came from.'

'Does that mean you can tell us where this flower grew?' Mary said.

'Possibly. I wanted to do a thesis on wild flowers at university, but it didn't fit my course. Now it's a hobby of mine. I know a few colonies around here.'

'Can you show us on a map?' Joseph asked. 'It's important we find this site.'

'Yes, but why don't I come with you? I can't guarantee finding where this *actual* orchid grew.' She smiled. 'They don't have fingerprints and I dare say there are clusters I haven't found yet.'

'Worth a try, sir,' Mary said.

'Definitely. I'll have a word with Old . . . your boss, and see if he can spare you.'

'Nice car,' Kimberley said, pushing her palm down on the leather seat.

'Why did a crushed flower upset you?' Mary asked. 'You said they were becoming scarce but –'

'You don't understand. The plant takes up to eight years to come into flower and then some idiot flattened it with a shovel.'

Joseph looked down at the map resting on his knees. 'Next left. Park where you can, then it's up to our expert.'

Joseph opened the car door for Kimberley. 'Right. Lead on, you're in charge.'

'It's quite a walk to the site,' she said, looking up the hill.

'Up there?'

'Yes. About half a mile.'

'Stay in the car,' Joseph said to Mary. 'This isn't the place.'

Kimberley looked puzzled. 'How do you know? We aren't anywhere near the plants.'

'Trust me. Get back in, we need to drive to the next area.'

The Rover pulled off the road onto a patch of shingle. A footpath sign pointed towards a church spire, visible on the horizon.

'This looks better,' Joseph said. 'At least the ground's flat.'

Kimberley bent and touched the ground. 'It's the soil which is important, and the weather. The rain this year has helped a lot.'

Joseph waited for Mary to lock the car. 'Which way, Kimberley?'

'Not far, over there, behind those Buddleia bushes.'

'Hidden from the path. That figures.'

Kimberley pulled a face. 'I don't understand.'

'Do you think we should all go?' Mary said. 'If this is a crime scene –'

'No. You and Kimberley wait here. I'm sure I can find a few flowers.'

'But I'd like to see the damage,' Kimberley protested.

'Please, just trust me.'

Turning left Joseph skirted the bushes. Clumps of soil littered the grass. 'Someone's been busy,' he said out loud. Stepping back, he waved Mary towards him. 'Wells, come here!' Joseph yelled. 'Kimberley, you wait there, stay on the path.'

'Sounds as though he's found something. Best do as he says. I won't be a minute,' Mary said.

'Why are you interested in orchids?' Kimberley asked.

Mary hesitated. 'We're not, but the spade is part of an investigation. Somebody may have buried drugs.'

'What did you find?' Mary asked, sounding a little out of breath.

'Not what I expected. Someone's been digging, but judging by the shape and size of the disturbed area I'd say it's more likely to be a grave rather than an attempt to hide drugs,' Joseph said. 'Make sure Kimberley stays where she is. These heel prints need protecting. Better call the station. And make sure the public don't enter this area.'

'Kimberley will be upset about her precious flowers,' Mary said.

'Tell her there's no harm done. The one on the spade must have been unlucky.'

Mary hurried down the path. 'Kimberley, don't let anyone near those bushes. This is could be a murder case now. We have to keep the public away.'

'Murder?' She put a hand to her mouth and stared down at her feet. 'At least I've proved my younger brother wrong. He always says plants aren't as interesting as tropical fish.'

Chapter 18

September 1986

Fighting to stay in control of the day, the sun gave clouds a golden outline. Mary made a pretence of studying them, anything to help ignore the tent and the human remains inside.

Joseph held out a circular tin. 'Here, use this Vaporub, put it under your nose. Helps clear the sinuses at the same time.'

'Thanks.' She dabbed the pungent jelly above her top lip. 'Wow, it's strong,' she said, dabbing her eyes with a tissue.

'Better than smelling our friend over there. Think what it's like for the Forensic boys.'

'No thank you. We've done our bit. Can't we leave them to it?'

'Yes. There's nothing more we can do here. Fancy something to eat? My stomach's rumbling.'

'Urghh. No, I don't. How can you even think of food at a time like this?'

'Okay, please yourself, I'll drop you off at your place. Looks like I'll be dining alone again tonight.'

*

Joseph handed Mary the autopsy report. 'As you'll see,' he said, 'the victim could be our mystery bike rider, one of the robbers at the bookmakers. Few people have eyes like this. Seems Samuel Beckworth has a lot more questions to answer. The spade links him to the burial.'

'Are we getting an arrest warrant?' Mary asked.

'No need. We've got enough evidence, let's pick him up.'

'Where?'

'First stop, Mark Payne's place. If he's not there, we'll try his home address.'

'After we've alerted Payne? He'll contact Beckworth.'

'He can try. Stop off at my house, there's something I need.'

*

Joseph slid the Ballester-Molina into its shoulder holster and fastened his jacket. 'This could cost me my job, but, *needs must when the devil drives* as they say.'

Sitting in the Rover, Mary used a pen to scratch her chin. 'Who makes these crosswords up? Oppressively strict? Thirteen letters.' She stared at the puzzle. 'Got it. *Authoritarian.* Right, that helps with fourteen across.'

The car door opened.

'Okay, let's go,' Joseph said. 'Time to arrest Beckworth. Hmmm, I wonder if I could persuade him to admit killing one of those prostitutes? Or even both of them. It would get Hughes off my back for a while, at least until the confession's withdrawn.' He grinned. 'Don't worry, I'm only kidding.'

'Good. I'm never sure with you sometimes.' She hesitated. 'I meant to ask. How did you know the first site Kimberley took us to was wrong?'

'If you wanted to bury something, would you lug it up a bloody great hill?'

*

Joseph held up an internal memo on the over-use of paper-clips in all departments. 'Warrant to search these premises,' he said. 'Tell your boss we'd like to speak to him.'

The door behind Julie opened. Mark Payne beckoned to the detectives. 'Now what do you want? Not more unpaid parking tickets I hope.'

Joseph followed Payne into his office, Mary close on his heels. Julie resumed filing her nails.

'We're here to speak to one of your employees, a Mr Samuel Beckworth,' Joseph said. 'He was arrested for a traffic violation but we have reason to believe he may have committed further offences.'

Payne gave a mock groan. 'It is, isn't it, more bloody parking tickets.'

Joseph ignored the theatricals. 'I must warn you, if you obstruct us in our enquiries, I shall arrest you.'

'Hold your horses. I'm not obstructing anyone. I'm a legitimate businessman and I've got connections.'

'I know. You're connected to a suspect in a murder case.'

Payne licked his lips. 'I don't know what you're talking about. And I've never employed anyone by the name of Beckworth.'

'I think you have. Let's take a look at your employee's records.'

Payne paused. Opening a drawer in his desk, he reached inside. 'Where's your warrant? I haven't seen it yet.'

Joseph moved around the desk and slammed the drawer shut, trapping Payne's hand.

'Aaagh! What are you doing, you stupid bastard!'

'Jogging your memory. Now, if you want your fingers back, tell me where he is.' Joseph placed his free hand on the back of Payne's neck and pushed. Mary winced at the sound of bone hitting wood.

Joseph jerked him upright. Blood trickled from Payne's nostrils. Using a knee, Joseph applied more pressure to the drawer.

'Enough! He's not here. I sacked him.'

'Then tell me where we can find the bugger.'

'I don't know.'

'Liar.' Joseph smashed Payne's forehead onto the solid mahogany desk. 'Where – does – he live?'

Julie attempted to open the door. Mary used her backside to slam it shut. The receptionist's knowledge of profanity impressed her.

'Go to hell.' Payne spat blood. 'Your job's on the line for this. I only need to make a phone –' The sentence died as his face attempted to smash through the desk top.

'Enough, sir.' Mary leaned against the door as fists pummelled the other side. 'We should go.'

'Not without an address. I've got all day,' he said, applying more pressure to the trapped fingers. 'Let me ask again. Where does Beckworth live?'

'Twenty-eight, Washerwoman's Row. Now let me go.'

'There, see, easy wasn't it.'

'Fuck you. I'll report this.'

'Feel free. Lack of witnesses may be a problem, but go ahead.'

'Fuck off. And take that bitch with you.' He pinched his nose. Blood dripped from his chin onto his shirt.

'I will. And you're coming with us.'

'Do what? Are you arresting me?'

'Not yet.' Joseph smiled as he watched Payne wrap bruised and bloody fingers in a handkerchief.

'You can't make me go anywhere. I know my rights.'

Joseph turned his back to Mary and opened his jacket, pulling it aside. 'Of course, you do, sir. Now, shall we go?'

Mark's face paled.

*

Washerwoman's Row could have supplied Charles Dickens with a suitable backdrop for another novel. Colourful ivy lazily climbed painted walls. Leaded windows blinked in the sunlight. A black cat lay draped on a windowsill, soaking up the warmth. Flowers dipped their heads in time to the soft breeze. A cobbled road threaded its way between houses.

The Rover shuddered in protest on a surface laid a century or more ago for the use of pedestrians and horses. 'Slow down, this road's rattling my teeth.' Joseph put a hand to his jaw.

Mary changed gear. 'Yes, sir.'

Mark Payne stared down at the handcuffs. 'You'll pay for this.'

'Make sure it's not you who does the paying when Beckworth answers our questions.' Joseph reached forward and touched Mary's shoulder. 'Park where you can, I'll walk from here.'

'Yes, sir.'

'I'm not walking anywhere, *sir*.' Payne leered at Joseph. 'And you can't make me.'

'You'd lose your money if you were to place that bet. Sit here and behave. When I've interviewed your employee, we'll all go down to the station.'

'Will we? We'll see.'

Joseph stared through the window. The room was empty. Walls stripped back to the plaster. Floorboards scrubbed clean. Light fittings and switches removed. He didn't need his detective training to tell him the occupant was not at home. The curtains of the adjoining property twitched. Joseph crossed the communal garden and knocked.

A woman in the late autumn of life opened the door.

'Good morning, madam,' Joseph said. 'Sorry to disturb you. I'd like to speak to your neighbour. Do you know where he is?'

'Good morning to you too, young man. He's moved up to Scotland, gone to live with his brother.'

'When was this?'

'Let me see…Monday? No, Tuesday, that's right, Tuesday. I remember because I had kippers for tea.'

'It looks like he took everything, including the wallpaper.'

'Bless you, no, he didn't do it. A big lorry came. The men were very nice. I made tea for them.'

'Did these men tell you what they were doing?'

'They said the new owner wanted it done up. Waste of money if you ask me.'

'Did they take the furniture away?'

'Most of it, yes. I asked if I could have the kitchen table. They said no, but they were very nice about it.'

'Did your neighbour tell you where his brother lived?'

'I never asked.'

Joseph looked back at the empty property. 'I see. Well thanks for your help. Goodbye.'

The woman partially closed the front door and pushed her face into the gap. 'Do you think you could ask the new people not to light bonfires? The smuts get all over my washing.'

At the rear of the property the garden gate hung drunkenly from a solitary hinge. Joseph squeezed through the gap.

Charred wood lay scattered on the scorched grass.

Peering through the downstairs window he could see the *nice* men had been thorough with this room too.

The back door put up token resistance, but yielded to Joseph's shoulder. Inside, the smell of damp clung to the walls and floors. Electrical wires protruded from power sockets and holes in the ceiling.

Joseph stood beside the open window of the Rover. Mary sensed something was wrong.

Payne held up his wrists. 'Take these off, then drive me back to my office. I've got calls to make.'

'We can't hold him. I'll explain in a minute,' Joseph said. Opening the rear door, he reached inside and released the handcuffs. 'Right, out you get. You're free to go.'

'Good. Now take me back to my office.'

'Bollocks. Get out.' Joseph grasped Payne's jacket and pulled. 'The walk will do you good.'

'You bastard. I'll get you for this.'

Mary and Joseph watched Payne walk away.

'He's not a happy bunny,' Mary said. 'Now, where's Beckworth?'

'His neighbour told me he's moved to Scotland. But not only isn't he here, neither is anything else. It looks like a biblical plague of locusts paid a visit. The place has been stripped bare.'

'Somebody's broken in?'

'Even thieves don't take the paper off the walls. I doubt if Misery Guts and his team will find a thing.'

'Seems extreme.'

'I agree, but somebody wanted to erase all traces of our man ever living there. A lot of stuff has been burned.'

*

Hughes paced back and forth behind his desk. 'Are you telling me there's been another murder? What is going on?'

Joseph shifted his weight from one foot to the other. 'There's only three –'

'But you said your suspect in the last case has disappeared in unusual circumstances.'

'Yes, but without a body we have to assume Beckworth has relocated, as his neighbour stated. I suspect he's responsible for killing one of the men who robbed the bookmakers. We just need to prove it.'

'And his motive?' Hughes' eyebrows arched up to nudge the furrows on his forehead.

'I think he was acting under orders, sir. I also think the dead prostitutes and the victim we found are connected.'

'Do you have anything to support this?'

'Not yet. But I believe two men can supply all the answers. Samuel Beckworth and Mark Payne.'

'It appears one of them has slipped through your net, but why haven't you arrested Payne?'

'I can't, sir. There's not enough evidence.'

Hughes tilted his head back to avoid looking at Joseph. 'I received a phone call from above. It would appear your Mr Payne has friends in high places.'

'He said as much to me, sir.'

'Unless you can prove something, I would advise extreme caution.'

'Do you mean stop the investigation?'

'Certainly not, but tread lightly. I may not be able to protect you against further complaints.'

'Thank you for the warning, sir. I'll make sure there aren't any.'

Chapter 19

September 1986

Sitting on a bench overlooking the waterway, Mary held open a crossword puzzle book, one hand clasping a pencil. Gazing into the distance she focused on the windmill, standing sentinel at the side of the river, hoping for inspiration to strike. Birds flew up from their gathering point in a tree. Black specks wheeled in the sky, performing an aerial dance based on instinctive choreography.

'Strange,' she said. 'That's what I'm stuck on. A group of starlings. What on earth's it called?'

'A *murmuration*.' Joseph turned a page of his newspaper.

'Thanks. Not much you don't know, is there.'

'No, apart from why you torture yourself doing those things. It's not as if you win prizes.'

'It keeps the grey matter ticking over.' She counted the squares. 'Eleven. You're right. Clever, I wouldn't have thought of that.'

'Lucky I'm here then. Any sandwiches left?'

'Yes.' She lifted the lid of the wicker basket. 'Here, you may as well finish them, I've had enough.'

'Okay, be a shame to waste them. Fish paste is good for you.' Taking a bite, he waved the sandwich towards her. 'Mmmm, this is the way to spend a day away from the office. Great idea of yours.'

'Graham wanted me to go to a boot fair. I told him I had to work. I'm not sure he believed me.'

'I think it's time we laid our cards on the table.' He folded his newspaper exactly in half. 'Perhaps we should get together and discuss the situation as adults.'

'I agree. What do you suggest?'

'Meet at a pub. Where does he drink?'

'The Cricketers.' She grimaced at the thought of the one and only time she had been there. 'It's where I made my first arrest as a beat officer. Definitely not my scene.'

'Okay, how about the Coxswain? They do a nice chicken-in-a-basket.'

'Trust you. Okay, I'll see what he says.'

'Let me know when it's arranged. I'll turn up and handle it with my usual diplomacy.'

'That's what I'm afraid of.'

*

Mary put her plate in the sink and turned on a tap.

'I could murder a pint,' Graham said, from behind his newspaper. 'Too much vinegar on those chips.'

'The pubs are still open. What's stopping you?'

'You're right. Why don't we nip down to the Cricketers?'

'For a start I don't want to drink with you. And on top of which, I don't like the place.'

He put his arms around her waist and pulled her close. 'Okay, what pub do you fancy? You choose. It'll be my treat.'

Mary gathered up the greasy paper. 'The Coxswain's not bad.'

'Suits me. If it's where you want to go, then fine.'

'Right, but I'm only having a couple.'

*

Outside the block of flats, Mary shook herself free from Graham's grasp. 'Blast. I can't remember if I turned the gas off. Walk on, I won't be a minute, I'll catch you up.'

'Okay, sweetheart. I'll wait here and have a ciggie.'

Mary let herself back in, and picked up the phone. 'Joe? Is that you? Are you eating? Never mind. Look, I know its short notice but he's taking me to the Coxswain. He's waiting outside – we're walking – about ten minutes. Okay, but sooner if you can.'

*

Smoke hung in the air, waiting its turn to escape whenever the door of the Coxswain opened. Customers at the bar engaged in friendly banter, most with a pint in one hand and a cigarette in the other.

Mary coughed. Graham nudged her forward. 'Grab the booth over there. It may be quieter.' He produced his wallet. 'What are you having?'

'White wine and some crisps, please. Plain if they've got them.' Taking off her light jacket she tossed it onto the bench seat and slid across.

'Do me a favour,' Mary said, when Graham returned. 'Get rid of these dirty glasses.'

'Sure, no problem. Won't be a minute.' Thrusting his fingers into them he picked up four in each hand.

Catching sight of Mary, Joseph pushed through the crowd. 'Been here long, love? Where is he?'

'Hello, Joe. Not long. He's taking the empties back.'

'How many have you had? I got here as quick as I could.'

'They weren't ours. This is my first.' She held up her glass.

Graham glared at Joseph. 'Oi! What's your game? She's my wife.'

'I know. We work together. I'm Joseph, but most people call me Joe.'

'Well, *Joe*, it's been nice to meet you, now sod off. We're having a drink and three's a crowd.'

Mary reached out and grasped Graham's jacket. 'Don't be like that.'

'Mary's right,' Joseph said. 'What are you drinking? Same again?'

'No. Bugger off.'

Mary opened her crisps. 'Take no notice. I'd like another wine, please.'

'Be right back,' Joseph said, heading towards the bar.

'What's going on?' Graham moved into the booth. 'I thought the idea was to enjoy an evening together.'

'We will. You'll like Joe when you get to know him.'

His expression changed. 'The penny's just dropped. I bet he's the new man in your life. Did you know he'd be here?'

'Let's say I'm not surprised.'

Joseph put both drinks down and sat beside Mary.

Graham took a deep breath. 'I think you'd better come outside,' he said.

'And I think you should calm down. We're all adults, let's talk this over.' He looked at Mary. 'I know she's your wife, but only until she gets a divorce. She's told me –'

Graham leaned across the table and jabbed his fingers into Joseph's arm. 'If you're scared to sort this out, man to man, sling your hook.'

'Okay. It's your funeral. Come on, let's get it over with.'

Getting to his feet Graham knocked his drink over. 'Shit.' Pulling out a handkerchief he mopped the table. 'Sorry, sweetheart, did I get you?'

Mary pressed herself back against the wall of the booth. 'No, I'm okay.'

Joseph got to his feet. 'When you've stopped playing barmaid perhaps –'

'Don't worry, I'll knock –' Graham paused. 'Oh . . . I get it. This is a set-up. You came here to start a fight. Then I get banged away for assaulting a copper. Very clever.'

'Don't be stupid. I only want to clear the air, tell you how I feel about Mary. But your idea sounds good. Do you want to finish what you started?'

'No. I'm not volunteering for prison. Forget it.'

Joseph opened his wallet and took out a ten-pound note. 'Here, take this, get some drinks. Let's start again.'

'How's life in the Falklands?' Joseph swirled beer around his glass. 'I wouldn't have minded getting into that myself.'

'We didn't need detectives. It was us squaddies who shoved it to the Argies.' Graham sniffed. 'And there wasn't any need to look for villains, they were all around us.'

Mary covered Joseph's hand with her own. 'Joe was in the army too.'

Graham lifted her hand off Joseph's. 'Yes, I know, you told me before. What mob was he with?'

'I can't tell you.' Joseph drew a finger across his throat. 'Our mob, as you call it, never existed.'

'Oh, one of the cloak and dagger boys, were you?'

'Shall we change the subject? Let's talk about you, me, and Mary. She says it's over between you, but I get the impression you don't feel the same.'

'You're right. Just because I slipped it to some silly bitch, doesn't mean a thing.'

'But it does to me,' Mary said. 'What would you say if I'd been letting someone slip it to me, as you so charmingly put it?'

'What? Like you are now, do you mean? With him?'

'Don't shout,' Mary said. 'We don't want everyone to know our business.'

Graham turned his head. 'Nosy sods. Where was I?' He looked across the table. 'Look, I love you, sweetheart. We've both played away from home, why don't we forget it and get on with our lives?'

'Because it's made me realize I don't love you. I'm not sure I ever really did. I think getting married was a mistake.'

'How can you say that? We were made for each other. Everyone said so.'

'My mother didn't, I should have listened.'

Joseph rested his head back and stared up at the ceiling. 'We're not getting anywhere. Can I make a suggestion?'

'No. Keep your nose out.' Graham banged his glass on the table. 'It's because of you she's being like this.'

'Oh, I see. It's got nothing to do with you shagging someone else?'

'Why should it? For all I know she's been sleeping with half the coppers at your nick.'

The sound of the slap stopped nearby conversations. Graham rubbed the side of his face. Mary's fingers tingled as she sat, tight-lipped. Joseph placed a hand on her arm and leaned toward Graham. 'You asked for that,' he hissed. 'Now apologise. Better still, get your sorry arse outside.'

Pushing his knuckles against the table, Graham raised himself up, looked around the pub and sat down again. 'Okay, you win.'

Mary turned to Joseph. 'What's your suggestion?'

'I think the best thing is a cooling off period. You and I continue to work together, but anything else has to stop.'

'You'll stop shagging my wife, you mean?'

'Don't be so coarse.' Mary blushed.

'Why? It's what he's doing isn't it?'

'I told you,' Joseph said. 'Mary and I will keep our relationship on a professional level. If you two bury the hatchet and make a go of your marriage, I'll respect your decision.'

'Very generous.' Graham sneered. 'I could get you sacked for what you're doing.'

Joseph looked into his eyes. 'Yes, and that would mean the end of Mary's career too.'

'Bollocks . . . yes . . . I suppose you're right. From what she's told me it's not easy for women in the police. Okay, we'll do it your way.'

Mary shook her head. 'Don't I get a say in this? Aren't my feelings important to either of you? Move out of the way, I want to go home.' She pushed her hips against Joseph. 'Come on, I can't get out until you do.'

'Sorry.' Joseph stood. 'I think I've made a mess of things. Maybe this wasn't such a good idea after all.'

A group of girls on the other side of the bar fed coins into the jukebox and swayed to the music, *Tainted Love.*

Graham held out a handkerchief. 'Don't cry, sweetheart, please. I'll take you home.' He glared at Joseph. 'If it's okay with you of course.'

Chapter 20

October 1986

The drizzle did nothing to improve the sight of boarded-up houses. Reflections in puddles were blown apart by a passing car. A teenager leaned against a wall, a clear plastic hood protecting her hair. Apart from this she was not dressed for the weather. Her partially open blouse and short skirt were working clothes, not fashion statements. From the meagre shelter of the alley, she watched and waited.

Mary stopped the Rover. Joseph got out and approached the prostitute.

'Looking for some action?' she asked.

Joseph produced his ID card.

'What's that for? I ain't doing nothing wrong.' Opening her handbag, she fumbled amongst tissues and packets of Durex for her cigarettes. 'What do you want?'

'Information. You must have heard about the murder in the park. Do you work for the same person?'

'I don't work for no one.' She sneered. 'It's against the law.'

'We interviewed a few of your associates and they all pass their earnings to a man.'

'If they do, why don't you arrest him for pimping?'

'Because they wouldn't give us a name. They didn't want to end up the same way as her.'

'Nor do I, so shove off.'

'If you tell me who he is, I can put him away for living off immoral earnings. You'll all be safe then.'

'No thanks. If he don't get convicted, we're all in the shit.'

'Sounds like you do work for him. I think you'd better come down the station and answer a few questions.'

'Might as well. Be nice to get out of this rain. You can buy me a cup of tea. But I ain't got nothing to say.'

Joseph grasped her arm. 'Didn't that girl's death teach you anything?'

'Yes. Keep my trap shut and stay alive. Come on, get it over with, arrest me. Never know, I might even drum up some trade, all those lonely policemen and cosy cells.'

'You'd rather risk your life than help?' Joseph looked up at the sky. 'I give up with you lot. What's the point? If I take you in, you'll spin me a pack of lies and I won't achieve a thing. Apart from more paperwork. But think about it. If another girl is murdered, you'll be partly to blame by protecting this man.'

She sniffed. 'Why? It's not me going around killing people. You're the police, why don't you catch him?'

'Did you learn anything?' Mary switched on the ignition as Joseph brushed the rain off his jacket before climbing in.

'No. She's like all the others, scared shitless. If one of them would break their silence, I could nail Payne.'

'Are you sure it's him?'

'Who else? I'm certain these women are working for him. Then there's the man caught carrying drugs and money. He disappears, and another man, who may also have worked for Payne, is murdered.'

'He must be getting short of staff,' she said, smiling.

'I think it's a safe bet . . . hang on, you've given me an idea. Why don't I get Kimberley to work for him?'

'She wouldn't agree.'

'I don't see why? She told us her brother kept tropical fish.'

'What's that got to do with walking the streets?'

'Pardon?' Joseph's brow wrinkled. 'Walking the streets? Oh, I see. No, I meant work in his warehouse. Who could be better? I'll speak to Misery Guts in the morning, arrange for her secondment to our department.'

'Before, or after you ask her? She may not want to do it.'

*

Kimberley looked away from Joseph to Mary, then back again. 'You want me to apply for a job in town? Why?'

Mary unclasped her hands. 'Shall I explain, sir?'

Joseph nodded.

'D S Fargough meant he would like your assistance in investigating a crime. It would mean applying for a position at Mark Payne Enterprises who trade as tropical fish importers. We suspect it's a front for drugs. You're not part of this department, we can only *ask* you to help.'

'In which case I'll say no. I enjoy what I do. If I'd wanted to be a detective, I would have applied when I left university.'

Joseph opened his mouth, but Mary spoke. 'And I'm sure you would have been a great asset to any detective team,' she said. 'We also suspect Mark Payne of being involved in four murders, two of them women about your age. We would appreciate your help in bringing him to justice, especially as you have the advantage of possessing some knowledge of fish-keeping, courtesy of your brother.'

Kimberley lowered her head and stared at the office floor. 'I don't think I can do it. I'm sorry.'

'Fair enough,' Joseph said. 'I understand. But you would have been perfect with your analytical mind. And as your brother keeps tropical fish, you probably have some useful knowledge. Your help could save lives.'

Inside the pockets of her white laboratory coat Kimberley screwed her hands into fists. 'Let me think about it.'

'Thank you.' Joseph held out a hand.

*

Opening a cabinet, Kimberley searched through the files. Removing two, she flicked through the photos, read the reports. The analytical pages lacked any compassion for the victims. She shuddered. 'This could have been me.'

The morning seemed to pass her by. Mechanically, she went through the motions. Images of the teenage prostitute in the park gnawed at her. The mutilated body. The battered face of the woman on the bed. Both returned time and again, swirling around in her head, distracting her from her work. By lunch-time she had made her decision.

*

Kimberley bit her lip. 'You asked me to make up my mind,' she said. 'And I have. If it'll help catch whoever killed those women, I'll do it.'

'Thank you. Come in. WDC Wells and I need to discuss this further with you.'

Mary set the coffee cups down and sat beside Kimberley. 'Are you sure about this?'

'Yes. I read the autopsy reports on both the victims. Somebody has to do something.'

Joseph spread his palms flat on his desk. 'Good for you. I wish I could do it, or WDC Wells, but we're both known to the suspect.'

'I understand. What exactly is it you want me to do?'

He gazed up at the ceiling. 'I wish I knew. All we can ask is you report anything which seems at odds with running a fish import business.'

'I know it sounds vague,' Mary said, 'but there really isn't much we can tell you.'

Joseph focussed his attention onto Kimberley. 'As we suspect him of drug smuggling, we're arranging to have his next shipment of tropical fish scrutinised by Customs and Excise. There's not a lot more we can do.'

'Which is where you come in,' Mary said. 'Working for us on the inside may give us the evidence we need.'

'I understand. But I'm not sure what you want, or how I'm supposed to get it.'

'A lot will depend on what you are employed as. I'd like you working in his office, but it's unlikely. You'll probably be in the warehouse.' Joseph sighed. 'Not ideal, but it's something. I want you to listen and watch. It'll take time, but it's our only hope.'

Mary sipped her drink. 'We can supply you with a credible reference from your last employer who you had to give notice to when your family relocated. If Payne checks, which I very much doubt, the pet shop will confirm it.'

'But I applied to join the Forensics team straight from university. I've never worked anywhere else. How can someone say I worked for them?'

Joseph tapped the side of his nose. 'Please . . . don't ask.'

*

Ignoring the wolf-whistle Kimberley crossed the yard to reception.

'Good morning,' she said. 'Do you have any vacancies?'

'No. I'm the receptionist and I also handle Mr Payne's paperwork. We don't need anyone.'

'I didn't mean clerical work. I'm used to looking after animals, fish and reptiles.' She thrust a brown envelope under the partition. 'This where I worked before my dad moved our family up here.'

The girl ignored the envelope. 'We don't have animals either. Try Banham Zoo.'

Kimberley retrieved her reference. 'Are you sure about a job? I really need one, I'm behind with my rent.'

'Which bit don't you understand? There – are – no – vacancies.' She flicked through the pages of her magazine. 'Bye.'

Stepping out into the low sunlight Kimberley shielded her eyes. A man stepped aside, but not quick enough to avoid the collision. 'Sorry,' she gasped. 'I couldn't see a thing.'

'No harm done,' Mark said. 'Are you buying or selling?'

'Pardon?'

'Have you come to buy fish? Or are you a sales rep?'

'Neither. I came to see if there were any vacancies, but the receptionist told me there aren't.'

'What sort of job are you after?'

'This place sells tropical fish. I thought they may need someone who knows the aquatic trade. Never mind, it was worth asking.'

Mark held out a hand. 'I *own* this establishment and I decide if we need anyone or not. I could do with some help in the warehouse, we're short staffed in there at the moment. Do you fancy giving it a try?'

'Yes, please.' Kimberley held out an envelope. 'This is my reference from the last place I worked.'

He waved it away. 'I don't take any notice of those. I'll soon know if you're worth employing. Shall we say a month's trial? Give me a chance to see what you can do?'

'What? I mean, yes, thank you. When would you like me to start?'

'Come with me. I'll show you around while we discuss things.'

Mark Payne listened as Kimberley identified many of the species.

'I have to admit I'm impressed, you certainly seem to know your stuff,' he said. 'The hard work starts when we get a new shipment. Getting all those fish to settle into tanks.' Payne lit a cigar. Smoke drifted from his nostrils. 'But that won't be for another six or eight weeks.'

Kimberley peered into the next tank. 'Wow. This red-tailed catfish. It's huge.'

'Which is why it's still here, none of the pet shops we supply have found a customer for it.' He sighed. 'If it doesn't go soon, I may have to offer it to a public aquarium or the zoo.'

'I think I'll enjoy working here. You've got some wonderful specimens.'

'Thank you. I find South America to be very lucrative, which is why I specialise.'

'The last place I worked at would love to see this lot. I can't wait to get started.'

'Good. Shall we say tomorrow?' He massaged an ear lobe between thumb and finger. 'About ten? Give me time to sort my post before you arrive. After that it's nine till six, with an hour for lunch, Monday to Friday.'

'Any weekends?'

'No, I've other staff to cover those. Now about your wages. I'll pay you whatever you've been earning to start, with a review at the end of the first month.'

'Lovely, thank you. I'll see you in the morning. Goodbye.'

Mark watched as she walked through the gates. *Nice arse. I think you'll fit in very well here.*

Chapter 21

October 1986

'That was easier than I expected,' Joseph said, sliding the page inside a folder. 'Kimberley starts work at Payne's place next Monday. I told her to contact me on my home phone, unless of course it's an emergency. I didn't give her your number in case your husband answered.'

'Probably best under the circumstances.' Mary held her powder compact close to her face. 'Not sure I like this colour.' She pressed her lips together and held up a lipstick. 'It must have been a present at sometime.'

'I think it suits you. And talking of presents, it's my birthday on Thursday.'

'Is it? I thought yours was the twenty-second?'

'No. It's the twenty-third. Well, it was last year, I don't see any reason to change now.'

She laughed. 'Touché. How do you plan to celebrate?'

'I thought champagne and a home-cooked meal should do the trick. What do you think?'

'Sounds nice.' Putting the compact back into her handbag she asked, 'Who are you inviting?'

'You of course.'

'I can't. What about Graham?'

'I didn't think about him.' Joseph sighed. 'I see what you mean.'

'Sorry . . . but next year could be different. I may be a free woman by then.'

He got up and put an arm around her. 'Not if I have anything to say about it. As soon as you two call it a day, I'll ask you to marry me.'

'And make an honest woman of me? That's nice. But nothing's decided yet. Sometimes I think I should give him another chance, but when he turns aggressive, I quickly change my mind.'

'Does he hit you?' Joseph's hands clenched.

'No. It's nothing I can't handle.'

'If he does, I swear to God, I'll kill him.'

'I believe you would.' She paused. 'I know in my heart of hearts the only answer is divorce.'

'I can't interfere. But remember I'm there for you.'

'I know you are.' She shifted in her chair. 'I wish I could be with you for your birthday –'

Joseph slapped both hands on his desk. 'Why don't I invite both of you? George and his wife are coming.'

'Are they? It's a thought I suppose. I could ask him, but you're not in his good books at the moment.'

*

'A birthday meal? With him? Are you joking? We'd end up throttling each other.' Graham screwed up his racing paper and hurled it across the room. 'Tell him to stick the invitation up his arse.'

'You're not making it easy. He is my boss.'

'And your lover.'

'It's over. He agreed, remember?'

'He can say what he likes. I don't trust either of you.'

'Huh, that's rich, coming from you. A new territory opens up and you can't wait to rush off and explore it.'

'That was different.' He dropped a hand to the area of his crotch. 'Oh, what the hell, tell him we'll go if it's what you want. But I'll be keeping an eye on you.'

'Please yourself. How about George, our desk sergeant, and his wife? Planning on watching them too?'

*

Joseph looked down at his apron; women's lace underwear printed in black against a pink background.

Mary sniggered.

Graham remained tight lipped.

'You're early,' Joseph said. 'Never mind, come in.'

'Happy Birthday, Joe.' She turned to Graham. 'Go on, give him the wine. He won't bite.'

Pulling a face, Graham reached into a carrier bag.

'Thanks.' Joseph attempted a smile. 'Nice thought.'

'And here's your card, Birthday Boy.' Mary held out an envelope. 'Hmmm, something smells good. What's cooking?'

'If you've finished standing on the doorstep, come in and find out. Let me take your coats.'

Graham ignored Mary's disapproving look as he let cigarette ash fall onto Joseph's carpet.

'Do you need a hand, Joe?' Mary called.

'No, I'm fine, it's nearly ready. Wine or beer, Graham? I've got red, white and rosé, or Newcastle Brown.'

'Beer's fine.'

'Take no notice of Mr Grumpy,' Mary said. 'I think I'll have white wine, please.'

'Could you get the door?' Joseph said. 'It's probably George.'

A bottle clinked against a pint glass. 'There you are, Graham. You can pour.' He turned to Mary. 'Let me get ours then we can get the evening started.'

'Happy Birthday.' Mary held out her glass. 'Twenty-one again.'

'I wouldn't mind being twenty-one, back in my unit and doing it all over.' Joseph said, touching his glass against hers.

Graham looked up. 'Where were you?'

'Not allowed to say. Most times, officially, we weren't. Other times we were only there to advise.'

Graham slowly poured his beer. 'Oh . . . right . . . yes, I remember now. The hush-hush mob. Who did you say your commanding officer was? James Bond, wasn't it?'

'Do you like your card?' Mary smiled. 'It's the best I could find. There wasn't a lot to choose from.'

'Yes. Thanks. I like humorous ones.'

'Me too,' George said. His wife smiled.

Mary sniffed. 'Is something burning?'

'Bugger. I thought I'd turned the oven off.' Joseph leapt from his chair.

Graham wrinkled his nose. 'I can smell it now. Looks like it could be fish and chips on the way home.' Holding up the bottle he let the last of the beer drain into his glass. 'Where's the toilet? Upstairs or down?'

'Next to the front bedroom.' Mary pointed towards the ceiling.

'The bedroom, eh? You seem to know your way round. If he comes back tell him I need another beer. I won't be a couple of shakes.'

Graham zipped his trousers and put out a hand to flush the cistern. He paused. *No, let's take a look at the love-nest first.* Outside the bathroom he stopped and listened. Joseph and Mary were laughing.

Stacked coins kept company with a comb and keys on the bedside table. Graham opened the wardrobe. Neatly pressed trousers, suit jackets, carefully ironed shirts and ties. Highly polished shoes beneath the hanging clothes. Graham picked up a pair of black brogues. 'Very nice. Bet these weren't cheap.' He put them back in place. 'Strange?' He picked at the remains of a large moth, trapped against the side of the wardrobe. 'How did you get squashed? This is weird. Is there a false bottom, or is it a dodgy bit of kit?' He listened. The sound of talking from below reassured him. Removing all the shoes he ran his hands over the shelf. It moved. He pushed down. With a click, the shelf lifted.

'A gun? What's he doing with this?' Removing it from its holster he aimed at the pillows on the bed, one at a time. 'Very nice. It's a dead ringer for the souvenir I left on the Falklands.'

With the holster back in place, he replaced the shelf, topped it with the shoes and closed the wardrobe doors. The pistol nestled against his chest, inside his shirt.

He entered the bathroom and flushed the toilet.

Tip-toeing down the stairs he placed the gun inside the off-licence carrier bag and hung it behind his coat.

George and his wife took turns to plunge their fingers into the bowl of peanuts.

Mary backed away from Joseph as Graham entered the room. 'Oh, you're back. I was beginning to wonder what you were doing.' She held out her glass. 'Joe's opened the champagne, I'll get you some.'

'No, don't bother. I'll stick to beer.'

Joseph prised the cap off a bottle and passed it to Graham. 'Cheers. Now, who wants *lasagne al forno*? Most of it's edible.'

Mary ran a finger around her plate. 'Lovely. Even the crispy bits. You can cook it again anytime, it was wonderful.'

'Did you like it, George? There's more if you want. How about you, Alice?'

'Not for me, thanks.'

'Nor me, thank you.' George pushed his plate away. 'It was very nice though. We have to make a move soon.'

'Okay.' Joseph turned to Mary. 'Can I tempt you? There's another glass of champagne I think.'

George toyed with his glass. Mary tried to sneak a peek at her husband's watch.

'Tell us, Graham,' Joseph said. 'How do you like Civvy Street? Mary told me you'd quit the army.'

'It's okay,' he said, pouring the rest of the beer into his glass.

'I know what you mean. It took me ages to adjust.'

'Shall I serve the Arctic Roll?' Mary said.

'Yes, please,' Joseph said, adding, 'There's a jug of cream in the fridge, if anyone fancies it.'

'I don't. It's time we went.' Graham put his glass down.

'You can go if you like, but I'm having dessert,' Mary said. 'How about you, Joe?'

'Yes, I'll have some, thanks. Can't let it go to waste.' Turning to Graham, he said, 'Getting back to the army, I bet you miss it.'

'Probably.'

'Have you tried getting a job with one of the security firms around here?'

'No.'

Mary held out a plate. Arctic Roll sat in a sea of cream. 'There you are, Happy Birthday again. I brought you a spoon as well as a fork, might save you licking the plate.'

Joseph grinned.

'Hurry up.' Graham grasped Mary's elbow. 'I told you I'm going.'

She shook herself free. 'Who's stopping you? I can find my own way home.'

'You'd like that, wouldn't you. Give you a chance to give him his birthday present. I'm not stupid. We're leaving together.'

'Please yourself. But you'll have to wait.'

'I knew this would be a mistake. I shouldn't have agreed to come.'

'I wish you hadn't.'

'Can you two save all this?' Joseph spread out his hands, palm side up. 'If I'd wanted an evening of aggravation, I'd have brought some paperwork home.'

Graham lifted his jacket from the hook and held it against his chest. Joseph held Mary's coat as she slipped her arms into the sleeves. He opened the door and stood aside. Mary turned and kissed him on the cheek. 'Thanks for having us, enjoy the rest of your birthday. I'll see you at work tomorrow. And thanks again, I really enjoyed it despite –'

'I know what you mean. I did too. Bye, Graham. We should do this again sometime.'

'I don't think so.'

Walking down the road, Mary shivered. 'Aren't you wearing your jacket? It's chilly tonight.'

Graham clutched his coat closer. The gun inside the bag pressed against his ribs. 'No, I don't feel the cold like you do.'

Chapter 22

October 1986

Kimberley checked the temperature and measured the pH of the water in the last fish tank. She recorded the values in her notebook and stifled a yawn. Her third day at work was proving as uneventful as the previous two. She yearned to be back with her colleagues in Forensics.

Yesterday, a young lad collecting an order had provided a welcome break from her chores. He had been friendly at first but changed when she attempted to accompany him to the store next to the warehouse. She thought he was trying to impress by refusing her offer of help to carry boxes labelled Water Balance.

That night she phoned Joseph to make her daily report. He warned her to be careful, but asked her to check the contents of the boxes. She told him it would not be easy as there was always a man in the storeroom. His sole job, she said, appeared to be handing out these Water Balance kits.

She asked Joseph why he hadn't applied for a search warrant. He said it would alert Mark Payne. Kimberley told him she realized she wasn't cut out for undercover work and asked permission to quit the job.

This morning, Julie had phoned in to say she would not be in today, citing women's problems. Mark called Kimberley to his office and asked her to take on the task of keeping his men supplied with tea and coffee while he was short staffed. She managed to refrain from asking why making tea was considered to be a woman's prerogative.

Carrying hot drinks, Kimberley entered the building where the mystery boxes were stored. A man sat slumped over a table reading a paperback book. She placed the chipped mug down. 'Good morning. You're Peter, aren't you?' she said, looking at her list. 'Four sugars, not too much milk?'

He jerked his head up. 'Thanks, sweetheart. Why are you doing the tea run?'

'Julie's off sick today, back tomorrow I think.'

'Oh.' He sipped the tea. 'Nice. Better than she makes it. They should let you have the job.'

'What are you reading?' She pointed to the pile of books.

'Westerns. Louis L'Amour and Zane Grey, mostly.' He frowned at the look on her face. 'I love them. I caught the cowboy bug when I went to Saturday morning pictures as a kid.'

'My dad told me about those, he especially enjoyed the serials.'

'They were okay, if you could scrounge the money to go every week. Otherwise, you had to ask your mates how the hero escaped.'

'That's where books win,' she said. 'All you have to do is keep reading.'

Peter stood up. 'Would you stay here for a minute to keep your eye on things? I forgot my fags. I'm gasping.'

'Take your time. I'll look at one of your books, if it's okay with you.'

Sorting through the pile he said, 'Here, try this one. It's great. You can borrow it if you like.'

She watched him walk towards the door.

Cardboard boxes kept company with polystyrene containers in the corner of the building. Taking one from the stack, Kimberley placed it onto the concrete floor. It was sealed with brown tape. She used her nails to pick at the end of the tape. *There's no way I'll manage to get all this back on. I'll have to hide this when I'm finished.*

Removing the lid, Kimberley stared. *Water Balance kits? It's plastic bags of white powder.*

She sensed, rather than heard the man behind her. Turning, she looked up at Peter.

'What are you doing? You know we mustn't touch these boxes.' He reached out and grabbed her. 'You'd better come with me to see Mr Payne. We'll both be for it now.'

'Why tell him? I won't if you don't.'

As Peter struggled to decide, Mark Payne entered. 'Tell me what?'

He pushed her forward. 'She opened one of the boxes. I caught her doing it.'

'How did she? You're paid to watch this lot. What were you doing?'

Looking down at his feet Peter mumbled, 'I needed some fags. She said she'd stay –'

'And you, what are you doing poking your nose into my business?'

'I was just curious. I've never heard of Water Balance kits.'

He scowled. 'And now you've seen inside what do you make of them?'

'Chemicals? Or is it marine salt?'

'I think you'd better come with me. We can talk about this in my office.' Putting an arm around her waist he dragged her towards the door. Turning to Peter, he said, 'And I'll deal with you later.'

Mark Payne interlaced his fingers.

Kimberley chewed the inside of her lip.

He unlocked his fingers. His eyes narrowed as he lit a cigar. 'Now, what have you got to say for yourself? Why were you in that building? Why weren't you doing what I pay you for?'

'For a start I *was* doing what you pay me for, making tea and coffee. Then I offered to wait while Peter went to buy cigarettes.'

Payne leant forward. 'He should have known better. But why tamper with one of our kits?'

'I don't really know,' Kimberley examined her nails, avoiding his gaze. 'Like I said, I was curious I suppose.'

'Were you? Well remember what they say, curiosity killed the cat. For all you know the contents may have been toxic. Did you think of that?'

'It's okay. I didn't get anything on my hands. The chemicals are all safe inside bags.'

'And you don't know what they are? You told me you worked in the trade. Didn't your last employer use anything like it?' Cigar smoke followed Payne's words across the desk.

'No ... I mean yes. I suppose they may have done.' Kimberley dabbed her mouth with a tissue. 'But they only sold fish like Angels and Neon Tetras. They had a few tropical marines, but due to cost, and the difficulty keeping them, they were a limited market.'

'I know. I spoke to your boss.'

Kimberley crossed her legs. 'Oh.'

'He said he'd try to come up here. I told him about the red-tailed catfish and he may be interested. Said it would make a nice display in his shop window.'

She relaxed. 'Can I go now? I've still got a few more drinks to make and I need to get back to my proper job.'

'Yes. But in future don't enter the other warehouse. Go and check the fish after you've fetched me a coffee.'

Kimberley stood up. 'Sorry, I thought I'd brought your drink. I'm not used to being the tea-lady.' She paused at the door. 'Thanks for giving me a trial, but I don't think I'll fit in here. I'd like to give in my notice please. I'll be leaving at the end of the week.'

*

Back amongst the tanks of fish, Kimberley put her hands on her knees to stop them shaking. She lowered herself onto the kick-along stool.

'Are you okay, darling?' a man pushing a broom called out. 'Can I do anything?'

She wiped a tear from her cheek. 'No, I'm fine, thanks. I've just got the start of a headache.'

'I get 'em all the time,' he said, 'it's all this heat. Bloody fish.'

'You're probably right. I've got aspirins in my bag. I'll take a couple.'

'You new here, darling?' He pushed his broom beneath the tanks next to her. 'Or do you work in the other building?'

'No, only this one. I got into trouble when I went next door. I was only taking Peter his tea.'

'I don't go in there. I'm not allowed. I sweep in here, Mr Payne's office and reception, Sometimes Julie lets me wash the floor. Oh, and I do the yard as well.' He looked at Kimberley. 'I don't know who cleans the other place.'

*

'Take this.' Mark Payne gave Peter a ten-pound note. 'Go into town. Buy a padlock and hasp and I want it fitted *now*. I'm not paying you to sit on your arse all day reading and going for a stroll whenever you feel like it. You're supposed to be dealing with customers.'

'Yes. I'm sorry. It won't happen again.'

'I know it won't. You're finished in there. I can't trust you. I need to think about this.'

Peter traced circles on the ground with the toe of his shoe. 'Where have Tom and Sam got to lately?'

'Tom said he was moving to London, a friend of his offered him a job. And Sam? Who knows? He didn't collect his wages, just disappeared.'

'I liked Sam. He was a boxer, like me.'

'The only difference being he kept more of his brain cells. I should have given you the sweeper's job, you might have been able to manage a broom.'

'Got you, boss. I'll go and buy a lock and put it on.'

*

Kimberley leaned against the inside of the call box with the phone pressed against her ear, picking at a flake of red paint with her nails.

'Hello? Can I speak to Detective Sergeant Fargough please?' She stared up the street towards Mark Payne Enterprises. 'Hello, it's me, Kimberley. There's boxes full of bags of white powder! I'm sure it's cocaine. Somebody at university tried to get me to snort it with him.'

'Whoa, slow down. Where did you find it?'

'The other building. Where he keeps all the polystyrene boxes.'

'We looked there. They must have moved it while we searched the fish warehouse.'

'Well, all I know is, it's not hidden now.'

'Can you get a sample? We have to be sure. We can't raid his place without evidence, he's already lodged a complaint with someone high up.'

Kimberley took a deep breath. 'I can try. But I'm really scared of Payne. He caught me with an open box. I think I convinced him I was only interested as part of my job but –'

'Don't take chances. If –'

'Sorry, got to go. No more change. I'll phone you at home tonight.'

*

Clutching her clipboard Kimberley walked around the yard, her shadow dancing attendance. The winter sun painted the window of Mark Payne's office orange, his Venetian blind acting as a reflector. Satisfied everyone must be at lunch she headed for the warehouse. A finger parted the slats of the blind and Mark peered out.

*

Unscrewing the lid from a jar she placed it beside the clear plastic bag. Using her pen, she made a hole and let the powder run into the container. A shadow falling across the bag startled her.

'What the fuck do you think you're doing?' Mark roared. 'I thought I told you this place is off limits.' He gripped her arm. 'It's time I taught you a lesson.'

She drove the heel of one shoe into his shin. He lashed out with the back of his hand, slapping her face. His diamond ring drew blood.

'Who are you working for, bitch?' He aimed a punch at her chin. The blow knocked her off her feet. He kicked out. 'Tell me who sent you. Was it the coppers?' His foot thudded into the curled up body on the floor. 'Or have you got a habit to feed?'

Blood dribbled from the side of her mouth as she tried to reply.

'What? What did you say?' He leaned down, spread his hand across her face and squeezed. 'You need time to think? Okay, I'll give you a day or two.'

He picked up an industrial tape gun. She tried to fight him off, but was no match for him. Brown tape secured her wrists and ankles.

She could taste iron. 'Help! Somebody! Anybody! He's going to kill me!' More tape silenced her cries.

An electric drill disturbed the silence. Kimberley struggled to sit upright, flopping around, a fish out of water. Polystyrene boxes formed a prison, hiding her from sight.

Peter finished his task. She heard him come in, walk to the table and gather up his books. She rolled against the boxes, desperate to attract attention. *Over here! Peter, help me!*

The lights went out.

She heard the padlock snap shut.

*

'Donald, I've got something for you.' Mark Payne grinned. 'Pretty young thing. I was planning on keeping her for a while, but I've changed my mind. She's yours if you want her. Pick her up from here ASAP. When you've had enough, dump her. But make sure she can't talk.' Putting the phone down he rubbed his hands together. 'Nice to have someone tidy up.'

Mark led his brother across the warehouse. 'Here she is. Trussed up like a turkey ready for the oven.'

Kimberley gazed up at the two men.

Mark sneered. 'Too nosey by half. I warned her.'

'You were right, she's a pretty little thing. I'll have a lot of fun with her.'

'Be my guest.' He took a knife from his pocket and bent down. 'I'll cut the tape so she can walk.'

*

Donald parked under trees, got out and looked around. Satisfied there were no witnesses he opened the boot and manhandled Kimberley out, her face contorted with pain.

'Come on, slut. No one will find you here, it's been deserted since the war.' Gripping her arm, he dragged her through the undergrowth and trees.

The Nissen hut was barely visible. Weeds and moss on the roof helped it blend into the trees.

Donald used a key to open the new padlock. The door opened. A rat scuttled off into the gloom.

'In you go.' He pushed her inside. 'Stand still while I light a lamp. Don't want you hurting yourself.'

Kimberley shivered. *He's going to rape me! Oh, please God, no!*

'There. That's better.' He held the hurricane lamp. 'Come on, let me show you to your room.'

The new bedding gave the camp bed an air of respectability it did not deserve. A length of chain lying on the bed terminated in a pair of handcuffs. Kimberley felt her stomach churn as she breathed in. The air, heavy with the cloying smell of chemicals from an Elsan toilet, made her stomach heave.

'Nice, isn't it? I'll get some curtains soon, make it a home from home. I tried painting the glass in the windows but I'm sure curtains are the answer.'

Kimberley held her wrists towards him.

'Okay, I can do that. And you can scream all you like. Nobody will hear you.' Taking a penknife from his pocket, he sawed at the tape.

Kimberley massaged her wrists. Looking past her captor she saw chains and leather straps hanging from hooks on the wall. Light from the lamps revealed clothing adorned with metal studs. Masks, whips, sets of handcuffs. Her eyes bulged. Losing control, she stood in a puddle of urine.

With both hands free, she ripped the tape from her mouth. 'You bloody pervert! Take me home!'

'You are home. Now, take off those wet clothes.'

'I won't!' Grabbing hold of his jacket she brought one knee up, hard.

He grunted. 'You want to play games, do you? Good.' With one hand firmly clamped around her wrist, he put his hand up under her dress and yanked at her underwear. 'I like ones who fight.'

Carrying her to the bed he threw her onto it.

'Don't! I'm a virgin,' she screamed. 'Don't do this to me. I won't say anything to anyone. Let me go.'

Her mind struggled to make sense of the surge of emotions racing around her brain. *This is not how I thought my first time would be. I'll pretend it's not happening. Think about work.*

Anything. 'Can't we talk about this?' she pleaded. 'I can get you money. Take me back, please.'

'You don't understand. You're not going anywhere. This is where you live now. As for money, forget it. We'll have fun. I'll show you things your mother couldn't even begin to imagine.'

Unzipping his trousers, he let them drop to the floor.

Kimberley looked away as he dressed. She heard buckles being tightened, zips being fastened. She could smell leather. Her heart raced. *Oh, shit!*

She trembled as he approached. Reptilian eyes peering through a studded mask, held a menace of their own. The strange paraphernalia Donald needed to satisfy his lust frightened her. He pinned her to the bed. 'My lady friends accommodate my wishes to a degree, but it's not enough. I need young girls like you.'

'Get off,' she yelled. The sound of her voice echoed around the hut, returning to mock her. She tried pushing him away. 'Help! Help! I'm in here!' she screamed, pummelling him with her fists.

'That's right, my dear. Fight. Try to stop me. Look what you're doing to my best friend.'

Clutching her hair, he forced her to see the effect her struggles had on him.

'Owww! You vicious sod!' Pulling at the mask, her fingers sought his eyes. 'Bastard! You'll regret this when the police find me.'

'I think the word is *if*, not when,' he said, pulling her hands away. His nails dug into soft flesh as he forced her legs apart, metal studs on fingerless gloves adding to the pain. Chains, joining leather straps, hurt her breasts as he bore down. Her face screwed up in pain as he entered her. Rocking back and forth he ignored her pleas.

Animal sounds filled her ears as he climaxed. She screamed. But not in ecstasy.

Chapter 23

October 1986

Graham sorted through the crumpled clothes on the bed. Socks and underwear. Tangled shirts. He frowned. *I can't wear shirts like this. Where is she?* The sizzle of bacon cooking drew him towards the kitchen.

Putting his arm around her waist he nuzzled Mary's ear. 'You forgot to iron my shirts, sweetheart. And my socks and pants.'

She pushed him away. 'I washed them. If you want them ironed, do it yourself.'

'Why would I buy a dog, then bark myself? I bet if they were lover-boy's you'd soon iron them.'

'We're not lovers. Joseph gave you his word.'

'It's what he's giving you that's my worry.'

'You've got a twisted mind.'

'I can't see the problem. You're a woman. You're supposed to iron things.'

'Chauvinist pig. You should have stayed in the bloody army.'

'Yes, you and your randy copper would like that, I bet. While I'm laying my life on the line, you –'

'You mean laying your officer's wife. If you'd stuck to serving your country instead of serving her, we wouldn't be having this row.'

'And if you weren't shagging your way to promotion –'

'Don't be so crude.'

Graham put his arm around her. 'Don't be like that, sweetheart. Let's not argue. I'll take you out somewhere, anywhere you like. How about shopping for clothes and shoes?'

'Forget it. Some of us have work to go to.'

'Which just about says it all. You'd rather be working with him than spending the day with me. At least I know where I stand.'

'Good. It's about time it sank into your thick head.'

*

'Are you sure Kimberley said she'd phone last night?' Mary asked.

'Yes.' Joseph put his hands behind his head, tipped back his chair and stared at the office ceiling. 'And I'm getting a bad feeling about this.'

'It's only one missed call. There's bound to be a reason. Perhaps she went out with friends and forgot. It was a Friday.'

He let the chair fall forward and thumped the table. 'If she's in trouble, I'll –'

'Joe. Get a grip. You're letting this get personal.'

'Maybe, but it was my idea to plant her there. I'm the one to blame.'

Mary reached beneath her hair and played with an ear-ring. 'Let's go to her place. She may have a hangover or maybe she's not feeling well. And if she's not there, we could try Payne's.'

'And tell him she works for us? Not a good idea . . . but we could send someone else.'

'Who?'

'The man from the shop where she worked before.'

'But you made it all up.'

Joseph touched the side of his nose. 'Payne doesn't know that.'

'True. But we can't use a member of the public.'

'I don't intend to. Our shop owner is PC Alan Jefferson. He can go in civvies. Payne has never seen him, so it should work.'

'He could read up about tropical fish before he goes,' Mary said.

'Good point. Now, let's see if Kimberley's at home.'

*

'She's not here,' Mary said. 'Stop banging on the door. You're making enough noise to wake the dead.'

Joseph looked up at a woman leaning from a window above Kimberley's flat.

'You're out of luck,' she said. 'She hasn't been home all night. Disgusting I call it. In my day –'

He managed a smile. 'Thank you. We'll call back later.'
Turning away he said to Mary, 'Let's get back to the station. It's time I organised a certain visit.'

*

The Rover pulled onto the police station forecourt. 'Are you sure about sending Alan Jefferson to Payne's?' Mary asked.

'Have you got a better idea?' Joseph frowned. 'I suppose we could arrange to have another officer phone and ask to speak to her on some pretext . . . no, I'll stick with my original plan.' He pulled at his Adam's apple. 'It's common knowledge Jefferson wants to move up from being a beat officer, he'll jump at the chance to play detective. Tell him to make an appointment to visit Payne tomorrow. I want this made top priority.'

'It's asking a lot. How's Jefferson supposed to become an instant fish expert?'

'He only has to know enough to get by, how difficult can it be?'

*

Joseph nodded appreciatively. 'You learnt all about catfish from a library book, Jefferson? Well done.'

'Yes, sir. Thank you, sir. Actually, I became quite interested and could tell you about some other species too.'

'Good man. Now, as I said, Kimberley from Forensics was working undercover at the suspects' premises but we've lost contact.'

'With all due respect, sir, you should have sent someone like myself.'

'Maybe, but I didn't.' Joseph cleared his throat. 'Now I want you to find her.'

'I understand, sir.' The constable pulled back his shoulders and stared straight ahead. 'You can rely on me. To tell the truth, I rather fancy Kimberley. I tried asking her out, but she wasn't too keen.'

Taking a deep breath, Joseph exhaled through his nose. 'When you find her, who knows? She may change her mind. But remember, observation only, no heroics. Report back and leave the rest to me.'

'Yes, sir.'

*

Next morning, Joseph held the door of the Rover open for Mary.

Peering through the window of the flat, Graham muttered, 'Keeping an eye on her would be easier if I had a car. Anything will do.'

*

'I shouldn't have had the second doughnut, you're a bad influence,' Mary said.

'Well, I did offer to eat it for you,' Joseph retorted. 'Anyway, you said you didn't want anything, remember?'

'But how can anyone resist freshly cooked doughnuts?' She licked sugar from her lips. 'The smell gets me every time.'

'Most food does it to me. I'm an innocent victim of my sense of smell and taste buds.'

'Talking of innocent victims, have we heard from Jefferson?'

Joseph brushed sugar from the front of his jacket. 'Not yet.' He pulled back his sleeve to check his watch. 'But he's due to report to my office shortly. Let's get back and find out.'

*

Mary shut her powder compact in response to the knock on the door.

'Come in,' Joseph called.

'Good evening, sir,' PC Jefferson said, as he entered.

Joseph leant forward onto his elbows. 'Did you achieve anything today?'

'Not a lot, although I did manage not to buy the catfish. I told him it was much too big for my set-up. He seemed to –'

'We're not interested in fish. Did you see Kimberley?'

'No, sir. Payne was waiting for me outside so I didn't get the chance to speak to his receptionist. He gave me a tour of the warehouse where he keeps the fish. He said Monday was Kimberley's day off when I mentioned her.'

'Did you get to see inside the other building?'

'Again, the answer's no. I asked if there were more fish inside but he told me it was only a storeroom. It's got a brand-new padlock on the door. Do you want me to go back tomorrow? Payne knows she was supposed to have worked for me. It shouldn't be a problem if I ask to see her.'

'Let me consider the options.' Joseph pointed to the door. 'Well done, Constable. I'll contact you later.'

Mary waited until the door closed. 'What do you make of it?'

'Time for action.' Joseph got to his feet. 'Kimberley doesn't get a day off in the week. And the other building wasn't locked last time.'

'Do you think he's holding her prisoner?'

'I wouldn't put anything past the scumbag. And there's only one way to find out.'

'Shouldn't we wait? In the morning we could take a team and pull the place apart.'

'No. I'm going now. Be best if you stay here. This will be strictly off the record.'

Mary was already on her feet. 'We're partners. I'm coming.'

*

Trying to decorate the late evening sky, stars fought against urban light pollution. Walking along the high wall, a cat stopped at the coiled barbed wire topping the gates, sniffed, and turned back.

'I don't blame you, puss,' Mary said. Turning to Joseph she added, 'And how exactly do you intend to get in?'

'Through the gate. Keep watch, I'll soon have this open.' He inserted lock picks into the padlock.

Mary stood back as the gates swung open.

Joseph handed her the open lock. 'Here, slip this back on while I'm inside, but don't lock it. I won't be long.'

'You never cease to amaze me,' she said. 'How on earth did you do that?'

'I had a good teacher.' He winked. 'And I've told you before, best not to ask.'

As the gates closed behind him, Joseph headed for the locked warehouse. Minutes later he was inside and fluorescent lights blinked into life. Moving boxes, he methodically worked his way around the building.

Outside the gates, Mary paced up and down. *Come on, Joe. Hurry up.*

Reaching the far corner, Joseph stared at the floor. Brown tape, several layers thick, had been cut through and discarded. Stains on the concrete catapulted his mind back to the Middle East. Memories of prisoners taken in for questioning during covert operations caused him to break out in a sweat. *You bastard!*

'I take it she's not here,' Mary said.

'She's in trouble. Real trouble. We need to search Payne's house and grounds.'

'Tonight?'

'No. Things are easier to hide in the dark. We'll get there bright and early.'

*

Graham switched off the lights and swung his Ford Escort onto the grass verge. He watched as Mary and Joseph approached the house. He nodded. *Now I've got a car I can keep my eye on you, sweetheart.*

*

Mary leant against the glass panel, resting her head on one hand. 'There's no one in the swimming pool.'

Joseph looked towards the house. 'Payne does well for himself. All this from importing and selling tropical fish? Who does he think he's kidding?'

'Inland Revenue? He must have a top-notch accountant.'

'Probably, but it won't help him if he's hurt Kimberley. I'll cut his balls off and stuff them down his throat.'

Mary winced. 'Shall we try the house now?'

'Yes. Let's hope we have better luck there.'

Knuckling her eyes against the early morning sun, a young woman in a silk kimono stood in the open doorway.

'Is he in?' Joseph held up his warrant card. 'Mark Payne. Is he in? We need to speak to him.'

'He not come home last night.'

'Who else is in the house?'

'No one.' She tried to close the door. 'Go away. Mark be crazy. You not come in.'

'I will. You invited us.' Joseph pushed past. 'My colleague can vouch for it, she heard you.'

As Mary turned the knob of the third bedroom door it was wrenched from her grasp. Mark Payne lashed out. She folded like a rag doll as the blow sank into her stomach. Pushing past, he took the stairs three at a time.

Joseph rushed from the room next door. Mary was on her hands and knees, retching. Downstairs Payne was shouting at the unfortunate girl who had opened the door to uninvited visitors. Ignoring him, Joseph hurried to help his colleague.

'Get him,' she gasped.

'He'll keep. Let's get you sorted out first. Can you stand?'

'I think so.' She spat to clear her mouth. Clinging to him she pulled herself up. 'Get after him.'

'Too late, listen, that's his Jag. He'll be long gone before I get down there.' He offered her his handkerchief. 'Here, use this.'

*

The Jaguar sped through the gates. Turning into the road, it narrowly missed hitting the car parked opposite his house.

'Christ. He's in a hurry.' Graham raised two fingers toward the departing vehicle. 'Looks like they flushed their quarry.' Leaning across, he opened the glove compartment, grabbed a handgun and pointed it down the road. *I should have shot the tyres like they do in films. Bugger.*

*

Back in the hallway, Joseph gripped the women's arms. 'Keys,' he demanded. 'Fetch the house keys. All of them.'

The young woman pulled her kimono closer. 'He kill me. You not know how he like.'

'You're wrong. I know exactly what he's like.'

'He does like security,' Mary said, shaking bunches of keys.

'Probably quicker than opening things my way,' he said. 'Let's use them.'

'Okay, we've searched his gym, swimming pool and garage,' Mary said, 'but no Kimberley, no drugs, nothing. So why did he run?'

'One thing's obvious, he's got her hidden. We need to pick him up and ask him nicely where she is.'

Mary flinched as she put a hand over her stomach. 'Yes, and I'd like to be there when you *question* him.'

'Now you're getting the idea. No good leaving it to judges. Do unto scumbags as they would do unto you, but do it first, that's my motto.'

'Why do you stay in this job if that's how you feel?'

'Why not? I'm being paid and I get to hand out a little justice of my own now and again.'

'I don't think I'll ever really understand what makes you tick.'

'You will in time. Wait until some smart solicitor gets a child molester or wife-beater off on a technicality. Wait until you see the smug look on their faces as they walk free to do it again.' He clenched his fists. 'Then you'll know.'

She looked thoughtful. 'Hmm, maybe there's something to be said for the way you work after all.'

*

Joseph banged on the glass partition. Julie looked up from a magazine. 'He's out,' she said, returning to her reading. Joseph used his shoulder to force open the door and strode through to Mark Payne's office.

'You can't go in there!' Julie protested.

'Too late.'

'Nothing,' Joseph said. 'She's not in here, let's try the outbuildings.'

As they went back through reception Julie backed into a corner, clutching her magazine. 'I told you he was out.'

'Does that thing have work vacancies?'

'Yes. What are you looking for?'

'It's not for me, it's you,' he retorted. 'Once we catch up with your boss, you'll be looking for another job.'

'And if you keep harassing him, so will you. He knows lots of people, some of them high up in the police. He said they'll come down on you like a ton of bricks.'

'Did he? We'll see. Even bent coppers shy away from murderers.'

Julie dropped the magazine. 'Murder? He wouldn't –'

'He has. If I were you, I'd watch my back. They can only hang him once, metaphorically speaking. You could disappear same as Kimberley.'

'Kimberley? Who's she? Never heard of her.'

'Well, it's your funeral and I'm *not* speaking metaphorically. Aiding and abetting a known criminal? How do you fancy a long holiday in Holloway at the taxpayer's expense?'

'Mark will look out for me. He always has.'

'We're wasting time, sir,' Mary said. 'Let's check the warehouses.'

Fish drifted against the sides of the tanks. 'They look hungry,' Mary said. 'I wonder when they were last fed?'

'Only Kimberley knows that answer.' Turning the corner of the last row of aquariums Joseph bumped into a man pushing a broom. 'Where's your boss, and the woman who feeds the fish? Have you seen them?'

The man leant on his broom. 'Depends on what you mean. Of course, I've seen them, I work here. But if you mean, "Have I seen them today," that's a different question.'

Joseph grabbed his overall and pushed him against the tanks. Water slurped up the side. Fish darted back and forth.

'Don't get smart with me or I'll shove your sodding broom up your arse. Where – is – he?'

The man's head ricocheted off the glass. 'I don't know,' he gasped.

'Let him go, sir. He's not the full ticket.'

'The woman who works in here, when did you last see her?' Joseph released his grip.

'Two days ago, I think. I only do part-time. Yesterday I was at my allotment, weeding. I've had some lovely –'

'I expect you have.' He turned to Mary. 'We're not getting anywhere in here, let's try next door.'

The padlock offered little resistance to Joseph.

'How do you open these things?' Mary said.

'Never mind. You take this side. I'll check over there.'

'Somebody's cleaned the place from top to bottom,' Joseph said, snapping the lock back into place. 'If Payne is here, he's doing a bloody good job of hiding.'

Chapter 24

October 1986

The plane hit the runway hard and bounced twice before settling onto the tarmac, engines screaming in reverse. Mark Payne joined the other passengers in a round of applause for the pilot.

A blanket of humid air hit Mark at the top of the stairs leading from the aircraft. 'Jesus, I didn't realize Spain would be this hot.'

The air hostess smiled her professional smile. 'Thank you for choosing to fly with us today, sir. We hope you had a pleasant flight and look forward to flying with you again.'

'Thanks, love, I will. Only here for a visit.' Clutching his bag of duty-free drink and cigars he clunked his way down the steps, stopped, removed his coat, undid the top button of his shirt and loosened his tie.

Sun-glasses resting on top of his head, garish, short-sleeved shirt, baggy shorts, toes parted by the strap of flip-flops, all contributed to make Samuel Beckworth stand out from residents of his newly adopted country.

Pushing through the throng of people he held out a hand across the rope barrier. 'You made it then, Mark. Good flight?'

'Bit lumpy. Not too bad, I suppose. You got a car?'

Samuel glanced toward the glass entrance doors. 'Yes, in the car park. Have to open the doors before we get in, not much shade out there.'

Mark handed him his luggage. 'Here, make yourself useful.'

*

The Fiat spluttered to a halt in front of a tall apartment building. Heat haze turned the view ahead into a modernist painting. Blurs of colour, indistinct shapes. White walls warding off the glare of the sun. Garden plants, nestling against the building, wore speckles of white paint. A bright-eyed gecko, defying gravity high on the wall, turned its head.

'Is this it?' Mark stared at the apartment block.

'Yes. There's a cracking view of the sea from the balcony.'

'What's special about it? I've seen the sea. It's where I live, remember?'

'Aah, but the women go topless out here. I've set up a telescope, helps pass the time.'

'No wonder you don't seem to be selling much. About time you took your hand off your cock and got grafting.'

Samuel got out of the car and lifted suitcases from the rear seat. 'It's not easy,' he said. 'Most of the Brits are too pissed to buy drugs.'

'I know, I read the papers back home. Bloody cheap booze, it's ruining things out here.'

'Oh, it's not too bad. I'm getting some regulars. You have to be patient. Nothing gets done in a hurry out here, everything's man-bloody-yarna with this lot. Come on. Let's get out of the sun, it's cooler inside.'

'Do you have to climb all those stairs every time you come in and out?' Mark mopped his forehead.

'No, there's a lift.'

'Why didn't we use it, you silly bastard?'

'It's not working. Some days it does, other days it don't. That's Spain for you.'

'Thank God I don't have to live here.'

'You get used to it. Anyway, how long are you staying? You didn't say.'

'Not long, a couple of days should do it while I think things out. The law's breathing down my neck. Nosey bloody lot, hounding legitimate business men like me. I don't know why we pay our taxes.'

'What's the problem this time?'

'A slut. She was working for me and I caught her snooping around. My guess is she was planted by the coppers.'

'What did you do about her?'

'I gave her to my brother.'

Samuel's expression changed. Despite the sun-tan, the colour drained from his face. 'What? You know what he's like. Poor mare, would have been better to top her.'

'No problem, Donald's got his instructions.'

'Then you'll go back?'

'She's not why I flew out here. I hit a copper. There were no witnesses, so Twyford will be able to handle it.'

'Was it the bastard who beat me up? I hope you gave him a bloody good going over.' Samuel grinned.

'No, not him, it was the bit of skirt he carts around with him. I gave her a good wallop, teach her to barge in where she's not wanted.'

'You and your brother. Like two peas in a pod.'

'Only in looks. I'm the brains of the family. I'm the one with a big house, swimming pool and American cars.' Mark walked onto the balcony and gazed down at the white sand. 'He's a wanker. What's he got? A wife he thinks nothing of. A poxy job with the council, and the few bob I bung him from time to time when I want things done.'

'I meant the way you both treat women.'

'What are you on about? Women should know their place, that's all there is to it.' Mark's stomach growled. 'Getting hungry,' he said. 'What you got to eat?'

'Biscuits, bit of bread. Not much, I eat out all the time. It's so cheap, it's not worth cooking.'

'You eat foreign muck? Bloody octopus and rice?'

'No, there's a couple of bars who sell British beer, fish and chips, egg and chips, spam fritters and chips, steak and –'

'Don't tell me, let me guess. Chips.'

'Well, you can always have a bacon butty if you don't want chips. Steve's place has got proper Heinz tomato ketchup and HP sauce.'

'I see you enjoy the good life out here, no wonder you haven't earned much for me. Speaking of which, how much have you got stowed away?'

'Not a lot. I have to live and you said it was easier to use some of the takings rather than keep sending me my wages. I only send you any English money I get.'

*

Stevie's Wonder Bar. Aluminium stacking chairs surrounded tables cluttering the black and pink marble promenade. The cloying smell of coconut sun-oil hung in the air. A young Spaniard, carrying plates of food on his outstretched arm, snaked around the tables, followed by a girl holding a tray of drinks.

Samuel watched Mark ogling her. 'I wouldn't if I were you. That's Francisco and Maria. He's her brother. They say he knifed someone for talking to her.' Samuel used his beer glass to redirect Mark's stare. 'Isabel, behind the bar is part owner with Steve. He's from London. All the Brits out here have to have a Spanish partner if they want to open a business. Francisco and Maria aren't her kids, they walked in one day and asked for jobs.'

Mark licked his lips. 'Mmm, I could fancy Isabel. Is she married to Steve?'

'No.'

'Has she got a husband?'

'If she has, I've never clapped eyes on him. Steve gets enough nooky without bothering her, always plenty of holidaymakers ready to shake the sand from their knickers.'

'I think I'll get to like this place, apart from the heat. Let's take a look at the menu.'

'That's something else out here. Don't make no difference where you eat, the menu's the same.'

'Not bad,' Mark wiped egg off his chin. 'Not bad at all.' Picking up his glass he held it toward the bar. 'Same again.'

'You should have had the steak, bloody marvellous,' Sam replied. 'Washed down with English beer. Like being back home, but with wall-to-wall sunshine.'

'Busy little place this, must be making money. Why is it taking so long to get my business off the ground?'

'Like I said, cheap booze. The clubs may be a good market for drugs, but I need youngsters to take it in. I get turned away. Too old.'

Mark moved his lips as he counted tables. 'What's the problem? If you know the answer, do it.' Turning his head, he continued counting.

'I wish it was as easy as you think. The British lads aren't here long enough to be of any use, and the locals don't speak bloody English.'

'How much does Steve make, running this place? That brother and sister never seem to stop. All this booze must bring in a decent profit.'

Samuel pinched the loose skin of his neck. 'No idea. I could ask I suppose. Why?'

'Because while we've been sitting here, I've been counting heads. Is it always busy like this?'

'Most of the time.' Samuel paused to drain his glass. 'They do well at breakfast and lunchtimes but evenings are best. In between it's mainly drinks.'

Mark rubbed the ends of two fingers against a thumb. 'Sounds good to me. There's more to Spain than I thought. Let's get back to your place. I could use a shower.'

*

'Jesus, that's bloody hot,' Mark said, swiftly removing his hand from the back of a plastic chair on Samuel's balcony.

Samuel moved into the only patch of shade. 'Try this,' he said. 'It's cheaper than the imported British beer, but you get what you pay for.' Peering down over the tops of palm trees dotting the edge of the beach, he grinned. 'Look at those silly bastards. Like a piano keyboard, more white ones than brown. They'll regret it. The sun's a real killer out here. It'll skin you alive if you're not careful, even at this time of year.'

'I see why Steve's bar does so well, this beer seems to evaporate. Get me another.' Mark held out his glass.

'Like some cheese with it?' Samuel said. 'It's proper Cheddar.'

'Not for me. How many English bars are there?'

'Only Steve's. Unless you count the Irish one. The rest are Spanish.'

'So . . . he's got the English all to himself. Very clever.'

'He is. Some of the holidaymakers do use the Spanish ones, and *The Cheeky Leprechaun*. But you're right, Steve does do well.'

'Perhaps I'd be better off investing in a bar. Drugs don't seem to be doing much.'

'Easier said than done. First, you've got to get yourself a Spaniard for a partner, and then you've got to find a place. When you've –'

'Don't give me all that crap. I've already found the perfect place. Stevie's Wonder Bar. May even keep the name. It wouldn't be my first choice but …'

'Steve's? He won't sell. Why would he? He's making a bloody good living.'

'Good for him. Now it's my turn.'

Samuel's expression changed. 'What do you mean? You're only out here for a few days.'

'I can change my mind, can't I? Does this place of yours have a phone?'

'No. I have to go into town and use a call box. You'll need a fistful of pesetas too. I'll come with you and show you how to do it.'

'Bloody hell. Is it far?'

'No, not really. Or you could ask Steve. He lets me use his sometimes.'

'And have him listen to my private conversation? Sod that. Tomorrow morning you can drive me into town.'

Chapter 25

October 1986

Mary pulled the net curtain aside and moved her face nearer to the glass. 'Military Police? What on earth do they want?'

Leaping from his chair Graham rushed from the room. The door to the rear garden slammed.

The soldiers knocked.

Mary shook her head. 'Now what's he done?'

'Mrs Wells? Is your husband at home? Corporal Wells has been declared absent without official leave.' They pushed past Mary. 'We have orders for his arrest.'

'I am WDC Wells to you, and no, he's not here.'

'We'll take a look all the same. Funny how many times men who aren't at home are found hiding in lofts or cupboards. Found one a couple of weeks ago dressed as a woman. Silly bleeder should have remembered to shave.' He laughed.

The second man disappeared into the bedroom. There was a lot of banging and scraping. 'Not in here, Sarge,' he yelled.

'Try the kitchen.'

'Yes, Sarge.'

The sergeant's eyes narrowed. 'When did you last see your husband?'

'This morning.'

'Why haven't you reported him? You of all people should know it's an offence to harbour anyone on the run.'

'Very true. But I didn't know he was. He told me he'd been thrown out. Something about an officer's wife.'

'Correct. He would probably have been dishonourably discharged if he'd attended his court martial. How he got off the Islands we don't know.' The sergeant pulled the sofa away from the wall and peered behind it. 'I take it he isn't exactly the flavour of the month with you, after playing away from home? Why don't you tell us where he is so we can get him out from under your feet?'

Mary sighed. 'I don't know where he's gone, and now you've set the hare running he's not likely to come back.'

'He may. Like I said, there's a lot of silly bleeders about. If you see him, tell him to give himself up. Save everyone a lot of trouble.' Walking into the kitchen he said, 'Check the garden, see if there's a shed.'

'Gotcha, Sarge.'

'I can save you the trouble, we don't have one.' Mary sniffed. 'He was abroad most of the time and the attraction of a shed beats me. It must be a man thing.'

'Search the garden anyway,' the sergeant snapped. 'And hurry up.' He looked at Mary. 'I think this is a fool's errand. He's had it on his toes I reckon.'

'Well, if he's not here, I'd agree it's a possible explanation.'

*

Joseph thrust his hands into his trouser pockets. 'AWOL? And you didn't know? Are you sure?'

'Of course, I am,' Mary protested. 'Do you think I'd harbour him if I knew?'

'Sorry, but this was the last thing I expected to hear.'

'Apology accepted. It was a shock to me too. Still, looking on the bright side, I think it's the last I'll see of him.'

Putting his arms around her he pulled her close. 'I'd like to think so too, but there's no guarantee.'

'Yes, a divorce would be a much cleaner solution.'

'I used to be good at clean solutions.' Joseph grinned. 'But it was legal then.'

Mary frowned. 'Not sure I like the sound of that.'

'If I were you, I'd change the lock. He'll be back, mark my words. Or, collect your stuff and move in with me.'

'He'd be daft to come back with those MPs looking out for him.' She smiled. 'Feels rather good actually. Almost like having a personal bodyguard.'

'You've already got one of those – me. Now, back to work. Kimberley's missing, and in my book she's top priority.'

'Agreed. The patrol cars and all officers on the beat have been informed,' Mary said, 'If she's around she'll be spotted.'

'Yes, "if she's around" being the operative phrase. For my money the best we can hope for is she's being held against her will. Failing that...' His words trailed off into silence. 'My god, if Payne *is* behind this, I'll make him wish the midwife had never slapped his arse.'

*

Mary opened the front door cautiously. 'Graham? Are you here?' She checked each room. 'Hmm, I can see you haven't taken much. Where on earth are you?'

Holding the phone, she waited. 'Hello, Joe, I only wanted to let you know you were right about him coming back . . . okay, don't rub it in. Anyway, he's taken some of his things, so it doesn't look as if he plans to push his luck. Pardon? A drink? Yes, . . . okay, I'll wait for you to pick me up. Love you too,' she said, touching her lips to the phone.

*

Joseph watched Mary as she walked towards him.
'Where are you taking me?' she said, getting into the Rover.
'How about Hornigolds for a change? We haven't been there for a while.'
'Sounds good to me. I could use a stiff drink.'

*

The woman serving behind the bar poured rum over crushed ice, added ginger beer, squeezed a lime then garnished the cocktail with a green slice. Placing it on a paper coaster she waited. A young man paid, picked up his drink and took it to his table.
'What was that, Sandra?' Joseph asked.
'Dark and Stormy,' she said. 'Ginger beer and rum. Would you like to try?'
'Yes, why not? We're not on duty.'
'Nice to see you, Sandra, been a while.' Mary smiled.
Sandra busied herself with the cocktails. 'Yes, I wondered where you'd both got to lately. There you are. Enjoy.'
'Thanks,' Joseph said. 'How's things?'

'Not too bad, thanks.'

'We noticed the poster outside. *Coming soon. Late night disco.* Since when have you had music nights? And who's Sam Bellamy?'

'The DJ. He named himself after the pirate. Even wears an eye-patch. And we haven't had music before. It's something the governor wants to try. He wants me to take out some of the tables to make room for dancing.'

'Good luck with that. Strange combination, cocktails and disco.' Joseph nodded toward a table. 'Let's sit over there, by the skeleton.'

Mary grinned. 'Anyone we know?'

'No. He just acts as a warning to anyone thinking about going on a diet.' He rubbed his stomach.

'Oh.' Mary grinned. 'Got nothing to do with the cutlass sticking out of his ribs I suppose?'

'Have to ask Forensics, they may be able to work it out if you give them long enough.'

Sandra collected the glasses. 'Anything else, you two?'

'How about a steak sandwich?' Joseph said.

'Is that a cocktail? I haven't heard of it. Only kidding, we don't do food. I've tried talking to the new owner but –'

'What new owner?' Mary looked towards the bar. 'Last time we spoke, you said how well this place was doing.'

'It was, and still is. I've no idea why he sold it. It was all over before I even knew about it.'

'Do you get on with your new boss? Okay, I assume, or you wouldn't be here.'

'Payne's –'

'Payne? Not Mark Payne?'

'Yes, that's him. Why? Do you know him?'

'We certainly do,' Mary said. 'Have you seen him lately?'

'No. He doesn't come in very often. The last time he came he was with two men, one looked like a boxer. He had a squashed ear. The other one had funny eyes.' She shuddered. 'I didn't like the look of either of them.'

'If you see Payne, would you give us a call?'

'I might do.' She turned to look at the entrance door. 'But on the other hand, I might not. He's not the type of person to upset.'

Joseph laced his fingers, rotating his thumbs. 'You always were a shrewd judge of character. Be careful. But if you do see him . . .'

'Okay. Now, two more of the same?'

'Payne owns this place now, does he? Quite apt really, the pirate theme I mean.' Mary gazed up at the crows-nest. Its occupant leered down at her through cavernous eye sockets. Tied to the mast, the dreaded black flag had lost some of its menace beneath the silken touch of cobwebs. 'One thing's certain, Sandra won't see the man with strange eyes again.'

'True, but she should be on her guard.' He put his glass down. 'Watch it, she's coming back. I'll have a friendly word.'

Coffee slopped from her cup as Sandra pulled a chair back. 'Mind if I join you? Bit quiet at the moment, give me a chance to take the weight off my legs.'

'Of course, you can,' Mary said. 'As a matter of fact, we were talking about you. And your new boss.'

'Oh. What were you saying?'

Joseph used the slice of lime as a paddle to stir his drink. 'For a start I'd like to warn you about the new owner of this place. He's got a lot of questions to answer when we find him.'

'Sounds ominous. Should I be worried?' She turned her attention to Mary.

'Yes, you should,' Mary said.

'Meaning? Is he dangerous? I know I said there was something about him and his friends I didn't like but . . .'

'I don't think you're in any immediate danger, but we do have to grab him as soon as possible.' Joseph swirled the last of his cocktail. 'Other people are certainly at risk.'

'I was thinking of handing in my notice,' Sandra said. 'I think you've made up my mind. I get enough hassle from the creeps who come in here, without working for one.'

'Can you think of anything of interest regarding your boss?'

'Such as?'

'Has he done anything strange? Anything unusual going on?'

'He does make me keep separate books. One lot for him, one lot for the tax man.'

'Best I didn't hear that.' Joseph winked. 'But I've got bigger fish to fry than somebody cheating Her Majesty's government.'

'Worth bearing in mind though,' Mary said. 'It's how they got Al Capone.'

Joseph looked at his watch. 'Fancy another?'

Mary smiled. 'Why not? I'll have a Stormy Weather, please, Sandra.'

'Close,' she said. 'But you mean, Dark and Stormy.'

'There you are, two Dark and Stormy.'

'Thanks, Sandra. These are good.' Mary licked her lips.

Sandra took a few steps back towards the bar, then stopped. 'I did think of something while I was slicing the limes,' she said. 'Payne had part of the cellar partitioned. He's put a lock on it. Bloody nuisance, it was cramped enough as it was. Where I'm supposed to keep the stock I –'

'Has he? Now that's more like it. Show me.' Joseph got to his feet.

Sandra looked towards the door. 'Supposing he comes in and catches me?'

'He won't. Mary will keep lookout. Come on, let's take a look.'

'Ouch!' The single light bulb swung back and forth after coming into contact with Joseph's head. Shadows danced across whitewashed walls. A lone moth entered into its courtship ritual. Bottles of all shapes and sizes occupied shelves on either side.

'Sorry. I should have warned you. I'm used to it down here,' Sandra said. 'Look, there it is, right at the end.'

Joseph tugged the padlock. 'Hmmm. I don't think he wants you in there.'

'He only had to tell me not to go in, no need for a lock.'

'Which begs the question, what's he hiding? I'd like to take a look, but I haven't got my tools. What time do you close tonight?'

'You've been gone a long time,' Mary said. 'Come here, you've got cobwebs in your hair.' She brushed at the dusty strands.

'Thanks. I've got to come back later. I've got a date with a lock.'

'Am I invited?' Mary looked towards the bar.

'If you want to help, yes. But it's strictly off duty. Hughes would never sanction it.'

'Shame. I thought we could claim these drinks on petty cash. I was thinking of having another.'

*

A drink can trundled down the road, propelled by an onshore wind. It came to a halt at the feet of a young couple cuddled in a nearby shop doorway.

The Rover glided to a halt.

'Let's hope Sandra's as good as her word. Wouldn't like this to be a wild-goose chase.' Joseph got out of the car. He tapped his jacket pocket. 'Shouldn't take long.'

Mary joined him. 'Let's hope it's worth the trouble.'

The door opened to Joseph's knock. 'Hello, Sandra. Thanks for staying on. We'll run you home as soon as we get finished.'

'Are you sure he won't turn up? I'm having second thoughts about this.'

'Don't worry. I'll stay here. No one will get past me.' Mary straightened her shoulders.

'Thanks,' Sandra said, 'I feel safer knowing you're on guard.'

Joseph handed Sandra the lock. 'Hold onto this a minute,' he said, pushing the door open. 'Now, let's see what he's hiding.'

'What's he keeping in there? Did you find anything?' Sandra called out.

'Nothing. It's only invoices and stuff. No hidden treasure.' Joseph snapped the padlock. 'Never mind, it was worth a look. Thanks, Sandra. I owe you a drink sometime.'

'I don't know whether I'm glad or disappointed,' she said. 'Are you sure there's nothing in there? Why would he keep it locked?'

'Why would he do lots of things?'

'Can we go now? I'm getting the creeps. He may turn up at any minute.'

'Yes. Lock up and we'll take you home. Thanks for your help.'

'Anything?' Mary asked when Joseph came back up the stairs.

'Nothing. Let's get Sandra home, it's way past mid-night.'

*

Mary watched Sandra close her front door, then turned to face Joseph. 'Right. Now tell me what you really found. I've seen that look before.'

'Can't hide much from you, can I.' He took an envelope from an inside pocket. 'Here, take a look at these.'

Mary turned on the courtesy light. 'Wow!' She held up one of the strips of negatives. 'Who's the woman? And all these different men? You told Sandra you didn't find anything. Why?'

'If she knew, she may not be able to hide the fact from Payne.'

'Makes sense.' She looked at another strip. 'Have you seen all these?'

'I saw enough. There was a camera there too, but as it didn't have any film, I left it. Knowing how smart he is, it's a fair bet we wouldn't find any fingerprints anyway.'

'Judging by what's going in these pictures I'd say there's a good chance they were taken in the dead prostitutes flat.' She held the negatives closer to the light. 'These look like Payne. Hard to tell in a negative. But if it is, they'll help put him away for life.'

'I agree. We've got the evidence, now all we have to do is bring him in.'

Chapter 26

November 5th 1986

Donald signed the cheques using his brother's name. 'Is that it? Anything else need doing?'

Julie finished tucking her blouse back into the waistband of her skirt. 'No, I think you've taken care of everything,' she said. 'When will Mark be back, do you know?'

'Not for a while, my dear. You'll just have to get used to me.' He fondled her backside. 'Must be off, don't want to be late to the office. I don't get all day for lunch despite what you hear about council workers.'

'Next time you speak to Mark, remember to tell him I'm doing extra hours. I don't want any fuss when he sees my wage slips.'

'Don't concern yourself. I'll make sure he knows you're giving sterling service.'

She scrunched up a tissue and dropped it in the wastepaper basket. 'Don't. He'll kill me.'

'Then do exactly as you're told. I'll be back later in the week. Don't forget the baby oil.'

*

Mary spat into the sink, placed her toothbrush in the mug and dabbed her lips on the towel. 'Great breakfast,' she said. 'I think you can have the job when we get married.'

Joseph grinned. 'The sooner the better as far as I'm concerned. I'll get a fresh shirt and see you downstairs.'

Closing the bedroom door, he jammed his wallet under it. Removing the row of shoes, he prised the shelf up. 'Bugger!'

'Are you okay, Joe?' Mary's muffled voice asked. 'Have you hurt yourself?'

'No, I'm fine. I stubbed my toe. Put the kettle on when you've finished, we've got time for a cuppa.' He continued to stare into the void. 'Who the devil —'

'Sorry, are you speaking to me, darling?'

'No, go on down, I'll be with you in a minute.'

*

Mary flicked the indicator to signal her intention to turn into the road leading to Mark Payne Enterprises. Joseph clutched her arm. 'Stop. Pull over. There he is, on the other side of the road.'

Further back in the line of traffic, a Ford Escort joined other vehicles braking sharply.

'Where's he going?' She pulled the hand brake on.

'Does it matter? Let's grab the bastard.'

Mary turned to Joseph. 'Aren't you going to radio in?'

He frowned. 'No. Later perhaps. I want to keep this strictly between him and me. Don't need smart-arse solicitors muddying the waters. Stay with the car, I won't be a minute.'

Before she could reply, he was out of the Rover and dodging between the traffic.

The Ford Escort pulled into the kerb. 'Now what's lover-boy doing?' Graham scratched the side of his head. 'Be nice if he stepped under a bus, but I suppose that's asking a bit too much.'

Joseph attacked his target from behind. A punch to the kidneys brought the man to his knees. A good Samaritan ran to intervene.

'Police,' Joseph said, producing his warrant card. 'Thank you, sir, but everything's under control. This man is wanted for questioning.'

'Get him off. He's robbing me,' the man gasped.

The would-be rescuer glanced at Joseph's card, looked at the man and walked away.

Joseph used one knee to pin the man to the pavement. Forcing his victim's arms up behind his back he snapped handcuffs on. His protests were silenced by Joseph's hand clamped over his mouth. Dragging him to his feet, Joseph pushed him into the traffic, frog-marching him towards the Rover.

Headlights flashed; horns blared.

Mary jumped from the Rover and opened the rear door.

Joseph pushed the man. 'Mind your head.'

Mary turned away as the man's head hit the car.

'Get off me, you maniac! What the hell do you think you're doing?'

Joseph pushed him again. 'I told you to watch your head.'
Turning to Mary he said, 'Give me your cuffs. I'll attach him to
the door. I don't want him falling out before he's answered my
questions.'

The Rover indicated and pulled out into the traffic. A bemused
Graham attempted to do the same.

'Take the next left turn,' Joseph said.

'That's a long way round,' she protested. 'It's quicker if –'

'Do as I say. I want a quiet word with our friend before we take
him in.'

Mary started to open her mouth but changed her mind.
Approaching the junction she turned the Rover, accelerated away
from the town and into the countryside.

With eyes wide open, the man stared out at the passing fields.
'Who are you two? Where are you taking me? You can't do this!'

Joseph pushed him against the car door. 'Pull the other one,
Payne. You know very well who we are. What's more to the
point, where's Kimberley?'

The man's face turned pale. 'Kimberley? I've no idea who
you're talking about.'

'I think you do.' Turning to Mary, he said, 'Pull into the next
lane, park in the yard on the left-hand side. It's an abandoned
farm, there's a barn there which will do just fine.'

She glanced sideways, but did as ordered.

Graham slowed his Ford Escort as he saw the Rover turn off the
road.

Passing the farm entrance, he pulled onto a grass verge. Opening
the glove compartment, he took out the gun and walked back.

Inside the gloomy potato barn the sound of a fist smacking into
a face scared pigeons from the joists overhead. Mary looked up as
the startled birds flew towards the open door.

'Where's Kimberley?' Joseph snarled. 'Tell me now and save
yourself a lot of pain.'

'Get stuffed.' The man spat spittle tinged with blood. 'When I
get to my office, I'll report this to the police.'

'Why don't you stop playing stupid games? We searched your premises, remember?'

'I heard. He was my –'

Joseph pulled the man towards him. He fought back and spun Joseph around.

Stepping around puddles, Graham approached the barn. His training took over. Pressing his body against the corrugated walls of the building he made his way towards the door. Leaning around the opening he waited while his eyes adjusted to the low light level inside the barn. Resting the gun on his forearm he took aim.

The gunshot reverberated around the building.

The man went limp in Joseph's arms.

Joseph let go of him and dropped to one knee, fumbling for a weapon he hadn't carried for years.

Mary rushed to help Joseph. He pulled her to the floor. 'Get down! Stay down!'

Graham turned and ran.

Joseph recovered and sprinted towards the door. A discarded length of rusty chain tripped him. His arms flailed as he fell to the floor. Getting back to his feet he ran through the farmyard into the lane in time to see his quarry throw himself into an estate car. The vehicle roared away.

Joseph chased after it. Arms working like pistons, lungs sucking in air.

As the lane bent to the right, the tyres lost traction. The car ploughed into a grassy bank. Chunks of mud and grass spewed into the air as Graham fought to reverse. Giving up he leapt from the vehicle and used the roof to support the pistol.

A pheasant took to the air as two shots disturbed the peace of the countryside. Instinctively Joseph threw himself to the ground. 'Right, you bastard, I'll catch up with you later.' Staying low and using the hedgerow for cover he worked his way back to the barn.

Mary released the man's handcuffs, felt for his pulse and looked up. 'I think he's dead.' She checked again. 'Yes, he's definitely gone. I know he's a villain, but why would anyone shoot him?'

'Because *he* wasn't the target. I was. We were fighting. He must have moved into the line of fire.' He looked down at his grazed hands. 'And if I hadn't gone arse-over-tit I'd have caught your husband.'

'Graham? It can't have been him. I don't believe it!'

'You'd better. I saw him in the lane, plain as day.'

'If it *was* Graham, where would he get a gun? Steal it from the army?'

'He didn't have to. I'm pretty certain it was mine.'

'My head's ringing,' she said, massaging her ears with the palms of her hands. 'Did you say it was your gun? You haven't got one.'

'You're right, I haven't now, but I did have. When I left the service, I hung onto a souvenir. It seemed a good idea at the time, but in hindsight it was a stupid thing to do.'

'I can tell you another stupid thing,' she said, staring down at the body. A shaft of light from a hole in the barn roof illuminated the body. 'This is *not* Mark Payne.'

'Don't be daft, of course it's him.'

'Well, I'm telling you it's not. Take a look at his hands. Mark Payne wears a chunky gold ring. Not only isn't this man wearing a signet ring, there's no white mark on any of his fingers to show he ever did.' She pointed. 'Whoever he is, he didn't deserve to die. And I shouldn't say it, but both our careers have just gone up in smoke.'

'That's madness. Let me take a look.' Rummaging through the dead man's pockets he pulled a driver's licence from a wallet. 'Payne. There you are, I told you. Wait a minute. Donald – bloody – Payne. What's going on?'

'My guess is he's Mark Payne's twin brother. It's the only explanation.'

'Do what? I never knew he had a brother.'

'Why would you?' Holding out her hands, she added, 'Look, I'm shaking. Do you realize how near you were to being killed?'

He put an arm around her and pulled her close. 'Seems my guardian angel is still watching out for me. I've had my share of close shaves, but this must be the pick of the bunch.'

'I still can't believe Graham shot this man. What the hell did he think he was doing?'

'It's the old old story, two men and a woman. The eternal triangle.' He brushed at the blood spatters on his jacket. 'This'll have to be burned. And my trousers.'

Mary took out a handkerchief, spat on it and wiped blood off Joseph's hands. 'Why? I know a perfectly good dry cleaners.'

'And how do I explain all this blood? He's leaked all over me. No, they'll have to go.' He shook his head. 'A victim's blood on my clothes and a gun still registered to me despite reporting it lost in action. Ballistics will match the bullet to the gun and, hey presto, yours truly is in the frame for murder. Get it?'

'But Graham's prints will be on the gun.'

'And so will mine, unless he's done a bloody good job of cleaning it.'

'Of course, they will. Sorry my brain's gone to sleep.' She swallowed. 'What are our options?'

'Plan A, I report the incident. But if your husband has thrown the weapon away, it may be found. And I can't prove it wasn't me who fired the shot.'

'Or?'

'Or, Plan B, we hide the body.'

His words brought a look of disbelief to Mary's face. 'No. We can't do that. We're serving officers, not criminals.'

'Back to the first plan then. But you have to realize it will probably cost me my freedom. If I'm convicted, it's the end of all our plans together.'

'But I'm a witness. I could tell them it was Graham.'

'You could, but think about it. The gun used was mine. How could I convince a jury I didn't use it?'

'You haven't got a motive for killing Donald Payne.'

'Agreed. But the gun will convict me if it's married to the bullet.'

Mary pointed to the body. 'Why don't we dig it out?'

'We could try. But there's no exit wound, it's probably lodged deep. We'd need to be surgeons to remove it. Let's face facts, we're in the shit, right up to our necks. I think disposing of him is the best bet. Will you help?'

'What choice have I got? What do you want me to do?'

'Go and see if you can recover his car.' He pointed towards the barn door. 'While you're gone, I'll try to find the cartridge case and something to wrap the body in. Keep an eye out, he may double back. And remember, he's got a gun.'

Pocketing the expended cartridge case, Joseph searched the barn. Rusty farm machinery vied for space with wood pallets, old sacks and general detritus. In a corner he found a crumpled polythene sheet, home to myriads of spiders and their webs. Dust filled the air as he pulled it free. He looked up as he heard a car reversing into the barn.

Mary flung open the vehicle door and scrambled out. 'What on earth have you been doing? You look as if you've seen a ghost. Sorry, that wasn't called for.'

He held out the plastic sheet. 'Get the gloves from my car. Then help me wrap the body and get it into Graham's car. I found some baling twine. We should be able to keep leakage to a minimum.'

'Where will we take him?'

'There's a wood not far from here.' Joseph held up a spade. 'I found this too.'

*

'This is it,' Joseph said, pointing. 'Follow the track until I tell you to stop.'

The Ford Escort bounced down between tall pines, tossing Joseph and Mary from side to side. As the main road became lost in the rear-view mirror, Mary slowed the car.

'Not here,' he snapped.

She turned to face him. 'I can't do this,' she said. 'We can't go burying people. I joined the force to protect the public.'

He looked away. 'I know how you feel, but think about the alternative. We don't have any other choice.'

'I don't agree, there must be another way. Why not make an anonymous phone call? At least he'd get a decent burial.'

'And when they perform an autopsy, they'll find the bullet, then, if your other half gets picked up by the Military Police with my gun, it's game over.'

'I don't like it. It's not right. I should never have agreed to help.'

'Fine. Reverse back or turn this thing around. Drive to the station and I'll report the whole incident. But don't say I didn't warn you. When the army catch up with Graham and my gun, I'll be charged with possession of an illegal weapon *and* be the main suspect in a murder case.'

Mary lowered her head onto the steering wheel. Hooking gloved fingers in her hair she rocked gently back and forth. 'It's all my fault. I shouldn't have let my feelings for you get out of hand.'

'Don't blame yourself. If I hadn't kept hold of the gun, Graham couldn't have stolen it. If he hadn't stolen it, Donald Payne would still be alive. If he was alive, we wouldn't be sitting here.' He put an arm around her. 'It's like when I was a kid. I used to stand dominoes up in a pattern then knock one over. A chain reaction starts and there's no stopping it.'

Turning towards him she said, 'I suppose you're right. We don't have a choice.' She put the car into gear. 'What's done is done and I can't face living the rest of my life without you. Let's get on with it.'

*

Joseph and Mary struggle to remove Donald Payne's body from the rear of the Ford Escort Estate car.

Laboured breath hangs in the cold night air as they carry the murder victim. Frost-encrusted leaves crunch underfoot. Every twig that snaps, jolts Mary's memory back to the gunshot which placed them in this situation.

Far above the woods, a sky-rocket explodes, sending balls of colour screaming across the winter sky, lighting up the shallow grave and Mary's tear-stained face.

Tipping the corpse into its final resting place, Joseph picks up his spade and shovels the excavated soil into the hole.

Mary watches in silence. Adjusting her gloves, she steps forward to help lift heavy logs onto the mound of earth.

Satisfied, Joseph nods towards the car.

'Now what?' Mary gasped, sinking into the driver's seat.

'Back to the barn to collect the Rover.' His fingers drummed on the dashboard, muffled by muddy gloves. 'We'll hide his car there. It's probably stolen anyway. Where would he get enough money to buy this?'

'Why not burn it, to be on the safe side?'

'We could, but gloves mean there's nothing to link us to this mess.'

'Does it mean we're in the clear?'

'Almost. The fly in the ointment is Graham. He knows where my gun is.'

Chapter 27

5th November 1986

Without light from the hurricane lamp, the Nissen hut was as black as night. Kimberley sobbed. A length of chain restricted her movements. The chemical toilet was within the boundaries of her confinement. The folding table, with its camping-gas stove, kettle, water and food were not. For these she relied on her jailer. Hunger and thirst slowly overpowered the feeling of revulsion at the price she knew she would have to pay for them.

'Where are you?' Her voice echoed back from the walls, mocking her. 'I need a drink, you bastard.'

Something scuttled in the corner of the room. Shuffling across the bed she pressed her body against the cold wall.

Chapter 28

5th November 1986

A firework screeched across the night sky, heading up towards the crescent moon hanging in the sky. The sky-rocket exploded. Golden rain and coloured balls fell back, reflecting in the sea.

Sitting in the sea-front shelter, Graham bit into a cold Cornish pasty.

'Got enough cash to keep body and soul together for a while,' he muttered. 'But not if I pay for bed and breakfast. Looks like I'll be sleeping under the stars tonight and it feels like it could be a chilly one.' Pulling his coat closer, the gun pushed against his ribs. 'Bit like being back on manoeuvres.'

Hooking a finger into his mouth he pulled out a piece of gristle and flicked it across the promenade. Taking another bite, he continued chewing. 'How did I miss lover-boy? And who was the silly bastard who took the bullet?' He drained the remains of a can of lager. 'Wonder if he's okay? Be a bugger if I've killed the wrong man.'

Rubbing his eyes, he glared at the illuminated dial of his watch. 'Two-a-bloody clock? It must be later than that. All these piss-heads wandering about don't help, how am I supposed to get any sleep?'

*

Graham rubbed his eyes and groaned as his body protested about sleeping on a bench. Memories flooded back. Off-duty time spent fishing for sea trout and mullet in the Falklands. The first day he too had been lured, but by bait of a different kind. The excitement of illicit love-making. Making plans for a new start. The adrenalin rush when surprised by a furious husband. Escaping custody and making his way back to England.

He stretched. His feet bumped against the end of the shelter. He tweaked his nose as a breeze carried the stink of cider and urine from a nearby shelter. 'Bloody drunks,' he muttered. 'Christ, it's cold. Time to get a brew and something to eat if there's anywhere open this early.'

Taking the gun from inside his pillow, a carrier bag stuffed with newspapers, he pushed it down the waistband of his trousers and buttoned up his coat. 'It's no good, I've got to get rid of this for the time being.' Putting both hands to the sides of his head he groaned. 'What a bloody mess. The army's after me. The wife's shacked up with a copper, and to top it all I've shot some poor fucker.' He looked up at the sky. 'You've got a funny sense of humour. What's next?'

A plastic bag scurried along the promenade. A puppet under the control of invisible fingers. It rubbed itself against Graham's legs, imitating the actions of a domestic cat. He bent down to free himself from its caress. The pistol dug into his ribs. Straightening his back, he looked up and down the promenade, picked up the bag and shook it open. Pulling the gun free, he dropped it inside.

Clutching the bag, he jumped from the promenade onto the beach. Waves washed around wooden sentinels, interlacing them with foaming swirls, mocking man's vain attempt to control the tides. Graham counted. Stopping at the fifth post he scanned the deserted beach. Using his bare hands, he scooped out a shallow hole. Sand and water filled in his excavation faster than he could dig. It didn't take long to realize this was not a good place to hide anything.

'I can't see any other way. One of us has to go.' Taking the pistol from its wrapping he placed it against his temple. Shaking his head, he said to a non-existent audience, 'But it's won't be me.'

With the weapon again concealed inside his jacket, Graham headed towards a café, the light from its windows a beacon for early morning customers.

Stepping inside, Graham looked down at his footprints on the wet floor.

'I don't need this hassle,' a man muttered, ramming a string-headed mop into a galvanised bucket.

'Sorry,' Graham said. 'What time do you open?'

'I am open, but my cleaner's not turned up again. Bloody waste of space. This was his last chance. He won't be working here again. Nor will his girlfriend.'

'Oh. Do you need anyone?'

'Of course, I do. I can't cope on my own. Do you know anyone? I need a cleaner and someone who can cook.'

'How about me? I can cook, and the army taught me how to scrub and clean if nothing else.'

'You ex-army? I don't mean to be rude, but I took you for a dosser. We get a few in here and you look like you've been sleeping rough.'

Graham looked down at his feet. 'I have. Had a ruck with the missus, been walking the streets since.'

'Been there, done that, got the tee-shirt.' The man grinned. 'If you want one of the jobs, it's yours.'

Graham held out a hand. 'Why not both? I could do with the money and long hours aren't a problem, I've got nothing else to do.'

'Suits me, if you think you can do it. The cooking's nothing fancy, mainly fry-ups, egg on toast, that sort of thing. I do the tea and coffee, cakes and sandwiches, and take the orders for meals. You'd be washing-up, as well as before and after-hours cleaning.' Wringing out the mop he passed it to Graham. 'My name's Charles, but friends call me Charlie. Be good if you can start right away. If you've nowhere to kip, you can make space in the store out back. It's not the Hilton, but it'll be better than a park bench.'

'Cheers, I appreciate it.'

'Get the floor washed, then we'll have a cup of tea and discuss your wages, *after* you do us both a Full English that is. I want to see how good your cooking is.'

Graham's stomach grumbled at the mention of food.

Chapter 29

November 1986

DCI Hughes tapped the sheet of paper with the end of a pen. 'Most unusual. I'm not certain I can allow the pair of you to take leave at the same time. Who will deal with your work?'

'May I speak off the record, sir?' Joseph tried to sound deferential.

'Go ahead.'

'Thank you, sir. I've placed a member of staff in jeopardy and would like to concentrate on resolving this. WDC Wells has agreed to help me. We'd be off duty from the official point of view, but in reality we will continue investigations into all our open cases.'

'I don't understand. Why apply for leave if you intend to carry on with your duties?'

'I did ask if this could be off the record. I feel –'

'And it is. Get to the point.'

'It would be better if my actions don't embarrass the force, should anything misfire.'

Hughes leaned back in his chair. 'I am not sure I like what I'm hearing. You've crossed the line in the past and I've had to call in a few favours.' Turning to Mary he added, 'And you? Why do you want to get involved?'

'We're a team, sir.'

'Good for you, I admire loyalty.' He sighed. 'Against my better judgement I will sign these applications. But for two days, not a week.'

'Thank you, sir. You won't regret it.'

'Off the record,' Hughes replied, 'I hope not. Do what you have to, but walk on eggshells.'

*

Mary separated hand written notes from the revised and typed versions, resting each pile on opposite arms of the armchair. 'I can't see this is getting us very far,' she said.

Joseph dunked a biscuit into his coffee as he sifted through the case-files on his coffee table.

'I have to admit you're right. We seem to be going around in circles. We have two suspects who have both gone to ground, and three murders which I'm certain can be laid at Payne's door.'

The tone of Mary's voice became sombre. 'And Kimberley could soon be added to the list.'

'You're right.' Scooping up the papers he stuffed them back into a folder. 'This lot will have to wait, our priorities have to be number one, find Kimberley, number two, find your husband and my gun. And number three, find that arsehole Payne and his stooge, Samuel Beckworth. Stuff all this paperwork, it's getting us nowhere, we need to be on the street.'

'Sounds better than sitting here,' she agreed. 'Where do we start?'

'Let's talk to Payne's receptionist. I'm sure she knows more than she's letting on.'

'Okay, but let me speak to her, woman to woman. It's possible she may drop her guard, it's worth a try.'

*

'Good morning,' Mary said, producing her warrant card. 'Have you heard anything from your boss?'

'He's on holiday.' Julie carried on painting her nails.

'Oh, is he? Somewhere nice?' She leaned forward. 'I like the colour, not seen that shade before.'

'The girl in the shop said it only came in last week.'

'It suits you.'

'Thanks.'

Mary looked around the reception area. 'Are you running the business while he's away?'

'More or less. His brother calls in from time to time, but he's not much use. He's keeping an eye on me I reckon.' She dipped a brush into a small glass bottle.

'What's he like, this brother?'

'Let's just say I prefer Mark. Donald is creepy. I hate him.'

Mary swallowed. 'When did you last see him?'

'He hasn't been around for a day or two.' She half closed her eyes as she concentrated. 'It was my lunch hour on firework day, I think. Yes, I'm right, it was. I went to the display in the evening.'

'How about Kimberley?'

'Kimberley?'

'The young woman who worked here.'

'There aren't any women here, apart from me.'

'Okay, if you're in charge while he's away, you're responsible for anything we may find.'

'The fish you mean? I don't have anything to do with them. It's the warehouse manager's job.'

'How about anything else?'

'I don't understand what you're talking about.'

'Don't try to be clever. This place can't support your boss's life style and you know it.'

'This? This is only how he got started. Now he's into property. Pubs and clubs mainly.'

'Who places the orders for stock? You?'

'No. Mark sorts all that out. I only deal with sales. Have you ever thought about having an aquarium?'

'Got enough in my life without worrying about a few goldfish.'

'We don't sell them. Mark specialises in fish from South America.'

'Why not Africa? A friend of mine collects those.'

Julie spread her hands and admired her nails. 'Don't know. You'll have to ask Mark.'

'If you tell me where he is, I will.'

'I could ask his brother, he may know.'

Mary drew a deep breath. 'Listen, between you and me, and I really shouldn't be telling you this, your boss is in serious trouble. And you could find yourself in prison for helping him.'

Julie's face drained of colour. 'Why? I'm only the receptionist. I don't know anything about what else goes on.'

'By saying that, you've confirmed these premises are being used for other than the trading of tropical fish. Now, let's start again. Where is Kimberley?'

'I told you. I've never heard of her.'

'If you want to play it like this, you only have yourself to blame. If she's come to any harm, painting your nails will be a thing of the past. Do yourself a favour, tell me where we can find Kimberley, no one need ever know it was you who told me. Us women have to stick together in this man's world. If you don't help me, you could be locked away for –'

'Okay . . . yes she did work here.' She looked straight at Mary. 'But Mark threatened if I ever mentioned her name, I'd be sorry.'

'Will you give evidence against him? I could arrange to have you treated leniently if you co-operate. He won't be able to hurt you once he's in prison.'

'But his brother will. They're as bad as each other.' Lowering her voice, she added, 'Donald was here the last time I saw her. If you want to find out where she is, you should ask him.'

Mary looked down at her feet. 'We will. In the meantime, help me to help you. Provide a statement. Make no mistake, Mark Payne is top of the list of people we wish to speak to in the course of murder enquiries.'

'I told you. I don't know anything. Even if I did, I couldn't tell you.'

'But you've got nothing to be afraid of. Help us convict him, then he'll be going away for a long time.'

'And if he gets off, it'll be *me* going away. Permanently. No thanks, I'll take my chances.'

*

Joseph leaned across to open the car door for Mary. 'Well? How did it go? Did you learn anything?'

'Yes, and no.' She swung herself into the driver's seat. 'Julie knows more than she's willing to admit, but Payne's got her wetting herself. She told me he's on holiday, but wouldn't say where.'

'Probably because she doesn't know. I think Payne's left the country. I'll speak to Hughes and request we issue International Arrest Warrants for Samuel Beckworth and Mark Payne.'

She turned to face him. 'I agree. But it's not *Mark* Payne who holds the answer to Kimberley's disappearance. It was *Donald*.'

Joseph thumped a fist against the car door. 'Bugger!'

Chapter 30

November 1986

Kimberley struggled to raise herself from the bed.

Where am I? I must be late for work. What day is it?

She fell against the wall as she tried to stand.

Wow, it's like being on board ship. I'm so dizzy. Have I been to a party?

She slumped back onto the bed.

I can't be bothered with the loo, it was only a dribble last time, not worth the effort. Mummy will get me up if I need to go. I'm so tired.

Her eyes closed. Drawing both knees up to her chest she locked her hands around them and slipped into a dark abyss.

Chapter 31

November 1986

The fragrance of sun-cream wafting from an adjacent table on the terrace of Stevie's Wonder Bar, would have provided a pleasant contrast to the ever-present smell of chips if Mark Payne had not been smoking a cigar.

Samuel ran a finger down the side of a cold beer glass, condensation raced ahead of it. 'Did you manage to speak to the bit of skirt running the place while you're away?'

'Yes, eventually. Bloody phones out here are next to useless.'

'How are things?'

'Not so good. She keeps moaning about how the police are giving her a hard time. Says they keep on at her about the nosy little cow I caught snooping around.'

'Is that all? Don't see why she's worried, they'll have a job to pin anything on you.'

'Keep your voice down.' Mark frowned. 'And mind what you say, most of these in here are English don't forget.'

'Sorry.'

'And so will my brother be when I go back. The lazy sod hasn't been around for a week and he's supposed to be helping out. It's another thing she's harping on about.'

'I bet sparks will fly when you get your hands on him.'

'You can say that again. We don't really get on, never have. Fought like cat and dog when we were kids. Not much better now. But we help each other out when it's in our mutual interest, as they say.'

Cigar smoke drifted lazily on the warm Mediterranean air as Mark Payne exhaled. Samuel poured another drink from a large bottle of San Miguel.

Mark grinned. 'This is the life. Pity the busybodies back home can apply for extradition now, otherwise it would be perfect.'

Samuel looked concerned. 'Extradition? When did that happen? You said I'd be safe out here.'

'Couple of months ago, July I think it was. But don't worry, the police aren't interested in you.'

'Then why did you send me out here? Not that I'm complaining, I love it.'

'Things were hotting up. Bloody coppers snooping around all the time, sticking their noses in, asking questions. I didn't want the added worry of having you taken in for an interview, never know what they'd trick you into saying. We're both safer with you out of the way.'

'Didn't money sort them out? You usually get what you want.'

'No. I didn't even offer. The two I've got on my back don't seem the type.'

'Oh.'

'The slut they planted in the warehouse isn't there now, so I thought it best to take a holiday.'

'Gone away, has she?' Sam winked. He waved his glass towards the bar. 'Two more when you're ready, Steve.' Leaning towards Mark he said, 'How's the new nightclub coming along? Can I come back for the opening?'

'Possibly. But now I'm setting up out here –'

'What? Are you serious? I told you, you need a Spanish partner.'

'Not a problem. I'll tell you what I've arranged when we're back at your place.'

*

Samuel paced back and forth in his apartment.

Mark re-lit his cigar as he sat with his feet up on the convertible settee. 'Sit down. You'll wear the tiles out.'

'I don't like the idea. Haven't I done enough already?'

'Maybe, but we've both got blood on our hands, so why not one more?' He brandished his cigar towards Samuel. 'I think all this sunshine's muddling your brains. I set you up out here and pay you good money, so do as I say.'

'Okay. I know. But I like Steve, isn't there another way? What about the Paddy bar? They don't do a bad trade.'

'No. I've made my decision and written to Twyford. He's preparing the papers as we speak. Steve's selling you his half of the business and going back to England.'

'Is he? I thought you said we were –'

Mark laughed. 'We are.'

'I don't like it. Why don't you give me more time to get the drugs thing sorted? I can find a young local lad who speaks English, I'm sure. Then we can get into the club scene, make some decent money.'

'You've had your chance and failed. Besides, getting the stuff out to you is costing me an arm and a leg. Those lorry drivers are getting greedy. No, it's time for a change, I'm giving up on drugs out here.' Mark paused. 'But if my bar idea doesn't work out, I may have to reconsider our working relationship. Do you catch my drift?'

'Yes, okay. I don't want to be left in Spain with no money coming in. If it's the only way, I guess you can count on me. I wish it wasn't Steve though. I get on well with him.'

'He's just another pawn in the game of life. If you want to get rich, you have to go for it. Anyone gets in the way, tread on them. And I do mean anyone.'

Chapter 32

November 1986

George, the desk sergeant, coughed and held out a scrap of paper. 'You're on your own today, Joe,' he said. 'Wells has phoned in sick. I made a note. She said she hopes to be in tomorrow.'

Joseph read the note, screwed it up and threw it towards the waste bin. 'Thanks. I wonder what's wrong? She seemed okay yesterday.'

George held out his splayed hands. 'Who knows with women? My wife's always having funny turns.'

'Perhaps she should have auditioned for Sunday Night at the London Palladium.' Joseph grinned. 'She may have been able to keep it going.'

The puzzled look confirmed the sergeant had missed the joke. Joseph shrugged.

'Something else,' George said. 'A Mrs Payne reported her husband went to work a week ago, on the fifth she said, and he hasn't returned home. She said she didn't worry at first as he often stays away on business. I got the impression she only phoned because she thought she ought to.'

'And?'

'The surname's the same as the fish place where young Kimberley went to work. I thought you'd like to know.'

'Thanks.'

*

A knock interrupted Joseph. He dropped a sheaf of papers back into the tray.

'Yes. Come in.'

'Good morning, sir, could I have a word? I've found something which may be of interest to you,' PC Jefferson said. 'It's to do with the prostitute murdered in her flat.'

Joseph straightened up in his chair. 'What is it?'

Jefferson took a deep breath. 'Well, sir, as I said when you asked me to help find Kimberley, it's an ambition of mine to transfer to being a detective. By the way, is there any news of her? I keep asking the mobile units and the other beat officers.'

'No. I'm afraid there isn't. Hughes has put all our resources into finding her, but there's nothing so far. Now, tell me what you found you think will prove interesting?'

'There was a complaint from a member of the public regarding a disturbance in a block of flats. I attended the incident and spoke to the parties involved, a tenant and his landlord.'

Joseph scratched the side of his chin. 'I fail to see what this has to do with a murder case. Can you get to the point? I've got mountains of paperwork to attend to.'

'Sorry, sir, but I'd seen the landlord before. He was interviewed about the murder in the flat. He was her landlord.'

'I admit it's a coincidence but why would I be interested? After we interviewed him, he was charged with allowing a property to be used for immoral purposes, but was cleared of any involvement in the prostitute's death. His case comes up next month, I believe.'

'Yes, sir, it does. But I did some investigating in my own time. I wanted to see how many other properties he owned in this area.'

'Good, shows initiative. And the answer is?'

'None. He's just a front man.'

*

Joseph's smile vanished as he gazed at Mary's unkempt hair, red rimmed eyes and ashen skin. 'Hello, my love. I was on my way home and thought I'd call to see you. Can I come in?'

'Of course,' she replied in not much more than a whisper.

Pushing aside the wine glass, Joseph put a cup of tea down in front of Mary. 'How are you feeling? I don't think you need me to tell you you're not looking great this evening. More like death warmed up than the woman I love.'

'Sorry, Joe.' She took a deep breath. 'I feel like somebody's stuck a needle into me and sucked out all my energy.'

'But you were fine yesterday. What brought this on? Has Graham been back?'

'No. I haven't seen him since the day he left. I've had a terrible night, that's all.' She sipped her tea.

'Why?'

'I had the same dream over and over again. It was terrible. I woke up soaked in sweat and feeling sick. Each time I got back to sleep I found myself standing beside the grave we dug in the woods. I could see his face through the plastic sheet.' She shivered. 'I was up most of the night. In the end I gave up, got myself a drink and listened to the radio.' She stretched her arms above her head and yawned. 'It helped stop the dreams from driving me mad.'

'My poor love, it's really getting to you isn't it. I know you didn't want to help bury him and I wish there was something I could do to change things. If only Graham hadn't used my gun things could have been so much different.'

'But he did. I feel as though I'm losing my mind, and it's not only at night. I find myself doing strange things in the daytime.'

'Oh? Such as?'

'The pork pie you lost? I found it in the filing cabinet, filed under P. Another day, at home this time, I found a pack of bacon in one of my dressing table drawers.'

He put his hand on hers. 'Why don't you go back to bed now I'm here? Get some sleep. You'll feel much better, I'm sure. I'll sit with you.'

'Thanks, Joe. I'd like that.'

Joseph tip-toed back into the bedroom.

Mary sat up. 'It's okay, Joe, I'm awake now. How long was I asleep?'

'About ten minutes too long for my bladder.'

She laughed and patted the sheet. 'I guess you letting go of my hand is what woke me. Get into bed and tell me what you've been up to today.'

'Are you sure? I thought you wanted to rest?'

'Now I feel better,' she murmured. 'I think you should call in every night, make sure I sleep.'

'Good idea, but I think it's time you moved in with me. After all, Graham's not in a position to object, he knows you can call the army if he shows up.'

'What about work? You always said it could affect us our careers.'

'I know I did, but to hell with it, I'm not having you live like this any longer.' Joseph sighed. 'Perhaps I should have dealt with Payne's murder differently, but it's too late now.'

'I know. He's sure to be found sooner or later, then what? It's such a mess, what can we do?'

'We can't turn back the clock, but we can bring the other Payne to trial. Get some justice for those women.'

'And Kimberley, poor girl. Where on earth is she?'

'I wish I knew. Hughes has pulled out all the stops, but we're still no wiser. I can't get her out of my mind. I know you're suffering nightmares, but can you imagine how I feel, knowing it's all my fault?'

'Sorry, I guess I'm being selfish. I didn't realize it was affecting you so much. Has anything come to light about our other cases?'

'Yes. PC Jefferson came to see me in my office. Seems he's a fan of Sherlock Holmes.'

Mary snuggled closer. 'So, what's Sherlock been up to?'

'He did some research following an incident he attended, an altercation between a landlord and one of his tenants. He'd seen the landlord before. He was the one we interviewed during the investigation of the murdered prostitute. He discovered both properties are registered in the name of Mark Payne.'

'Brilliant. Now we can show a connection between Payne and a scene of crime. Anything else?'

'Yes. It would appear Mark Payne has other properties too. A fish restaurant, pub, a –'

'Sounds like he's a busy man.'

'I spent today trying to find the landlord. I want to know about other properties he's involved with.'

'Didn't Jefferson find them all?'

'He may have done, but he didn't ask the landlord.' Joseph glanced down at his fists. 'It will be a lot quicker my way.'

'Don't be too hasty, remember what Hughes said. If Payne is involved, we need to be careful.'

'I will. Now, shall we move your things tonight?'

'It would be nice … but I think we should give it more thought. Don't get me wrong, I like the idea, but let's leave things as they are for the time being.'

'Pity. Still, I suppose you know how you feel. I don't want to rush you into doing anything you're not ready for.' He swung his legs off the bed. 'I think it's time I wasn't here. By the time I get into my own bed it'll be time to get up. Will you be in tomorrow?'

'Yes. I can't keep taking days off. I'll be fine, you'll see.'

Leaning down he kissed her. 'Sleep well, my love.'

Closing her eyes, she turned over and pulled the duvet around her, assuming the foetal position in a vain hope of protection against the horrors that dwelt in her dreams. *'If I'm not asleep in ten minutes, there's another bottle in the fridge,'* she whispered to herself.

Chapter 33

November 1986

'Are you sure this is the place?' The young boy said, swiping at ferns with a stick. 'It's bloody dark in these woods. Why would anyone build anything here?'

His companion, a freckle-faced girl, waved him forward. 'Go on, keep going. It can't be far now. My aunt said there used to be roads and everything, but they've been overgrown since the war.'

The boy renewed his attack on the waist-high vegetation. 'My arm aches. Can't you do some whacking?'

'No, there might be spiders. You do it.'

'Only if you keep your promise,' he said, peering into the gloom.

'I said I'd show you, didn't I? But only if we find the hut, not in the woods.'

'If it gets any darker, I'll have to use my torch. I don't want to, because the batteries aren't much good.'

'Then keep them until we find the place. It'll be darker inside, I bet.'

'I could buy some new ones and come back another day.'

She stuck her tongue out at him. 'Go home if you're scared. I'll find someone else to take me.'

The boy pulled a twig from his hair and frowned. Staring at her prepubescent body he lashed out at the undergrowth once more.

'I didn't say I was scared.' He shielded his eyes against rays of light penetrating the trees overhead. 'What's that?' He pointed with his stick. 'Look, over there.'

'Where? I can't see anything, show me.'

He turned and hacked a path at a different angle. 'Over there. I saw something. The sun's shining on it.'

'You were right,' she said. 'We've found it. My aunt was right after all. And there is a path. Why didn't we see it?'

'The building looks old,' he said, staring up at the moss-covered Nissen hut. 'But I bet the padlock's what I saw. It's new.'

'Is it?'

'Got to be. It's not from the war.'

'How do you know?' she retorted.

'Because it would be all rusty, not shiny.'

'Well, as it's locked, we may as well go back. Come on, it's getting on for tea-time, I reckon. It's getting dark, my mum will be getting worried.'

'What about what you promised? I found the place, didn't I?'

'Yes, but I said only in the hut. I'm not pulling them down in the woods. Tough luck.'

'I can get us inside. The windows aren't much good. It'll be easy.'

'No, leave it, I've seen enough.'

'But I haven't, and you did promise, "*Cross my heart and hope to die,*" you said.'

'Oh, go on then, climb in. But hurry up, I want my tea.'

The boy got a grip on the rotten window frame and heaved. He staggered back as it freed itself from the building and crashed to the ground. 'Bum holes,' he said, grasping her arm. 'Give me a bunk up so I can get in, then I'll find another door.'

'I can't. You're too heavy for me to lift. Let's go back.'

'No. I'll manage.' Clinging to the rotting window sill, he pulled himself up.

She heard him drop to the floor. 'What's it like in there? Have you found a door?'

'Give me a chance. This bloody torch isn't much good, it would have been better to bring candles.'

'Okay, come back out then.'

'Not likely. You wait there, I'll soon let you in.'

The girl stood with her back pressed against the wall of the building, the slightest rustle in the trees adding to her growing fear of this dark and dismal place. 'I hate this. I wish I'd never heard about it.'

A scream from deep inside the hut sent shivers down her spine. Hairs on the back of her neck stood up.

'What's going on?' she shrieked, standing on tip-toe, trying to see inside. A weak orange light headed in her direction, bobbing and weaving in the dark. The boy's face appeared. 'Get me out! Quick!' He was sobbing. His face as white as snow. She could hear his feet kicking at the wall as he desperately pulled himself up. 'Get me out! I want my mum!'

She grasped his arms and pulled with all her strength. He toppled out and landed on top of her.

Jumping to his feet he ran down the path, ignoring his missing shoe.

Picking herself up, she chased after him.

Inside the building, rats, startled by a torch beam, returned to their feast.

Kimberley's parents would not recognise their child now.

Chapter 34

November 1986

'What do you mean, he hasn't been around?' Mark took the phone from his ear and glared at it. Replacing it to the side of his head, he raised his voice. 'I gave Don strict instructions he was to help you out. I can't expect you to run the business on your own. When I get back, I'll have his balls for a paperweight.'

On the other end of the line, Julie swallowed. 'The man in Brazil phoned,' she said. 'He sounded really pissed off.'

'If he phones again tell him I'll be in touch.' Mark ground his teeth. 'No, I can't get back any sooner. He'll have to wait.' He frowned as he struggled to hear her next question. 'What? The fish? Okay. Get hold of the shop keeper who came in about the catfish. Tell him I'll pay him double what he makes at the moment to look after the stock.'

*

A blue oily haze hovered above sardines, as if reluctant to depart. Mark and Samuel hurried past the man cooking on the beach.

The Spaniard pointed to the fish and flashed nicotine-stained teeth.

Mark shook his head.

Samuel pinched the sides of his nose. 'Urghh, I hate the smell of them things, turns my stomach.'

The two men walked closer to the edge of the sea, increasing the distance between them and the barbecued sardines. Crystal clear water rushed to wash their footprints from the sand. Mark undid his shirt. 'Is it always this hot? Back home I'd be having the electric fire on.'

Samuel laughed. 'You get used to it. Steve said he ate Christmas dinner on the beach last year.'

'Let's hope he enjoyed it.'

The smile on Samuel's face vanished.

Taking out a silver case, Mark turned his back to the onshore breeze and lit a cigar.

Samuel inhaled deeply as smoke leaked from between Mark's cupped hands. 'I prefer your cigar to those stinking fish,' he said, pointing back along the beach.

'I do too. Now, let's get back and see if the so-called postal system out here has managed to deliver any letters. But I won't hold my breath.'

*

Mark kicked off his recently acquired flip-flops. The cold marble floor tiles provided a welcome contrast to the hot sand of the beach. He opened the fridge and took out two bottles of San Miguel as Samuel entered the kitchen holding out a large envelope.

'Just the one,' he said.

'At last. Been quicker to fly home and collect it myself.' Inserting a knife under the flap, Mark sliced the letter open.

'Is it what you were you expecting?'

Mark stepped out onto the balcony. Laughter from the beach echoed back from the buildings as he continued reading Steve's death sentence.

Samuel joined him. Scanning the beach with the telescope he pointed with his free hand. 'Look at the size of those. She'll end up with two black-eyes if she tries to run.'

'If you say so,' Mark grunted. 'Fetch me another beer, this one's evaporated.'

'What's in your letter?' Samuel pointed. 'You must have finished reading it by now.'

'It's your future. And another source of income for me. It's the legal transfer of Steve's bar to you. This top copy,' Mark tapped his finger on the paper resting on his knee, 'is in Spanish. Twyford's sent another in English so I can check it. It's not signed or dated as there's no hurry.'

'You'll never get Steve to sign it.'

'Who said I would? I'll do it when the time comes. Do you think anyone out here will query a poxy signature? This document can be backed by enough pesetas to convince anybody. Money talks, my friend, always has, always will.' Mark sneered. 'I was listening to the wireless in bed last night. Mostly crap as usual, but there was one good song. *When the going gets rough*, I think it was. It should be my theme tune.'

'I must admit,' Samuel said, 'running a bar does appeal.' He ran his tongue across his top lip. 'All those English girls out here for a good time. Nice one.'

'You'd do well to remember who you're working for.' Mark tapped his chest. 'And don't ever forget it. Now, let's start thinking about how to bring this off. First thing we need to do is get on friendly terms with Steve.'

'Easy for me, I already am. When I first came out here, I saw his collection of scarves behind the bar. I told him I supported Arsenal.'

'You wouldn't know your Arsenal from your elbow. I've never heard you say you were a fan.'

'That's because I'm not. I read the sports pages to get an idea of what's been going on, try to remember a few names and what the score was.'

'I sometimes think you're not as daft as you look … but only sometimes.' Mark held out his cigar case. 'Have one of these. You can smoke it now, or keep it until we walk to Steve's. Talking of Steve, we need get him on his own. Don't worry, I'll think of something, I usually do.' He grinned and rubbed his hands together. 'But it can wait. This evening I think I'll have double egg, ham and chips for a change.'

'But you had the same last night.' Samuel lit his cigar and exhaled. 'And the night before.'

'I was joking, you clown. There's nowhere else to go, is there.'

'There is, but as I told you, the menus out here are pretty much the same all over. If you want to explore the area, Steve was telling me about El Torcal. Sounded like a load of rocks to me, miles from anywhere. He said it's a great place.'

'Hmmm, could be a good place to seal a business deal.'

'Why? We could talk in the bar.'

'With everyone listening? Use your common sense for a change. I think you, me and Steve should visit this El Torcal place.'

'I still don't get it.'

'Which probably explains why I'm the organ grinder and you're the monkey. Just do as I tell you, leave the thinking to me.'

*

The evening promenade was in full swing. Ladies in fine clothes, on the arms of men in smart suits, meandered along the marble tiles. As they passed Steve's bar, conversations took on a different tone. Tourists making the most of happy-hour drinks was abhorrent to their values. A woman, sitting on the floor, slumped against a table, held up her glass in a drunken salute. The sight of her Union Jack knickers did nothing to enhance her image as an ambassador for the British on holiday.

'Embarrassing, isn't it?' Steve said. 'Wait until the morning. She'll be asking her friends if she had a good time.'

Samuel shifted his chair to get a better view. 'I think she's the one I was watching on the beach. Why do you keep serving her? She's absolutely legless.'

Mark tapped his cigar against an ashtray. 'Why not? As long as she can pay for it, let her have it.'

'I will,' Steve said. 'This is a bar, not a kindergarten. If they don't know their limits it's their problem. I'm out here to make money. A few more years and I'll be going back home, buy myself a nice house and settle down.'

Samuel coughed and spluttered.

'What's up?' Mark thumped him on the back. 'Beer gone down the wrong hole?'

'Something like that.' Samuel looked across the table at Steve.

'Sounds like a plan to me, Steve.' Mark lifted his glass. 'Here's to making money, and all it brings.'

'Cheers. What do you do for a living, Mark? Samuel tells me he works for you, does he?'

'Yes, he does.'

'Doing what? I see a lot of him in here, he can't always be busy.'

Mark scowled at Samuel. 'Do you? He tells me he's run off his feet.'

'Perhaps he is. What exactly is your line of business?'

'Buying and selling, a few property deals, nothing exciting. Keeps the wolf from the door, so to speak. But I think your bar's got the edge. All these people with money to burn. All this sunshine. You've got it made, my friend. I envy you.'

Steve laughed. 'Huh. You wouldn't think so if you knew what goes on out here. Bribes to this one, free meals and drinks to another, just to keep the place open. The officials in town aren't much better.'

'Sounds like home from home to me. Greasing palms keeps the economy running, and the money coming in. I don't worry about paying for services rendered, do I Sam? It's peanuts compared to what I get back in return.'

'I think you and I are from the same mould,' Steve said with a wink.

Mark turned towards the bar. 'Another round, Isabel.'

Steve stood up. 'You're wasting your time. She doesn't like you, and she's conveniently deaf when it suits her.'

'She should be careful who she upsets, there are plenty of villains who've moved out here to escape the long arm of the law.' Turning to Samuel he said, 'Settle up for these drinks. I'll wait in the car.'

Samuel held out his hand.

Mark ignored him.

Chapter 35

November 1986

Joseph picked up the phone on his desk. 'Yes, sir. Right away, sir.'

Pausing to straighten his tie, Joseph knocked on the door.
'Come in,' DCI Hughes called.
'You wanted to speak to me, sir.'
'Yes. Take a seat.' Hughes glanced down at a note-pad. 'The receptionist at Mark Payne Enterprises phoned our fictitious pet shop owner. It appears they need a temporary warehouse manager.'
'Did she say why?'
'Yes. Apparently, Mr Payne has a brother. He was supposed to be covering for him while he is on holiday but has let them down.'
'Oh.' Joseph chewed the inside of his top lip before replying. 'That's good. We can send PC Jefferson again. This time, with luck, we'll be able to pin something on Payne.'
'Only if he's guilty. None of your maverick methods. I've got people breathing down my neck, waiting for us to slip up. Mark Payne has friends in very unexpected places. We're both in the firing line, so get it right.'
'Trust me, sir. I'll work strictly to the rules.'
'Good man. I'll leave it with you. Brief PC Jefferson on exactly what he should be looking for, then get things moving. The woman said she couldn't guarantee the work lasting for more than a week or two, so time is of the essence.'
'Yes, sir, thank you, sir. I'll get onto it right away.'

*

PC Jefferson held out his hand as Julie looked up. 'Good morning,' he said. 'Fred, Fred Watson, I was here before, I came to view the catfish. Dad said you needed help for a while. Where would you like me to start?'
'Hello, Fred. I'm Julie, Mark told me about you. You'd better feed the fish first. I keep on at our cleaner but I'm sure he forgets.'

She sniffed. 'One other thing, let me have a list of any dead ones. I have to keep records of the stock.' Looking at Jefferson she played with the buttons on her blouse. 'You're a lot younger than I expected. You've doing well to have your own business.'

'It's my dad's actually, but he gives me a free-hand most of the time.'

'Oh, I see. Well, best get started. You can have a lunch break anytime around mid-day, does that suit you?'

Jefferson raised his head a little, desperately trying to stop staring at her fingers as they moved from one button to another.

'Yes, fine.' He loosened his tie. 'It's warm in here, isn't it?'

'Wait until you get inside the warehouse, that's almost tropical.' She undid the top fastening of her blouse. 'But you're right, it is getting hot, I'll turn the heater off for a while.'

'Where do I find the fish-food and things?'

'Let me show you. I'll switch the answerphone on in case anyone calls.' She took her coat from a hook and slipped it on. 'I bet it's cold out there,' she said.

'It is.' He opened the door to the yard. 'After you.'

'Okay, now you know where everything is. If you see the cleaner, ask him to come to the office.' She tapped one of the tanks. 'Are you sure you can't give this one a home? He looks so sad in there, all on his own.'

The large catfish swished its tail, scattering the mixture of sand and gravel it was resting on.

'No, Dad gave me strict instructions. I'm not to buy anything.'

'Not even lunch?' She fluttered her eye lashes. 'There's a nice pub down the road. The Artillery Arms.'

Jefferson grinned. 'Sounds good to me. What time?'

'I'll come over for you when I'm ready. Have you got a car?'

'No, sorry, I haven't.'

'Never mind. It's not far. The walk will do us good.'

'Okay, I'll see you later.'

He watched the warehouse door close behind her. 'This detective work is more interesting than I thought.'

*

'How long have you worked there?' PC Jefferson looked up from his ploughman's lunch.

'Too long, probably. My mum says I'm wasting my time. Sometimes I think she's right,' Julie said.

'Then why not give notice? I bet there are lots of jobs you could get. How about a Personal Assistant? Or –'

'Or a rocket scientist?' She laughed. 'I don't seem to stand much chance of becoming either those. I've tried for other vacancies but no luck so far.'

'Something will, it always does. Hmm, this cheese is really good. How's the sandwich?' He sipped his lager. 'Would Payne give you a decent reference?'

'Mark? No chance. He can be funny sometimes.'

'Oh? In what way? I take it you don't mean funny ha ha.'

She smiled. 'No, not like that. It's … I don't know how to put it … he . . .'

'Scares you?'

'Are you reading my mind?'

'It was a guess. I was speaking to the cleaner earlier. Don't say anything, but he's on the lookout for another job. Says Payne scares the crap out of him.'

'Me too,' she said.

'Was Kimberley frightened?'

'Who's Kimberley?'

'The cleaner said she brought the tea round the day you were off sick.'

'Must be a friend of Mark's then. I don't know anyone by the name of Kimberley.'

Julie smiled. 'Good,' she said, turning the answerphone off. 'No missed calls.'

'Nice lunch. We should go there again,' Jefferson said, closing the office door.

'Why not? I'm glad you enjoyed it.'

'Right, I'll get back to work. There's a lot of water changes to be done. Perhaps I could have my afternoon break in here with you as Payne's not around?'

'Yes, good idea. Gets boring stuck in here on my own. I'll see you later, Fred.'

*

The man pushed a mixture of dirt and cigarette-ends along the floor with a broom. 'Excuse me,' he said. 'I need to get there.'

PC Jefferson stepped back. 'Go ahead, don't mind me. I think I'll take an early break. I swallowed some water.' He held up the syphon by way of explanation.

'Oh. I bet it wasn't nice. All those fish pissing and –'

Jefferson spat on the floor.

*

'Don't suppose you've got any biscuits have you, Julie?' Jefferson stirred his tea.

'No, sorry.' Julie patted her stomach. 'I have to watch my figure.'

'I don't mind watching it for you. I could sit here all afternoon and do that.'

'I bet you could.' Taking a deep breath, she looked down at her breasts. 'You men are all the same, one-track minds.'

'Guilty as charged. But I do follow football as well.'

'Huh. Typical. You're making things worse for yourself.' She shifted position. 'I need the loo. I knew the last drink was a mistake. Do you think you could look after things while I go? Save me having to return any calls.'

'No problem. I'll keep your chair warm.'

As she reached the door, the phone rang. She glared at it. 'Answer it for me. I *really* do need to go.'

Jefferson picked up the phone. His forehead wrinkled. 'The next shipment? You're doing what? Oh, yes, I understand. You're changing your bank account. Use the old one for now. I see. How many kilos? Okay. Yes, I'll pass it on.'

The door opened. Jefferson put a hand over the phone. 'Got a right one here,' he said. Removing his hand, he continued. 'Yes, I will tell my boss. I'm sure the money will be there. Okay, goodbye.'

Julie resumed her place behind the desk. 'Who was it?'

'Only someone calling about money.' He waved a hand dismissively. 'He said he'd call back later. I suppose I'd better get back to the warehouse, still got a lot to do.'

*

PC Jefferson nodded. 'Yes, sir. He said the next shipment wouldn't be sent until the last lot had been paid for. I wish I'd been able to record the conversation.'

'That would have nailed the bastard,' Joseph agreed. 'Are you sure Julie didn't know who you were speaking to?'

'I told her it was someone chasing money. She didn't seem surprised, sir.'

'Did you get the caller's number?'

'No, sir. I thought it may give the game away.'

'Agreed. Payne would know it. He wouldn't need to ask. You did well.' Joseph placed the tips of his thumbs and fingers together in silent prayer. 'There doesn't seem a lot more you can do there. I think it's time to pull you out.'

'But, sir. Why not let me see what else I can find? Maybe Kimberley –'

'No. Give your notice in tomorrow. Tell them there's a health problem in the family. Let's quit while we're ahead.'

Chapter 36

November 1986

Graham stacked the last plate into the rack then ran his hand around the sink full of soapy water. 'Got you. There's always a teaspoon trying to escape.' Placing it with all the other cutlery, he dried his hands on a tea-towel. 'Now, time to get my head down for a while.'

Charles, the café owner, had been correct when he told Graham it wasn't the Hilton, but it served its purpose.

Graham had placed an old door on top of drums containing cooking oil to make a bed, and purchased bedding from a charity shop. Clothes brought from his flat were neatly folded and placed on a chair. Instead of wallpaper, he was now surrounded by racks of tins and boxes. The only box that was his, contained a secret which had the potential to continue destroying lives.

He lay back on his make-shift bed with one hand beneath his head, smoke from a cigarette dangling from his other hand drifting upwards.

'Sorry to disturb you, I know you're finished for the day but I need a favour,' Charles said.

Swinging his legs off the bed, Graham ground out his cigarette. 'No problem, Charlie, what is it?'

'The Christmas decorations. I've been meaning to see to them all day. Do you think you could put them up? Most of the shops around here have been decorated for weeks.'

'Sure, it'll give me something to do. Show me where you want them.'

'Thanks. I'd stay and do it myself but I've got a darts match tonight, the semi-finals. Tomorrow's usually our busy day, what with the market and things. I'd like to see the place looking festive.'

'You go and sling your arrows. I owe you more than a favour, leave everything to me.'

Graham pushed the plug into the wall socket. 'Shit.' Removing the plug, he used a dinner knife as a screwdriver. 'Hmm, the wires are okay. Could be the fuse I suppose.' He returned the plug to the socket. 'Oh well, it'll have to wait until the morning. Wait a minute . . . I didn't check the bulbs.'

Beginning nearest the plug he twisted each bulb in turn. Suddenly the Christmas lights sprang into life.

'Not bad, not bad at all, even if I do say so myself. I'll nip outside and take a look.'

Despite the fluorescent lights, the decorations held their own, blinking on and off, giving the place a welcoming atmosphere. Peering back inside, he smiled.

'Hello, Graham.'

Peering into the dark, shielding his eyes from light spilling from the window, he said, 'Mary? What on earth? Come to turn me in have you?'

'No. What are you doing here? Is this place open? Joe would love a cuppa.'

'I work in this café.' Graham's eyes narrowed. 'Is he here too?'

'Yes. He's waiting in the car around the corner, we've been talking to a prossie. I said I'd get us a brew, but I certainly didn't expect to find you.'

'Oh, if he's here it means trouble.'

'It usually does. But only for people like you who stick their necks out.'

Graham pointed inside. 'How about coming in for five minutes? I'll put the kettle on.'

'Why should I?'

'No real reason, I suppose. I don't know about you, but life's not great at the moment.'

'I could tell Joe I've met an old school friend.' She hesitated. 'But you'll have to get me a taxi. I can't ask him to wait.'

'Okay, it's a deal. Go and talk to him while I make the drinks.'

'What did he say? Did he believe you?' Graham stirred a mug of tea.

'Not sure, I never really know with him.'

'Thanks for coming back. I had my doubts. If you'd brought him with you, I was ready to run.'

'Perhaps you should have. I'm tired, not thinking straight.'

'I think about you, well, us really, every day. Do you miss me?'

'No.'

Graham sighed. 'I don't really blame you. I've made a real mess of things haven't I.'

'If you mean shooting somebody, then I have to agree. Running away from the army wasn't one of the smartest things you've ever done, but murder?'

'Oh, bollocks, so he did die.' He looked away. 'Why aren't you arresting me?'

'We will when we're ready.'

'Oh yeah? I don't think so. You're bluffing. I mean, how will you explain what the two of you were doing there when he was shot? And the fact he was killed with your boyfriend's gun?'

'I think for all our sakes the least said the better.' She banged her mug onto the table. 'A lot hinges on the weapon. Have you still got it?'

'That's for me to know, and you to find out.'

A man shuffled past the café window. Graham got up and turned the sign on the door around and flicked the lock.

'I reckon the best thing we can to do is get back together. That way you can protect him and I can start to get my life back.'

'Dream on. How many more times do I have to spell it out?'

'Be careful, sweetheart, I'm holding the trump card in all this. All I have to do is put the gun in the post with a letter and everything will go tits-up for you and lover boy.'

'It's you who should be careful. Joe's the last person to upset.'

'Then it's a stalemate. I can't get you to change your mind about coming back, and you can't arrest me all the time I have his gun.'

*

'What did he have to say for himself?'

Mary squirmed in her chair. 'Who? Who are you talking about?'

'Graham of course. Being inquisitive I wanted to see your school friend, so I walked back. You never told me you two were at school together.'

'We weren't. Sorry, Joe. Why didn't you join us?'

'I thought it best not to. At least we know where he is. Perhaps I should –'

'Don't. We've enough on our plate as it is.'

'Enough on our plate? Meeting in a café? Very good.'

'It's not funny.'

'I know. Did you ask him about you know what?'

'Yes. He tried to use it as a lever to get me to forgive and forget.'

'Did he now? Smarmy little git. I really think –'

'I can guess. I'll think of something. I'm in this as much as you are, don't forget.'

*

The tranquillity of the woodland was disturbed. A small crane on the back of a truck dropped its claw onto a pile of logs.

'Bit like the one in the amusement arcade. Go on, Jim,' the man yelled, 'looks like you've got a winner!' His workmates joined in the laughter.

Again, and again logs were hoisted into the air and dropped onto the truck. With a final flourish, Jim scooped up the last of them.

'Whew, what's that stink?' The man studied the bottom of his working boots. 'It's not me. I haven't trodden in anything.' Approaching the area where the crane's fingers had scoured the earth, he said. 'It's coming from here. Smells like something crept under the logs and died.'

'You may be right,' one of the others agreed, 'but what is it?'

Jim jumped down from his cab. 'Strewth, what's the pong? Either of you go for a curry last night? Jesus, it's bad!'

He picked up a branch and prodded the ground. The smell increased.

'There's something not right here,' he said. 'Don't mess it about. I'll drive back to the road, try to find a phone box.'

'Not without me.'

'Nor me. I'm not stopping here. It's turning my guts.'

*

DCI Hughes looked as if all the troubles of the world had descended onto his shoulders. Joseph and Mary knew better than to speak at a time like this. Eventually Hughes broke the silence.

'I find this hard to believe. Another body's been found. We had three unsolved murders and now there is a fourth.'

Mary shifted her gaze towards Joseph.

'Male or female, sir,' he asked.

'I don't have that information yet. It would appear the cadaver was wrapped in heavy duty polythene and buried on Forestry Commission land.' He passed Joseph a piece of paper. 'This is the location. You will need identification to gain access.'

At the mention of the word, Forestry Commission, Mary slumped forward.

Joseph reached out to her. 'Do you feel okay? Would you like a glass of water?'

Instead of answering, she stood and left the room.

'Sorry, sir.' Joseph said. 'If that's all, I'd like to make sure she's all right.'

Hughes flapped a hand towards the open door. 'Yes, go ahead. Then join Forensics at the crime scene.'

*

Mary leant against Joseph's car. 'I can't drive. And how I'll cope when we get there, I dread to think.'

'I know how you feel. At first I thought Kimberley had been found, but when he said about the woodland it was like being hit in the stomach with a sledgehammer. I thought you were about to faint.'

She clutched his sleeve. 'What are we going to do, Joe? I honestly believe I'm losing my mind.'

Joseph put an arm around her and pulled her close. 'No, no you're not. It's stress. I've seen what it can do to grown men. I'll drop you at your place, put in a request for sick leave for you, and then go to the woods on my own.' He squeezed her. 'It'll be okay, trust me.'

'Thanks. Can you stop at the off-licence on the corner, near my place?'

*

Winding down the car window, Joseph held up his warrant card. The young constable saluted. 'Follow this track, sir,' he said, releasing the tape tied across the access road. 'Forensics have set up a tent. You can't miss it.'

Joseph held up a hand in acknowledgement as he eased the car forward.

Approaching the site, Joseph tightened his grip on the steering wheel. 'Christ, it seems like only yesterday. How did they find him so soon?'

'Good morning.' The greeting from the man in white protective clothing failed to carry any warmth. 'We've had a preliminary look. Bullet entered the back of the victim, no exit wound. Probably lodged in his rib cage.'

'Thanks. I'll get my coveralls on and take a closer look.'

The area was surrounded by a spider's web of yellow and black tapes winding from tree to tree.

Donald Payne's bloated body lay alongside a pile of excavated earth.

'Not a pretty sight,' the man from forensics said. 'Here, this should get you started. Whoever did this must have either been in a great hurry, or believed the body would never be discovered.'

Joseph carefully separated the paper concertina. 'Thanks, at least we have a name.' Walking away he muttered, 'How did we miss this? His bloody bank statement. Where the hell did he have it?'

*

Hughes passed Joseph the preliminary report. 'As you know, a gun was used, so there may be a connection to the robbery at the bookmakers. Forensics will be able to check the bullet against the ones retrieved from there.'

'Do you think it was gang related, sir?'

'No. In my experience our local gangs wouldn't go to such lengths. The victim would probably have ended up in an alley somewhere.'

'Perhaps we should visit his wife. Could be a domestic.'

'Are you serious? A housewife with a gun? And how could she bury her husband in woodland beneath a pile of logs?'

'Sorry, sir. I agree, she couldn't have. Not without help.'

Hughes took a sheet of paper from amongst the pile on his desk. 'A constable interviewed Mrs Payne after she reported her husband was missing. Have you looked at his report? Did he have any suspicion she may have been involved with his disappearance in any way?'

'Yes, I have read it, sir. And no, he didn't.'

'I suggest you speak to her yourself now his body has been found, she will have to identify him. I want results and I want them now. Do I make myself clear?'

'Perfectly, sir, I'll get onto it right away. Anything regarding our International Arrest Warrants?'

Chapter 37

November 1986

Mary's hand trembled. 'It's all getting out of hand, Joe. You said he'd never be found.'

Wine threatened to spill from the glass as she raised it to her lips. Extra make-up did little to hide the pallor in her cheeks. She uncrossed her legs then crossed them again for the third time.

'Don't get yourself in such a state,' Joseph said. 'I told you, I'll get it sorted. If only your darling Graham didn't have the gun –'

'We don't know he has. He may have disposed of the wretched thing.'

'I hope so. Anyway, I've done my bit. I took my wardrobe to the council tip and watched their machine make short work of it. The new one's coming tomorrow. I've got shot of all the ammunition. No pun intended. If anyone comes looking there's nothing to find.'

'We really are in up to our necks, aren't we?'

'Me, possibly. You, no. It was my gun, and if push comes to shove, I'll deny you were involved in any way.'

'Thanks for calling in, Joe. I'm feeling better now, but do you mind if I have an early night? I feel shattered.' She yawned. 'I'm sure a good night's sleep will do me good.' Reacting to his grin she added, 'No you don't, on my own I meant.'

'Can't blame me for trying. Best cure for sleepless nights ever been invented.'

'Not tonight. I want to rest.'

Pulling the curtains aside she waved as Joseph drove off. She was not sure he saw her through the rain speckled glass. 'Right, now you've gone I'll see what I can do to sort out this mess.'

*

The drizzle did little to brighten up the seafront. Mary pulled the strings to tighten her rain hat. The café had its lights on.

Graham busied himself clearing cups and plates, a hint to the last few customers it was time to go.

He turned and glared at the sound of the bell above the door. 'We're just closing.'

The woman took off her hat and shook it. 'I know. It's why I'm here.'

'Mary? I didn't expect to see you out on a night like this. Sit down. I'll make you a coffee.'

She hung her raincoat on the stand. Ignoring the stares, she sat at a corner table and waited for Graham to return.

'There you are, sweetheart. Just as you like it. Hot and strong,' he said.

She resisted the urge to smack the leer off his face.

Graham moved away, gathering up sauce bottles and cruets, making a great show of looking at his watch. One by one the stragglers said good night and left to battle the elements.

Graham shot the bolts on the door. 'Thought they'd never go,' he said. 'I don't like to be rude. Most of them are regulars.'

'I thought you handled it well. I half expected you to toss them out by the scruff of the neck.'

'I can't say I haven't been tempted.' He sat down. 'Now, why are you here at this time of night? What do you want, apart from coffee?'

'Charming. I come in for a drink and you automatically assume I'm after something.'

'I know you too well, sweetheart. You may as well come out with it, save all this sparring.'

Mary turned away and stared through the window. 'Pull the blinds. I feel like a goldfish in a bowl.'

'Better? Now, out with it.' Graham lit a cigarette, turned his head and blew smoke across the room.

'Okay, I'll come straight to the point. What did you do with the gun?'

'Oh, so lover boy sent you. Well tough luck. I'm not saying anything.'

She fluttered her eye lashes. 'Don't be like that. It's a simple enough question.'

'Why should I tell you? If he's worried, he should have come himself. I assume you've told him where I am?'

Mary edged her chair closer. 'I didn't have to. He saw us.' She lowered her voice. 'But he doesn't know I'm here tonight.'

'Oh? Okay, supposing I did tell you. What then?'

'Depends on your answer.' She licked her lips.

It was a sign he recognised. 'Don't do that.' He gulped. 'I thought you said it was all over between us?'

'Like I said, it all depends on your answer.' She pulled her jumper off over her head. 'Getting warm in here. Must be all these lights.'

Graham looked up at the fluorescent tubes, then back to Mary. He placed a hand on her knee. 'If I tell you, would –'

'Why not tell me and find out?'

'Okay, I've still got it.'

Silence.

'Where? Show me,' she said, undoing the top button of her blouse.

Graham pushed his chair back and left the table.

Mary could hear things being moved around. A minute or two later he returned.

'Here it is.'

Mary reached out. 'Taking a chance, aren't you? Suppose Joseph came looking?'

'I don't know. I'm only hanging onto the bloody thing for insurance.'

'Against what? How do you think it'll protect you? If the shit hits the fan, you could be going away for a very long time.'

Graham stared back up towards the ceiling. He moved a hand into his lap and gently squeezed. 'I answered your question, now what?'

'At the risk of sounding repetitious, it all depends.'

'On what?'

'Let's put it this way.' She finished unbuttoning her blouse. 'You've got something I want, the gun, and I think I've got something you want, right?'

Graham stood up. He didn't need to reply, the answer was obvious. He unzipped his trousers. 'Take the sodding gun. Tell him to stick it up his arse and pull the trigger.'

*

Joseph rang the front doorbell. The WPC standing next to him adjusted her hat. 'Thanks for asking for me to assist, sir. I hope WDC Wells feels better soon.'

Edna Payne had made an effort to be presentable. 'Come in,' she said. 'I've got the kettle on.'

The WPC stood aside, allowing Joseph to step in.

Furnished in a style which would bring joy to the eyes of any budding film director, the room harked back to the Sixties.

Joseph sank into an armchair. The chair's upholstery wrapped itself around him.

The WPC decided against sitting.

Edna pushed a mahogany veneered tea trolley into the room. A teapot took centre stage, its gleaming metal cover encasing white china. Plates, cups, and saucers, many of them matching, surrounded it. On the shelf below, a Victoria sponge cake was displayed on a stand.

'Thank you,' Joseph said, attempting to gain his equilibrium. 'Now, let me first extend my condolences for your loss. It must have been a great shock.'

'Not really.' Edna sniffed. 'I always expected him to come to a sticky end. Mind you, I didn't think someone would shoot him. That's a turn up for the books.'

Joseph tweaked an earlobe. 'Why aren't you surprised your husband was murdered? Wasn't he popular?'

Edna laughed, but it was a dismissive reaction. 'Oh, he was popular all right. Women loved him. Tarts, the lot of them. You wouldn't believe what I've had to put up with over the years.'

'Have you any idea who may have killed him?'

Edna shrugged. 'A jealous husband? Boyfriend perhaps? He didn't mind what age they were.'

'You'll forgive me I'm sure, but you don't appear to be upset about your husband's death.'

Edna produced the cake stand. 'Help yourself to a slice. It's very nice.'

Joseph reached down. 'Thanks. I'm partial to cream cake.'

The WPC shook her head. 'No, thank you.'

Wiping his lips, Joseph continued. 'Is there anything else you would like to add? For instance, do you know the names of any of his –'

'Floozies. They're who you're talking about. No better than prostitutes, any of them.' Edna bristled.

'That's as maybe, but names would help our enquiries.'

'If I knew I'd tell you. But I don't.'

'Did he bring any of them here?'

'No, he didn't! I wouldn't stand for it.'

'How do you know he was involved with other women? Have you caught him?'

'No, but be sure your sins will find you out. I've got friends who tell me things.'

Wiping cream and jam off his plate with a finger, Joseph transferred it to his mouth. He motioned towards the WPC. 'Time to go.'

Edna helped herself to another slice of cake. 'Are you going? You haven't drunk your tea.'

Staring at clots of cream floating in his cup, he grimaced. 'Sorry, we've got a busy day today, but thanks for the cake.'

'Don't you want to see his stuff? He had it in his room.'

'Would it be of interest to us? What is it?'

'Filth. Pure filth.'

The WPC turned her attention away from her notes to look across at Joseph.

He struggled to release himself from the clutches of the armchair. 'I may be able to arrange for it to be taken away. Would you like to show us?'

Edna brushed crumbs off her ample bosom. 'Don't bring her, she's too young. She shouldn't know about such things. I didn't, until I saw them in his room. Disgusting. What's the world coming to?'

Joseph helped Edna from her chair. 'As you wish.' He winked at the WPC. 'Come along, Mrs Payne, let's see what you've found.'

He followed her up the stairs, the swaying of her backside reminding him of the baby rhino on the news last night.

With a dramatic flourish she threw back the door and pointed. 'There you are. As I told you. Filth.'

The sight of leather masks, whips and chains, magazines and books took him by surprise. 'Oh my god. The dirty bast – sorry, I meant to say –'

'I know what you mean and you're right. Whoever shot him did the right thing.'

Joseph moved towards the bed. 'It appears there's more to your husband than we thought. If you have no objections, I'll have all this taken away for examination.'

'Take it. Burn it. Good riddance, I say. Makes my flesh creep. I'll have to bleach this place from top to bottom.'

'I see why you didn't want my colleague to see these.' He thumbed through one of the magazines. 'Talk about a picture being worth a thousand words.'

Chapter 38

December 1986

'That's settled, then.' Mark Payne tapped the ash off his cigar. 'El Torcal here we come.'

Steve raised a glass. 'Cheers, mate. Great idea of yours, do me good to get me arse out of this place, even if it's only for the rest of the day.'

Samuel turned and gazed at the beach.

'What's up?' Steve said. 'You don't seem very happy. Found a fiver and lost a tenner?' Turning his attention to the girls splashing around in the water, he smiled. 'Oh, I see. You'd rather be watching the talent with your telescope. Pervert.'

'It's not that. I don't see the fun in driving all that way to see a pile of rocks.'

Steve looked towards the bar and snapped his fingers. 'More beer, Francisco.'

Mark held up a hand. 'No more for us. He's driving.'

'Is he? He said he didn't fancy going.'

'And I heard him say he's driving.' Mark's eyes narrowed. Leaning across the table he held Samuel's arm and squeezed. 'That's right, isn't it?'

'If you say so.'

'I do. Now, go and get the car.'

*

Samuel took one hand off of the steering wheel and ran it across his forehead. The car moved closer to a steep drop lining the edge of the road, narrowly missing one of the white painted rocks. Behind the front seats, empty bottles clinked as Samuel pulled the car back onto the road.

'Stop fidgeting. Keep your eye on the road,' Mark said. 'What's up with you?'

'Nothing. I just don't like all these hairpin bends. We should have come up by donkey.'

'Ha, bloody, ha.' Steve unscrewed the top of another San Miguel. 'Don't give up the day job, mate. You won't make it as a bloody comedian.'

'You're right there, Steve. I keep telling him, with a face like his, he should have been an undertaker.'

Samuel's knuckles whitened. 'It's okay for you two, you should try driving. I didn't bring any spare trousers.'

Steve leant forward and burped. 'Now that is funny. Better than the donkey.' He wiped his mouth. 'Pull over when you can, I need a piss.'

Mark watched Steve approach the edge and unzip his trousers. He nudged Samuel. 'Go on. Get out and give him a push.'

Samuel opened the car door.

'Coming to join me?' Steve asked, turning back to finish watering the rocks below.

Samuel stepped towards him, both arms reaching out. Two steps brought him within touching distance.

Mark ran his tongue across his lips as he watched.

Steve staggered backwards, colliding with Samuel. 'Sorry, mate,' he slurred.

Samuel looked towards the car.

Mark shook a clenched a fist.

*

'How far you fancy going?' Steve pointed. 'The easy route's half an hour. The other one's got a cracking view of the valley. You up to it?'

Samuel turned and walked back towards the car.

'Where are you off to?' Mark grabbed his arm.

'I don't fancy the walk.'

'But I do, and I'm calling the shots. Right?'

'I guess so.' Shuffling his feet, Samuel followed Mark and Steve up the track.

*

'There, wasn't bad, was it?' Mark put an arm around Samuel and looked down into the valley. 'You've got to admit, it's some view.'

'Even better from up there,' Steve replied, indicating a stand of eroded rocks. Losing his balance, he staggered. 'It's not the beer,' he said. 'It's the altitudal height.'

'If you say so.' Mark smirked.

'I do.' Moving closer, he held onto Mark and leaned forward. 'Fancy climbing?'

'No. Not for me, but Sam will.' Mark propelled Samuel forward.

'I suppose I'll have to.' Samuel followed Steve's lead. 'But I'd have worn better shoes if I'd known we were mountaineering.'

Steve stood on top of the rocks and beat his chest, Tarzan style. Samuel scrambled the remaining few feet before struggling to his feet behind him. As he reached out, the sound of a Christmas carol filled the air. Down below, a group of walkers approached Mark.

'Good afternoon,' the man leading the group said. 'Do you come here alone?'

Instinctively Mark turned towards the rocks and looked up.

'Your friends?' The man used a walking-stick to point upwards, enamelled badges reflecting the evening sun. 'They desert you here?'

'No, they decided to climb, but it was too difficult for me.' He tapped the side of his leg to indicate an excuse.

The stranger turned to his group. 'Let us climb, *ya*?' Three young men took off their rucksacks and dropped them to the ground. The leader joined them and soon all four were halfway up.

Mark groaned. 'Bloody Germans. That's twice today Steve's got away with it. He must have the luck of the devil.'

Steve turned and saw Samuel lunging towards him. 'What's up? Careful, it's a long way down.' Throwing both arms around his attacker he held him close. 'Got yer. Hang onto me, mate. You're safe now.'

The German hikers joined them. 'Is good climb, *ya*? And the view, she is beautiful.' Taking a bottle from his jacket he offered it to Samuel. 'Schnapps. *Frohe Festtage.* Happy Christmas.'

Reaching for the bottle Steve stumbled. 'Merry Christmas.'

'Your friend, he is much celebrating, *ya*?' the hiker said to Samuel, pocketing the bottle. 'I think too much.'

Samuel nodded in agreement. 'Sorry, yes, he's been drinking nearly all day. I'll take him back to our car.'

'And part of us help you.'

*

'Steve could snore for bloody England,' Mark said, glancing over his shoulder at the back-seat. 'Look at the pair of them. Don't know how your spic mate can sleep through it.'

'You might have helped get Steve down off those rocks. He was like a drunken soddin' octopus, all rubbery and arms and legs.' Samuel sniffed as he changed gear. 'If those walkers hadn't helped me, we'd probably still be stuck there.'

'And then maybe you could have managed to do what I said. With the amount he's drunk today the police would have accepted it as an accident all day long.'

'It wasn't my fault. I never saw those Germans until they were on top of us.'

'I should have known not to send a boy to do a man's job.' Mark sneered. 'And another thing, why did you bring Pedro with us?'

'I think his car radiator's had it, there was rusty water everywhere. And his name's not Pedro, it's Pino. He's a relative of Isabel. I've met him in the bar a couple of times. He speaks good English.'

'Oh, so now I'm paying you to run a taxi service, am I? You're pushing your luck.'

*

The car crawled behind a donkey cart piled high with carpets. When the road straightened Samuel accelerated past. 'About time,' Mark said with a shake of his head. 'Bloody peasant. You should have nudged him off the road.'

Bright illumination from sprawling shops and bars contrasted with the mauve of the evening sky. Outside Stevie's Wonder Bar a group of teenagers were dancing. Hands on the hips of the girl in front, the line of revellers snaked along. One of the party tripped, taking two others with her as she fell. Shrieks of laughter filled the air as a flashbulb caught the moment for posterity. The girls turned their backs on their friend with the camera, bent over and raised their skirts. 'It's me best feature, Lisa. Make sure you get it all in,' one of them yelled. Glittery stars on Lisa's bopper headband shook on springs as she giggled. The flash on her camera lit up the row of pasty white backsides, emphasising the difference to the girls' sunburned legs.

Samuel stopped the Fiat short of the bar. 'Look at them,' he said. 'Pissed as farts. If I was a few years younger—'

'But you're not, so forget it. Get Sleeping Beauty and the prince out of the car.'

'Aren't you going to give me a hand?' Samuel opened the car door.

'What for? Pedro's okay, he hasn't had a drink. Dig him in the ribs, that'll get him going. You can manage Steve, surely. Hurry it up. I want to go back to the apartment for a wash before we eat.'

Mark watched in the rear-view mirror as Pino walked ahead. Steve escaped from Samuel's grasp, took a step forward, two sideways and then one back as he headed toward his bar. A girl came forward and put her arm around him. Lisa laughed as another flashbulb popped, capturing the drunken embrace. Steve pushed the girl away. Sinking to his knees he put out both hands to steady himself.

Mark slid across into the driver's seat. Looking back over his shoulder, he slammed the car into reverse.

The impact was illuminated by a flash of bright light.

Changing gear, Mark roared away from the scene leaving Samuel and the drunken girls staring in disbelief at the grotesque mannequin sprawled in the road.

Pino ran back to help. Isabel rushed from behind the bar. She held one hand to her mouth. The other hand touched her forehead, stomach, left and right breasts, offering up a prayer. Samuel swallowed hard as he looked away from the body. He watched the rear lights of the car disappear.

Lisa and her friends stood in stunned silence.

*

The refrigerator hummed as Mark closed the door. Carrying a large bottle into the lounge, he dropped onto the sofa. 'Don't just sit there,' he said. 'Do something useful.'

Samuel pushed himself up from the chair. He returned with two glasses.

'That's better. Now drink up. You look as if you've got all the worries of the world on your shoulders.' Mark unscrewed the beer and poured.

'Why did you do it? Steve didn't stand a chance.'

'So? He's dead, isn't he? Now you're part owner of his place.'

'You nearly killed me too.'

'Don't talk shit. I wouldn't do that. You're the goose who will lay the golden eggs for me.' He held up his glass in salute. 'Here's to the future.'

'What if someone recognised the car?'

'I doubt it. Most of them were pissed. Anyway, I didn't hang around did I.'

Samuel sipped his drink. 'I don't like it. There must have been an easier way.'

'There probably was. I could have let an old woman like you bore him to death I suppose.' Mark took an aluminium tube from his pocket and extracted a cigar. 'But dead's dead whichever way you look at it. Life is for the living so let's get on with it. As soon as the funeral is over, you can take the agreement to Isabel and start the ball rolling.'

Chapter 39

December 1986

Joseph pushed a pile of papers to one side as Mary entered.
'Bloody paperwork,' he groaned. 'Sorry. Are you feeling any
brighter?'

'Yes, thanks.' She smiled. 'And I've got a present for you.'

'Why? I've had my birthday.'

'I know. But wait until you see what I've brought you.' She held
out a carrier bag. 'Here you are. Happy Christmas.'

'Thanks. Hmm, let me guess . . .' He weighed the bag in his
hands. 'It's heavy, is it a cake?'

'Trust you. No, it's nothing to eat.' She turned and locked the
door. 'Now, unwrap it.'

He grinned. 'Is it something for the bedroom? I saw you lock
the door.'

'No, but if anyone comes along, they'll wonder *why* it's locked.
Hurry up.'

Joseph took out a shoebox and lifted the lid. 'It's my gun!'

'Now you know why I didn't leave your office open.'

'How did you get it? Did Graham give it to you?'

'That's one way of putting it.'

'I see. Best not to ask I suppose. But this is brilliant. Even
Forensics can't match a bullet to a gun they don't have.'

'You can dispose of it, then we'll be in the clear.'

'You're right.' Opening a drawer, he pushed the gun towards the
back. 'But first, when I get back to my place, I'll strip and clean it
to within an inch of its life.'

*

Joseph looked at the gun parts attached to fishing line and lead
weights. 'Seems a pity after all we've been through,' he muttered.
'But I can't risk it. All Graham has to do is make a phone call.'
Dropping the pieces into a pillow case, he left the bedroom.

*

On the deserted beach, birds marched back and forth, searching the mudflats. Joseph turned the collar of his jacket up. Reaching into the makeshift bag he took out one of the carefully prepared objects. Drawing back his arm he sent the missile out towards the oncoming tide and watched as it dropped into the mud. Walking slowly, he stopped at regular intervals and repeated his actions until the pillow case was empty. Screwing it up, he rammed it into a coat pocket and turned toward the promenade.

*

'Morning, Mary,' Joseph said. Looking up from the pile of paperwork he frowned. 'Have you seen yourself in the mirror? You shouldn't be at work. You should be in bed.'

'Why? I'm okay.' She touched her cheekbones, beneath her eyes, moving puffy folds of skin. 'Although, to be fair, I didn't get much sleep.'

'Was it those dreams of yours?'

'Yes.'

'Take the day off. I'll square it with Hughes.'

'No. I've used a lot of my sick-leave, I'd rather stay.'

'If it's what you want, fine. Get us both a coffee and give me a hand with this lot.' Lifting a third of the files off the top of the pile he pushed them across his desk.

'Boring, isn't it.' Joseph put the cup to his lips. 'Want another? No, don't get up, I'll go, I need to stretch my legs.'

'Yes, and some biscuits, please.' She yawned. 'I think my energy level needs a sugar boost.'

'Fresh air would do you good. Let's carry on for a while then go down to the sea-front.'

As the office door closed, Mary crossed her arms on the folders in front of her, rested her head on them and closed her eyes.

'Wakey, wakey. I know I said paperwork was boring, but I didn't expect to find you snoring.' He passed her a cup. 'Here, drink this, then we'll go. I got you a KitKat. I know how much you like chocolate.'

Mary rubbed her eyes. 'Was I really snoring? Sorry.'

'Don't be. This lot's enough to put a glass eye to sleep.'

She blinked. 'You're right, it is, and I've been thinking. Maybe it's time I changed my life around, chuck this in, get myself a job without all the hassle.'

'Give up your career? Have you thought about your pension?'

'I must admit that's partly what's stopping me, but a pension's not everything.'

'Easy to say now, but you may regret it later.' He placed a hand on her shoulder. 'Come on, let's go and investigate the mystery of the missing hamburger. If it's not missing now, it will be when I get my teeth around it.'

'Silly sod. Thanks, Joe, you do make me laugh.'

'Excuse me, sir.' The desk sergeant put down the phone as Joseph passed. 'Just received a strange call. Seems a young lad arrived home missing a shoe and scared out of his life. His mum said he'd found something horrible.'

Joseph opened the station door for Mary. 'Meet you in the car. I'll see if there's anything in this for us.'

'Right, now tell me what his mother said.' Joseph leant on the sergeant's desk.

'He went into the woods with an older girl, sir. She'd heard about an abandoned building and dared him to go with her to find it. They did, and it's where he said he saw something. Said it stunk.'

'Dead fox probably. Or a badger. I haven't got time to waste on kids and what they get up to. Just log it in.'

'Are you sure, sir? The woman did sound concerned.'

'Okay, George, I'll tell you what, why not send PC Jefferson? He fancies himself as a detective. See what he makes of it.'

'Will do, sir. Are you sanctioning the search?'

'No. Tell him I asked him to do it in his own time. He'll jump at the chance.'

*

'I need to phone someone,' Joseph said, thumping his desk. 'Why didn't I think of it before?'

'Who? What? You're talking in riddles,' Mary replied.

'The army. Graham hasn't got a hold over me any more.'

'Of course. I should have thought of that. He was a fool to part with you-know-what.'

'On second thoughts, let's bring him in ourselves. It's time him and me had a chat.'

Mary put a hand on his arm. 'Don't. Please. Leave it to the army, he's their problem now.'

'But look at all the aggravation he's caused. To both of us. Surely he should pay the price?'

'Please, Joe. If we're ever to get our lives sorted out, we should avoid antagonising Graham.'

Placing a hand over hers he said, 'Okay. We'll do it your way. I'll get on the phone right away.'

*

The café owner smoothed out the piece of paper. Scratching his head, he read the scribbled message. "My brother has been let down and needs help with his business. Shop keys are on my bed. Happy Christmas." He screwed the note up. 'Thanks a lot. Selfish git. I take you in off the street and this is all the thanks I get. How am I supposed to find a cleaner and a cook at short notice? Happy Christmas? Not sodding likely.'

*

Joseph picked up the phone. 'Yes, I'm DS Fargough. Yes, correct. Say that again? But he was working there. Oh, did a moonlight flit did he? No, sorry, I've no idea where he may have gone. Yes, of course. Thanks for letting me know. Goodbye.'

Mary stopped doodling on her note-pad. 'I take it that was the army? I –'

'Yes. When they got there, Graham had gone.' He tapped the ends of his fingers together and stared at the ceiling. 'Seems he was quicker off the mark than me. Any idea where he would go?'

'I know he had friends in London when we met, but I don't think he kept in touch with any of them.'

'Hmm. Okay. Well, he's gone now. I think our best bet is to leave it to the Army.' He looked back at the ceiling for inspiration. 'Do you know where his friends live? Did you ever meet any of them?' Opening a drawer, he took out an address book. 'I did a few years in the Met. It's been a while, but I'm sure they'll remember me.'

'I can't help, I'm afraid. I did meet some of them, but they weren't my type. All beer and football, you know the sort I mean?'

Joseph smiled. 'I get the picture. Oh, well, he's not our immediate problem. We should –'

A knock interrupted him.

'Come in.'

The desk sergeant entered. 'PC Jefferson's in hospital. I thought you ought to know.'

Mary jumped up from her chair. 'What happened to him? How bad is he?'

'I can't tell you much,' George said. 'His mother said he went out last night and when he came home, he was in a terrible state. She phoned for an ambulance and they took him to hospital.' He held out a slip of paper. 'Here are his ward details and the visiting hours.'

*

The pale features of PC Jefferson blended into white pillows supporting sagging shoulders. Beneath a bandage circling his head, eyes, surrounded by bruising, stared at his visitors. He opened his mouth to speak, but nothing came.

Mary rushed to his bedside. 'Alan! You look as if you've been in the wars.'

Jefferson licked his parched lips. Mary reached for a water jug and poured some into a glass. 'Here, drink this,' she said. 'Don't speak until you're ready.'

Joseph approached the bed. 'What happened? Were you attacked?'

'Kimberley,' he croaked. 'I saw her.'

Joseph gripped his shoulder. 'Where is she? Is she okay?'

Jefferson sipped at his drink. 'No. She's dead.' He dropped the glass onto the bed. The water soaked into the bed cover. He slumped forward, covered his face and sobbed. Mary put an arm around him and pulled him close.

'Shit!' Joseph glared around the ward.

'A boy found her. In an old Nissen hut in some woods.' Jefferson sniffed. 'He didn't tell his mother everything he saw. I think the shock was too much for him. But she had the sense to report it all the same.'

'Poor Kimberley.' Mary put a hand to her mouth. 'And her parents. They didn't even know she was missing.'

'I expected to find a dead fox or something. I certainly wasn't prepared for what I did find. It was horrific. I left in a hurry, fell from the window, bashed my head on a brick and knocked myself out.' He shuddered. 'I think I must have been in shock when I got home. Somebody has to go and collect her. I only recognised Kimberley by her clothes. I bought the blouse for her birthday.' Reaching for a kidney bowl he retched.

Mary took it from him. 'Lay back. You need to rest.'

'Do you know what gets to me most?' He pointed at Joseph. 'You! You set her up. It's your fault she's dead.'

Joseph turned away. 'I need a coffee. Be back soon.'

Mary bit her lip as she held Alan's hand. His fingernails drew blood from her palm.

'Sorry,' he said. 'But I'm so angry. It was stupid to send her in the first place. Why did he do it?'

'He made a bad decision, but for all the right reasons. Now he has to live with it. I do too, I agreed with him. I should have said something.'

*

Do they know it's Christmas? Band Aid asked on the hospital radio. Tinsel and fairy-lights around the canteen answered the question.

Joseph banged his tray down. Hot coffee erupted from a mug. A slice of Genoa cake caught most of it. Ignoring the mess, he slammed a fist into his empty hand. 'Shit, shit, shit and more shit. Kimberley, I'm so, so sorry. Payne, you bastard, I'll have you for this.'

Visitors sitting at an adjacent table took their tray and moved across the canteen. The manageress came out from behind the counter.

'Would you please be quiet,' she said. 'This is a hospital. I'll have to ask you to moderate your language.' She spun on her heels and marched off before he could react.

Joseph pushed the tray away. Pictures of the young girl, so eager to please, so keen on her work, flashed through his mind. White coats, orchids, rows of fish tanks. A kaleidoscope of objects and colours spun in front of his eyes. The colours vanished. Blackness replaced them. The sounds in the canteen were replaced by an insistent buzzing noise in his head. He felt himself spiralling down into a dark pit.

'Sir, sir, are you okay?' The voice from miles away filtered through. He felt hands pulling at him. His vision returned.

'What happened?' He rubbed his eyes and stared around the room.

'You must have passed out. I saw you,' the man said. 'You hit your head on the table. Are you feeling okay?'

Joseph sat back in the chair. Smashed crockery, scattered cake and a plastic tray lay on the floor. 'Yes. I'm fine. Thanks.'

*

'You look worse than Alan,' Joseph said, staring at Mary. 'He's sleeping now, why don't you get a breath of air. It's stuffy in these places.'

'I feel so guilty,' she said. 'What will we tell her parents? We took out of her comfort zone and put her into the hands of a murderer? Or suspected murderer I should say,' she corrected. 'We still have to prove it in court.'

'Maybe. But he has to make it to court in the first place. Getting back to you. You really do look all in. Are you feeling sick?'

'A little. Nothing to worry about. What I really need is a drink. Like you said, it's stuffy in here.'

'Coffee?'

'No, I need something stronger. I've got some wine at home, want to join me?'

*

Joseph sat down hard. Mary's sofa protested. 'I feel I need to make it up to Jefferson in some way.' He looked down at his shoes. 'I should have gone myself. Not asked him.'

'He can't dodge life. It has a way of smacking you in the face now and then. If you join the force, you need to harden up.'

'Yes, I agree. But even so …'

'You didn't know he'd find her body. No one could have known.'

'He wanted to be a detective. I wonder if he feels the same way now?'

'I expect he does. He's a good officer. Very conscientious.'

Joseph bobbed his head in agreement. 'Tomorrow, I'll have a word with Hughes. I'll try to get him attached to us for a while. He could prove useful.'

'Yes, we've got a lot on our hands at the moment. But you do realize Alan holds you responsible for Kimberley? He may not want to join us.'

'It's possible. I'll have to have a word with him, explain my actions. I'm certain he'll see what I did was right. We could assign him to finding Payne's drug cache.' Joseph held out his wine glass. 'Pour me another, please.'

'When do you plan on setting this up?'

'Jefferson should be discharged from hospital tomorrow. The nurse I spoke to said they were keeping him in overnight for observation. I'll check with him first, then approach Hughes.'

'While you're seeing Hughes, don't forget to hand in the report about finding Kimberley. He can call off the search now and concentrate our forces where they're needed most.' Mary grabbed her glass as her hand brushed against it, causing it to teeter on the edge of the table.

Mary shook the wine bottle over her glass. Her lopsided grin turned to a frown. 'Empty,' she slurred. 'Good job there's another in the fridge.' She attempted to push herself up from the sofa. Her knees buckled. She fell back. Turning to Joseph, she said, 'You get it. My legs are on strike.'

'No. You've had enough. We've got work in the morning.' He pulled her to her feet. 'Bedtime for you. Come on, let's see if I can get you up the stairs.'

Chapter 40

December 1986

Green paint must have been on special offer when *The Cheeky Leprechaun* was decorated. Anything and everything which could take a coat of paint, had.

Posters extolling the virtue of Ireland's favourite tipple plastered the walls. The newly acquired CD player kept up a constant supply of Irish folk music.

'It's not as nice as Stevie's Wonder Bar,' a girl whispered. 'But I agree with you, I don't fancy drinking after what happened.' She fanned her face with a menu.

Lisa frowned. 'Apart from the fact it's shut, you mean?'

'Is it?'

'Of course, it is. Until they've had the funeral.'

Two more girls joined them at the table, clutching fizzy drinks.

'Not trying the beer then?' Lisa smiled. 'Supposed to put hairs on your chest.'

'I know,' one girl replied. 'I don't want to risk it.'

They all laughed.

'Did you bring the photos, Lisa?'

'Naturally. I haven't looked at them yet. I thought I'd wait until we were all together.'

'Come on then, let's see them.'

Lisa took an envelope from her bag. She smiled as she shuffled through the prints, then handed them around. 'Sorry about the red-eye. But there's some good ones amongst them. Look at you, you drunken lot!'

'I am. Don't you dare show this to anyone. Look at the size of my arse.'

'Who will know it's yours? There's four of you in the picture.'

'True, but I'm going on a diet when we get back home.' She pushed her bag of crisps away.

Lisa gave a cry and dropped the last photo. 'Shit! I don't believe it.' Picking it up she held it out. 'Look at this!'

'Oh my god,' her friend gasped. 'You shouldn't have taken that.'

'I didn't realize I had.' Lisa held the photo closer. 'You can see the driver. Christ! What was he thinking? He's looking over his shoulder. It wasn't an accident. He meant to kill him!' Turning her head, she emptied her stomach onto the floor.

'Oi! You lot! Out!'

Everyone on the terrace stopped talking.

A line of teenagers sitting on the floor, their legs around the person in front, singing *Oops, upside ...* stopped in mid verse. 'What's up?' one of them shouted. 'What do you mean, out? We're only having fun.' His inebriated companions shouted their agreement.

'Not you.' The man pointed. 'Them. Look at the fooking mess.' Carrying a mop and bucket he approached the girls. 'If you lot can't hold your drink, keep away from my bar.'

Lisa dabbed her mouth with a tissue. 'Come on, let's get back to the hotel. I need to lie down. Poor Steve, I really liked him. What shall we do?'

'Take the photos to the police I suppose.' The girl gulped at her drink. 'I wish one of us spoke Spanish.'

'I think it's obvious. We need to show them to our Holiday Rep. Let him earn his money.' The girl, whose backside challenged the chair she occupied, tore one of the photos into pieces. 'But not this one. I don't want him, or any hot-blooded Spanish policeman, seeing me with no knickers.'

*

Lisa waved the poolside waiter away. She picked at a dish of mixed salted nuts. A man in his late twenties approached her, mopping his forehead.

'Sorry to keep you waiting, had an emergency. I keep telling everyone not to lay in the sun too long. Anyway, how can I help?'

The Oxbridge accent jerked her back to reality.

Pushing the packet of photos across the table, Lisa said, 'This is one of my holiday photos. I warn you, it will come as a shock.'

Tossing the hair from his eyes, he smiled. 'Take a lot to shock me. I doubt you can show me anything I haven't seen before.'

Lisa spat out the shell of a pistachio nut and wiped her lips with the back of her hand. 'You couldn't be more wrong.'

Pulling a chair from beneath the table, the holiday rep pinched the creases and hitched up his white trousers before sitting. Opening the envelope, he stared at the photo. 'Shit! I don't believe it. What on earth made you take this?'

'Oh, cheers. You think I took it on purpose? Are you a complete dick-head?'

He swallowed and beckoned the waiter. 'Brandy. Double. No ice.' Looking at Lisa, he asked, 'I need to steady my nerves. Can I get you one?'

She nodded. 'The same, please. And one for my friend.'

'Make it three.'

The waiter headed towards the outside bar.

'Sorry, it's just . . . I don't know . . . it's the shock of actually seeing somebody being killed. It must have been terrible for you, being there, I mean.'

'I need you to take it to the police for me,' she said. 'I don't speak Spanish. Apart from ordering a beer.'

'We'll go together. Let's have our drinks, then I'll organise a taxi to take us into town.'

Lisa scowled. 'Before we do, take a closer look. The girls and I don't believe it was an accident.'

Taking a pair of reading glasses from his blazer he turned the photo, holding it close, avoiding the glare of the sun on the glossy print. He inhaled deeply, then let the breath out in a rush. 'You're right. Forget the drinks, the Guardia Civil need to see this right away.'

'I should think so,' Lisa's friend said. 'I nearly shit myself when the car hit Steve. If he hadn't pushed me away when I tried to help him, I may have been killed.'

'It certainly was scary. I never want to see anything like it again.' Lisa shuddered. 'I wanted a picture of you and Steve, but not like that.'

*

The holiday rep pushed open the police station door. Standing aside he waited for the two girls to enter. 'Don't worry,' he said. 'Leave all the talking to me.'

Lisa held her friend's hand as they approached the desk.

The officer on duty smiled. *'Buenas tardes, Señor. Buenas tardes, Señoritas. ¿En que puedo ser de ayuda?'*

Lisa looked at the rep.

'He asked if he could be of help. If he wants you to explain anything, I'll translate. But I'm sure I can manage. The photo says it all.'

Lisa pointed to a bench against one wall. 'Let's wait over there,' she said to her friend. 'There's not much we can do to help.' Lowering her voice she added, 'I wouldn't kick him out of my bed, would you?'

'Who?'

'The film star behind the desk. Who do you think?'

'Oh, yeah, I see what you mean. Bit of a change from the lads back home.'

The rep turned away from the desk. *'Gracias, Señor, has sido de gran ayuda.'* Indicating the door to the street, he said, 'That's it, ladies. All done. Shall we go?'

'What did he think?' Lisa frowned. 'You two seemed to have a lot to say.'

'Actually, he was very interested, he was one of the two policemen who attended the accident.'

'It was no accident. You saw the photo, the driver *meant* to do it.'

'And the officer agrees with you, I mean with us. Actually, I'm sure he does speak English, just prefers not to. Anyway, he'll pass it to the Policia Nacional. They deal with serious crime. These are just the local guys.'

'Is that all?'

'No. He'll make sure all his officers have a photo-copy. They'll be looking out for your man, whoever he is.'

'Do you think he lives around here?'

'No way of knowing. He doesn't look Spanish. Probably a visitor. I don't recognise him, so he's not staying in one of our hotels. I've got a good memory for faces.'

*

Mark Payne put his feet up on a chair and took in the view. The beach shimmered. Waves gently threw themselves against the shore. Holidaymakers swam and played in the water.

'This is the life,' he said to Beckworth. 'The best thing I ever did was sending you out here.' He picked up a glass and held it against his forehead. 'Mind you, I think the summers might be too much for me. This can be my winter retreat. Get away from all the cold and wet.'

'It's not too bad,' Samuel replied. 'Unless the electric goes off. Without any fans it's hard to sleep. A lot of people walk on the beach, it's cooler by the sea.'

'Isabel took it better than I expected.' Mark pointed over his shoulder, towards the bar. 'I don't think she understood why you gave her the cash, but she seemed happy enough with the situation.'

'She didn't have a lot of options, did she? The document you and Twyford came up with looked the bee's knees.'

'Shame it took you so long to read. I should have told Twyford to put pictures in it.' Mark smirked. 'Never mind, it's done now. All I have to do is sit back and count the money.'

'While I do all the work I suppose? No change there then.'

'Don't push your luck. How many other people get the chance to dodge the law and lay in the sun?'

'According to what Steve told me, quite a few. Anyway, if they do get me, you'll have a lot of explaining –'

'Don't be too sure. Obviously, I wouldn't want anything to harm my new business, but you know the consequences when things don't go my way.'

Beckworth swallowed, hard. 'I was only saying. I wouldn't drop you in it. You know me.'

'I do, and it worries me at times. Maybe I should have become Isabel's partner.'

Chapter 41

December 1986

Clutching his holdall, Graham stepped off the London Transport bus. He looked around, trying to get his bearings. Shops had closed down. The cinema had also failed as a bingo hall, its windows boarded up. Things had changed. Not a lot, but enough to throw him for a minute.

He headed for the Rose and Crown.

*

In the corner of the pub, lights on a gambling machine blinked on and off, racing around, enticing punters to deposit coins and win a fortune. A dart board had its share of devotees, pints in hand. Serious drinkers huddled together, close to the bar.

Graham used a foot to push his bag further under the table and sipped his drink.

'Wotcha, mate. You made it then.' The new arrival pulled up a chair. 'How was the journey? Bet you're glad to get away from all that fresh air.'

'Hello, Roger.' Graham patted his stomach and pointed. 'You putting on weight?'

'Cheeky bleeder. Its relaxed muscle.' He looked across the bar. 'Going to get meself a wet, what you having?'

'Still got this, thanks.' He held up his glass.

'Drinking halves? Blimey, I know you said you were brassic, but halves?' Roger stood up. 'Anything with it? They do handsome rolls in here. Don't worry, I'll pay. Had some luck on the gee-gees.' He patted his jacket. 'I fancy cheese and onion. That do you?'

'Thanks. My treat next time. But I need to get a job first.'

'There you go, mate. Cheese and pickle. She's run out of onion, dozy bitch.' Roger held up his pint. 'Cheers. Almost like the old days. Squidgy was coming but his bird's dragging him round

Muvvercare. Silly sod. I told him he was playing Russian roulette riding bareback, but you know what he's like.'

'Sounds like Squidgy.' Graham laughed. 'Any of the others still around?'

'Depends what you mean by around. You can visit Jack if you fancy it, he ain't going far.' Roger grinned. 'He's got another seven years to do.'

Graham toyed with his glass. 'How's Annie? She still with him?'

'Yeah. Well, she was last time I heard. Why? Do you fancy her?'

'No, even if I did, the thought of Jack would put me off my stroke.'

Roger grinned. 'You ain't changed much have you. But I thought you was serving Queen and country? How'd you get out so quick?'

Graham lowered his voice. 'I was being economic with the truth when I phoned you. I'm not on leave, I'm on the run. Got caught doing what comes naturally.'

Roger held up his hands. 'Don't tell me, mate. Let me guess. You was in the wrong bed, right?'

'Got it in one. But that's the least of my problems. I'll tell you more later, too many ears in here.'

'Right. Drink up. Let's get back to my place. The missus has got a room ready for you. I've warned her what you're like, so no funny business, right?'

'Come off it, Roger. I got enough on my plate without starting a fight with you.'

*

Mavis shut the fanlight. 'That's enough to blow the cobwebs away. Switch the fire on, it'll soon warm up in here.' Her breath lingered in the air. 'How long are you staying, Graham? I need to know when to wash the sheets and how much grub to get in.'

'Give it a rest. He ain't moving in permanent, only until he gets his act together. Let the poor sod catch his breath.'

'Keep your hair on, I only asked. I'm going back downstairs, have you two had enough to drink, or do you want something?'

'Cup of Rosie for me,' Roger said. 'How about you, mate?'

'Tea's fine, thanks.'

Mavis clunked down the bare wooden stairs. 'About time you got this carpet put back,' she called over her shoulder. 'Be time to paint these stairs again before you get around to it.'

'Yeah, yeah, yeah,' Roger mouthed.

Graham looked through the window. 'Nice garden, Roger. Bet it looks a picture in the summer.'

Roger shrugged. 'Ain't too shabby. Lot of graft though. Don't know how she manages all the digging. I did offer once, but she told me to piss off up the pub. Said I was about as much use as a chocolate tea-pot.'

'Bloody women. We can't live with them and we can't live without them.'

'Ain't that the truth.'

'Nice room. Right next to the loo, very handy.' Patting the bed, he added. 'And this looks comfortable.'

'Be careful with the wardrobe. Got one corner balanced on some beer mats, these bleedin' floor boards are all cock-eyed.' Roger used his hand to indicate a slope.

'Okay, thanks. What's the chances of getting a job around here? Much going on?'

'Not a lot. Bloody recession's ballsin' everything up. Factories are laying off, even the bakery. Said on the box the other night fings is improving, said we got less than three million poor buggers out of work now. Huh, as if that's anything to be proud of.'

'Any idea what I do to earn a crust? Shit. I was better off in the army.'

'Bit of ducking and diving I suppose, like yours truly. Don't worry, mate, things will sort themselves out. I'm going down to see what's happened to our brew, back in a shake.'

Graham sat on the bed, blew on his hands and rubbed them together. 'What's this all about? Here I am, sitting in front of a one bar electric fire in a room not big enough to swing a cat. And that bitch, Mary? She's got my flat and lover boy to keep her warm.' Turning, he punched the pillow. 'Cow. One day . . . I swear . . . one day I'm going to get even with those two.'

Roger nudged the door open with his shoe. 'Here you go, mate. Two teas. Mavis is bringing up the biscuits. And there's sausage and mash tonight, with lashings of Bisto and onion gravy. Handsome.'

*

'That was great. Thanks.' Graham used a slice of bread to clean his plate.

'How about a pint to wash it down?' Roger mimed lifting a glass to his mouth. 'Plenty of time before they call last orders.'

'What about the washing up? Shouldn't we do it before we go?'

'No, it's okay,' Mavis said. 'I can manage. You go.'

Roger stood up. 'Come on mate, I'll lend you some clothes. We'll go down the market in the week, get you sorted.'

*

Light from shop windows bathed the pavement. The sky, dark as ink, provided a suitable backdrop for illuminated Christmas decorations spanning the road.

Graham ran a hand down the raincoat he was wearing. 'Christ, it's turned chilly tonight. Thanks for lending me this. And the fisherman's jumper. Been too cold to come out otherwise.'

'You're right, they said on the telly it's only just above freezing. I pity any brass monkeys out tonight.' Roger pulled the collar of his overcoat up to reach his ears. 'Now, come on, spill the beans. What you really been up to? What were you about to tell me? You know, when we was in the Rose this afternoon?'

'Not a lot.'

'Leave it out. You said you was giving it to some bird, but there must be more to it. You've had more women than I've had hot dinners. What's special about this one?'

'She was married to my commanding officer.'

'Oh.' Roger banged his gloved hands together. 'Thinking with your dick as usual. No change there then. Is that it?'

Graham took a deep breath and coughed as the cold air assaulted his lungs. 'I wish it was. Going AWOL's bad enough but . . .'

'Come on, mate, it's me you're talking to. Fill me in.'

'It's bad, Roger. I'm not sure I should.'

'After all the things we've done together? How bad can it be for Christ's sake?'

'Try murder.'

Roger stopped, turned and grasped Graham's arm. 'Piss off! You ain't have you?'

'It was an accident. I didn't mean to kill the bugger.'

Roger pulled Graham into an alley between the shops. 'How can you kill someone by accident? You taken a page from Jack's book?'

'It was Mary's fault. She's been shagging her boss. I took umbrage and decided to sort him out.'

'It was manslaughter then. You must have hit him too hard.'

'No. I shot him. Well, not him actually. He was the one I aimed at, but he must have moved, someone else took the bullet.'

'You shot another geezer? Who the fuck was he?'

'No idea. Does it really matter? I topped him, whoever he was.'

Roger frowned. 'I don't believe this. Where did you get the bleedin' gun?'

'It belonged to her boss.' He held up a hand. 'Don't ask, it's complicated. Let's just say I nicked it.'

'Have you still got it?' Roger looked back down the road. 'It ain't in my house, is it?'

'No. I was daft enough to give it to Mary. It was a sort of swap.'

'You daft sod. Why on earth didn't you get rid of the bloody thing? Now she's got a gun with your prints all over it.'

Graham shrugged. 'I suppose so. I don't know what she'll do with it. It must be registered to him, so it could make things difficult.' He paused. 'It's all her sodding fault. Her and her fancy man.'

'Like you said, mate, bloody women. Been giving us grief ever since Adam and Eve. Come on, let's get a couple of swift pints. Things never seem so bad looking through the bottom of a glass.'

'You're not wrong there, Roger.'

Chapter 42

December 1986

Joseph scraped a cup against the rim of a saucer as he looked at the constable standing on the other side of his desk. 'I understand your reticence, Jefferson, and I understand your problem with me.' He held up a hand as Jefferson opened his mouth. 'No, let me finish. As I say, I know you think I acted unwisely in regard to Kimberley, but we have to put personal feelings to one side. To solve her murder, and three others, we need evidence. That's where you come in. You said you'd like to work your way up to becoming a detective. Now's your chance. I'd like you to join our team on a temporary basis. Naturally your salary will be adjusted accordingly while you're with us.'

'It won't be easy,' Mary said. 'Mark Payne is behind all this and he may have skipped the country. There are International Warrants out for Payne and Samuel Beckworth, who we think is an accomplice. The murders are our top priority, but it would assist us greatly if you would concentrate on locating the large quantity of drugs linked to at least one of the murder victims. Find those and we'll have the proof we need to lock Payne up and throw away the key. Kimberley found what she was sure was cocaine in boxes marked Water Balance Kits. It's probably the reason for her disappearance.'

PC Jefferson turned his attention back to Joseph. 'I owe you an apology, sir. I shouldn't have said what I did in the hospital. I know Kimberley was aware of the danger, we spoke about it. She is . . . sorry, she was brave to do it. I want to do all I can to catch the man responsible for her death.'

'No apology needed. We all say things we come to regret.'

Mary suppressed a smile.

'So,' Joseph said. 'I take it you'll join us? After I clear it with Inspector Hughes of course.'

'Yes, sir. I appreciate the chance. Where do you want me to start?'

'I think we need you back at Mark Payne Enterprises. Call in, tell the receptionist you're moving into this area for a while and looking for a job.'

'And say your aunt died,' Mary said. 'You did give family reasons for leaving when you helped out before.'

*

Julie slid the glass partition back. 'Good morning, Fred. How's your aunt? Feeling better, I hope.'

'Hello Julie. No, sad to say, she died.'

'Oh. I'm sorry.'

'Thanks. But I didn't really see a lot of her.'

'Still a shame though.'

'Yes. Changing the subject, I've staying with my uncle for a while, help get things sorted out, and I was wondering, are there any vacancies?'

'Yes, we certainly have.' Julie smiled. 'I'm going crazy trying to run this place on my own. God only knows when Mark's coming back, and I haven't seen his brother in ages. When can you start?'

'How about today? I haven't got anything to do that can't wait.'

'Brilliant! We've had so many fish die I'm finding it hard to keep up. We need more stock. I'm turning business away every day. Do you think your father would help?'

'What? I mean yes, I'll phone him tonight. He's got contacts, hopefully one of them will deal in South American fish.'

'Thanks.' She smiled. 'But why wait? Use this phone.'

'I can't. He's away for the day.'

'Oh. Okay.'

'Why don't you use your usual supplier? Surely he must be the easiest option?'

'I don't have his number. He either phones us or Mark calls him.'

'Sounds like a strange way of working. No wonder you're in a mess.'

'Mark's always been the same. You do things his way, or not at all.' She looked at her watch. 'Fancy a cup of tea? I could do with one.'

'Why not? Then I'll take a look at the fish.'

*

PC Jefferson pulled the chair closer to Joseph's desk.

'I got the job, sir. She was desperate. I got the impression Payne's lost interest. She hasn't heard from him for days.'

'He's enjoying the good life in Spain, that's why. We examined the phone records for Mark Payne Enterprises, he phones her from a public phone. We know the town, but not where he's staying.'

'How about extradition, sir? It's possible now.'

'Yes, it's all in hand. Not that it will happen overnight. I've had experience of the way the Spanish do things. They can organise a bull-fight, but anything else . . .?'

'At least you know where the suspect is, sir. Is there no other way?'

'There's always another way.' Joseph tapped the side of his nose.

'I know it was only your first day,' Mary said, 'but did you make any progress?'

'No. I was too busy removing dead fish, doing partial water changes and sorting out treatments. The place is beginning to stink. It desperately needs re-stocking. I told Julie I'd find a supplier.'

'Don't concern yourself, I'll get you some numbers to call.' Joseph put his hands behind his head and leaned back. 'Where's their usual man?'

'That's the strange part, sir. Seems she has to rely on him phoning. When Payne's around he contacts the supplier. Julie isn't allowed to do it.'

'He doesn't trust her, that much is obvious. I'm certain she knows much more than she's told us so far, but how much?'

Jefferson nodded agreement. 'I get on well with Julie, we hit it off straight away.' Seeing the look on Mary's face he continued. 'Nothing like that. I was hoping to form a relationship with Kimberley at the time.' He swallowed. 'Julie and I are friends, no more, no less.'

'I understand,' Joseph said. 'But you have to exploit this friendship if we are to bring Kimberley's killer to justice. It's not nice, but neither is murder, running prostitutes and drug dealing. Do whatever you need to do to help this investigation.'

Taking a deep breath, Jefferson stretched himself to his full height. 'You can rely on me, sir. I'll do my very best.'

Mary smiled. 'It's all that can be asked of anyone. Until we can arrest Payne and Beckworth, your friend Julie is all we have. We've searched his house, his office, and his premises. Nothing was found. He's very clever at covering his tracks.'

'Yes,' Joseph said. 'But everything comes to he who waits. Be patient, be thorough, but above all don't let your feelings interfere with the job you're there to do.'

'You needn't worry, sir. If Julie's involved, she deserves to go down with the others.'

'Glad to hear it, Jefferson. Anything you find, no matter how trivial it may appear, I want to hear about it, understood?'

'Yes, sir. Perfectly.'

*

Julie polished the front of a glass tank. A shoal of red bellied Piranhas nudged the barrier between them and a possible meal. 'These look really good,' she said. 'Where did you find them? The rest of the consignment's are great too, your dad certainly came up trumps. It was all getting me down, but now you're here there's light at the end of the tunnel.' She put an arm around his waist and kissed his cheek. 'Thanks, I appreciate it.'

Jefferson fought to erase the picture in his mind of Julie, in a prison cell. 'Glad I could help. Dad did all the work though.'

'I hope he told you what they eat,' she said. 'We've never had these before. I haven't got a clue.'

'Don't worry. Frozen vegetables, raw potato, prawns, that sort of thing is all they need. Forget Hollywood, these make good pets if you look after them.'

'How about letting me look after you? Let me treat you to a pub lunch at The Crown.'

'Sounds good to me, but you don't have to. I'm only doing what you pay me for. Besides, I enjoy my work.'

'I wish it was like this all the time. You know, just you and me, no Mark or his creepy brother.'

'Don't know what Dad would say. He expects me to take over when he retires.'

'Perhaps I could come and work for you. I'd love to get out of this place.'

Jefferson frowned. 'Then why don't you? Give in your notice and find something else.'

'We've had this conversation before, remember? You don't know what he's like. If I tried to leave . . .'

'How long have you worked for him? And if he's that bad, why have you stayed?'

'Since I left school. This is the only job I've had. He used to be fun to work for, but he's changed.'

'I must admit when I first met him, I wasn't impressed. Arrogant bastard I think sums him up. But surely he can't make you stay?'

She touched her cheek. 'He can.'

'You say he used to be different. When did he change?'

'I came to work for him the year he started. He worked a lot of hours but it paid off. Money seemed to come from nowhere. He took me out to restaurants, bought me anything I asked for. It was a good time. Then he bought his big house and I began to be left out. He had all sorts of buildings added to the house which caused a lot of bad feeling around the local area. It's a listed building.' She shook her head from side to side. 'He took me there once, to show off. I swam in his pool, saw the gym, sat in all those gorgeous Cadillacs.'

'I'd love to see those. Do you ever go back?'

She swallowed. 'No. I've never been asked again and I wouldn't want to.'

'Why?'

'I prefer not to talk about it.'

'Does he still –'

'You don't understand. I don't have any choice. But at least it's only now and then. I just close my eyes and let him get on with it.'

'It's not right. You should go to the police. That's rape.'

'Is it? It would be his word against mine. He's got people who look out for him. I haven't. It could be worse, I suppose.'

'How?'

'I don't know. It was a silly thing to say.'

'Sounds to me someone should bring him down a peg or two.'

'How? He told me once he's untouchable. Even got the police in his pocket.'

'Has he? Has he mentioned names?'

Her derisive laugh made him feel uncomfortable. 'Do you think someone like him would be that daft?'

'Probably not. Do you know how he makes his money? I mean, buying and selling fish hasn't made my dad rich. He earns a good living, but gyms and Cadillacs? Dad must be doing something wrong.'

'Mark has got other things. He bought the lease for Hornigolds, you know, the cocktail bar in town. And the Mariner's Arms. He's going to build a night club there. I've seen the plans. Then there's the fish restaurant and a lock-up garage. It's anyone's guess what he'll get hold of next.'

Jefferson stopped watching the piranhas. 'A lock-up? Bit down market, isn't it? Where does that fit in?'

She spread her fingers. 'No idea. More cars perhaps?'

'Do you think so? Perhaps we could go together and have a look. Have you got a key?'

'No, but there's probably one in his office. I'll try to find it as I owe you a favour. But don't ask me to come with you, I've seen enough of his cars to last me a lifetime.'

*

'Call it a day now, Fred, please,' Julie said. 'Nobody will be calling this late. I want to lock up and get off home.'

'Suits me. I'm about done in here. The rest can wait until the morning.' He got off the push-along stool. Light from the fish-tank gave his face a strange hue. 'Supposing your boss phones? Won't he be annoyed if there's no answer?'

'He's had all day. I told you before, I haven't heard from in ages. Why would today be any different?'

'Did you find the key to the lock-up? If we're closing early, I could go and see what's inside.'

'No, I'm not sure.' She opened her handbag and passed him a keyring. 'But there's four on here I don't recognise. It could be one of them, you'll have to try them all.'

'Thanks. Are you sure you don't know what any of them are for?'

'I told you. No. If you don't want them, I'll put them back.'

Jefferson closed his fist around the keys. 'Let me keep hold of them until tomorrow. I'm keen to see what he's got under lock and key.'

'Please don't touch anything.' She held out a hand. 'Perhaps I shouldn't have given you those. If he sees anything's been disturbed, there'll be hell to pay.'

'I won't touch a thing, scout's honour.' He raised three fingers to the side of his head. 'Besides, I don't suppose there's anything there.'

*

Jefferson stared at the up-and-over door. Metal angles, welded to the frame and secured by padlocks, ensured any opportunist thief would give up trying.

'Four locks? What the hell's he got in there?' Grasping one of the padlocks he tried the keys. The second one opened it. Bending down he tried the other keys. 'Got you, two to go.' Crossing to the other side he took off the remaining locks. 'Now, let's see what's so important.'

Taking hold of the handle, he tugged.

The door opened.

He switched his torch on.

'Oh – my – god!'

Slamming the door, he attached the locks and ran.

*

Inside the phone box Jefferson's breath condensed on the glass around him as he spoke. 'Yes, sir, and I need you to come at once.' He repeated the address of the lock up garage. 'There's more than enough evidence here. We'll need a van. Okay, sir, but . . . shit! Why is it I never have enough change?'

*

The Rover stopped at the entrance to the cul-de-sac. Headlights dimmed, then died. Joseph hurried towards Jefferson. Street-lights sent his shadow ahead of him.

'Good evening, sir. Sorry I ran out of coins. It took ages for them to put me through to you.' Jefferson cupped his hands, blew into them and rubbed them together. 'Getting chilly tonight.'

'It certainly is,' Joseph said. 'Now, what exactly have you found? I would have got here sooner but someone wanted dropping at the off-licence.'

'Wait until you see this, sir. I couldn't believe my eyes. You won't either.'

'Give me the keys. We'll soon see.'

Jefferson held his torch as Joseph fiddled with the locks.

'I hope this isn't a fool's errand,' Joseph muttered.

The door swung up. Torchlight reflected back off of polythene wrapped packages stacked along one side of the garage. A stack of boxes labelled Water Balance Kits lined the opposite side of the lock-up.

'What the . . .? This lot must be worth a king's ransom. Help me take a sample, we need to get it back for testing. If it is what it looks like, we've got the bastard!' Joseph pulled a penknife from his pocket.

'Now you see why I said we'd need a van, sir,' Jefferson said, walking to the rear of the building. Reaching over he pulled a parcel wrapped in paper towards him. 'Look at this, sir. It's heavy, but this one's different from the others. Shall I open it?'

'No, I'll do it. Hold the torch.'

The brown paper ripped apart as Joseph tore at it. If it were possible, Her Majesty the Queen would have blinked in the light.

'Christ!' Jefferson let the torch beam waver. 'Look at all this cash!'

'My guess is it's the money found when Beckworth was arrested. This gets better and better.'

'We'd should get it to the station, sir. It's more evidence.'

'Is it? I'd say it was a bonus for work well done.'

'Pardon? Do you mean to say you're not handing it in?'

'No, I most definitely am not. This is money gained from crime. I don't intend for it to be returned to Payne if we don't get a conviction.'

'How can we fail, sir? It's all here. Drugs, probably cocaine, and more money than you could shake a stick at. He'll go down for sure.'

'I wish I had your confidence. I've seen bastards like Payne walk away scot-free many times. This money can be put to better use. Help yourself.'

Jefferson took a step back. 'I can't, sir. It's not right. We should hand it in.'

'Don't be naïve. Do you really think it will all be there on the day of the trial? If we don't take it, someone else will.'

'Who? Who'll take it?'

'The police holiday fund, probably. Do yourself a favour. Nobody knows we found it, and Payne's not likely to complain it's missing, is he?'

'I can't, sir. It's tantamount to stealing.'

'It's your choice. I admire your integrity, but you've got a lot to learn about life. In our line of business, it pays to have funds which don't have to be accounted for. People expect to be paid when they supply information. Petty cash doesn't interest informants.'

Jefferson reached down at the contents of the parcel. His hand hovered over the banknotes for a second or two before retracting it. 'No, I can't. I assume you'd rather I didn't report this part of the find, sir,' he said.

'Yes. Just treat it as a case of *malum prohibitum*. Sometimes the end justifies the means.' Joseph placed a hand on Jefferson's shoulder. 'Get in the car, we'll go back to the station and organise the collection of this lot. DCI Hughes will be pleased with your work tonight.' Picking up the parcel of money he headed back to his car. 'Make sure you lock up,' he said. 'Don't want anything else to go missing before SOC arrive.'

*

Next morning, DCI Hughes looked up from photos of men in white coveralls and packages of drugs. 'Well done. PC Jefferson, you did well. I'll grant the newspapers access to some of these.'

'With respect, sir,' Joseph said. 'I don't think we should. I suspect this haul to be connected to Mark Payne. We should conceal its discovery until we apprehend him. If he knows we have this, he'll know the game is up.'

'Which leads me to this.' Hughes held out a fax. 'This came from London earlier. It's not a good picture, but the Spanish police think it could be the same man we arranged an International Arrest Warrant for. They want him in connection with a hit-and-run accident and have asked us to confirm identification.'

Joseph stared at the paper. 'It is Payne. He's the driver. And if I'm not mistaken, that's Beckworth in the background. We need to chase up those requests for extradition.'

'I agree.'

'One more thing, sir, if I may.'

'Yes, Fargough. What is it?'

'Next year's holiday leave, sir. I'm in need of a break. Would you sanction it if I request taking a week off? I know I'm not entitled until April, but I would appreciate it.'

'I quite understand. WDC Wells, PC Jefferson and you have all done sterling work lately. I think I can sanction it. When were you thinking of?'

'As soon as we get confirmation the Spaniards have our suspects under lock and key, sir. Then I can relax a little.'

'That's understandable. Have you finished with PC Jefferson? Will he be returning to his duties?'

'With your permission, sir, I would like to extend his stay with us. He would be of great help to WDC Wells while I'm away, which, hopefully, will be very soon.'

'Permission granted. I think the young man shows great potential.'

*

The choir singing Christmas carols in a cathedral were silenced by Mary waving the remote control. She moved along the sofa, away from Joseph. 'Bit sudden, isn't it? You haven't said anything to

me about a holiday. What brought this on?' She sipped her wine.
'Are you planning another few days, snooping around off the
record?'

'Nothing like that. Hughes told me the Spanish police are close
to arresting Payne for a driving accident. Seems he's responsible
for yet another death.'

'Well, there's a surprise. The man's the *Grim Reaper* brought to
life. But what's all this got to do with you asking for holiday
leave? Am I invited?'

'Not this time, I'm afraid. I need you to hold the fort while I fly
out to Spain.'

'I see.' Tipping her head back, she drained her glass. 'I can
guess why.'

'I don't intend for him to slip through our fingers. As soon as
he's arrested, I'm off. I'll stay until the necessary paperwork is
signed off then bring him back to the UK. I'm hoping they nab
Beckworth too. They know he's wanted by us.'

Offering the wine bottle to Joseph, she said, 'Won't you join
me? It sounds like we've got something to celebrate.'

Joseph frowned. 'You seem to be finding lots to celebrate lately.
I haven't mentioned this before, but I think you're drinking is
becoming a habit. I almost fell over the pile of bottles on your
kitchen floor. I need you to be fully functioning while I'm away.'

'Cheek. I don't drink much. It helps me relax at the end of the
day.'

'And at the start of the day as well. I know you've been
indulging before you come to work. I've smelt it on your breath.
It's got to stop.'

'Is that an order?'

'If it's what it takes, then yes, it is. But try to see it as a friendly
warning. Drink has cost people their jobs in the past.'

'Okay. I know you're right. I'll cut down.'

Putting his arm around her he pulled her close. 'Thanks. It
means a lot to me. We're a team. I rely on you.'

'I hope I don't let you down, but I'm not sure I can live like this.
We should have reported Donald Payne's death, it's really getting
to me. The wine dulls it for a while, but when I go to bed the
nightmares return. Isn't there anyway we can resolve this? Make a

clean breast of it? We didn't kill him. Now your gun can't be found, there's nothing to implicate you.'

'We could, but I'd still have to explain why I took an innocent man to that barn. It could look as though I set him up.'

'Don't be silly. Why would you?'

'I wouldn't. But, in the cold light of day, it wouldn't look good. I'm sorry, my love, but we'll have to leave things as they are. Now you've explained about the drinking, I'll try to be more supportive. I'd still like you to cut back though.'

Chapter 43

December 1986

Graham put the bags down, banged his gloved hands together and stamped his feet. Voices filled the air, extolling the virtues of goods for sale. Smoke from pipe tobacco and cigarettes vied with exotic spices.

'Christ, I think it's getting colder.' His breath seemed reluctant to go very far. 'What time is it? Are they open yet?'

Roger pulled the sleeve of his overcoat back. 'Yeah, ten minutes ago. Fancy a pint?'

'Does a bear shit in the woods?' Picking up the bags, Graham walked on. 'I don't know when I can pay you back for this lot. Thanks, mate.'

'As long as you can buy a round or two, we'll call it quits. You helped me when I needed it. I gotta ask though, why the knife? Got a wicked looking blade, going to use it for gutting fish being as you live by the sea?'

'Something like that.'

'Mavis asked if you've got any plans? You know, where are you going next?'

'I think I'll make a move in a day or two. I've outstayed my welcome I expect. She's a diamond, your Mavis, but I don't want to push my luck. Think of all the extra cooking and washing.'

'You ain't got to go,' Roger said. 'That's not what she meant.'

'Maybe. But I think I will just the same. I've enough for my train fare back at the moment, but if we keep propping up the bar in the Crown –'

'You going back? What for? It sounds as if your bleedin' marriage is on the rocks, why bother? There's plenty more fish in the sea. And pulling birds always was one of your specialities.'

'It's not so easy. I love the cow. And I can't say too much about her having it off with someone can I? Not with my track record.'

'I think you should cut your losses, mate. If I was you, I'd move to the other end of the country, change me name and start again. If you don't, the poxy army's bound to catch up with you sooner or later.' He pulled his wallet from inside his coat. 'Come on, the first round's on me.'

Graham lifted his glass. 'Cheers, Roger. Apart from us getting cold it's been a good morning.'

'Cheers. Yeah, you got some bargains. I fancied one of them jumpers, but I got a load already.'

'I keep thinking.' Graham lowered his voice. 'You know, about the army and how to get Mary to come to her senses.'

Roger put both hands around his drink and studied it as if the answers to all Graham's concerns would be answered by this alcoholic version of a crystal ball. He leaned toward Graham. 'I think you're in deep shit. If I was in your shoes, I wouldn't go making any waves.'

'Thanks, you're a great help, I must say. I thought you might have some ideas. Anyone could state the obvious.' He motioned toward the bar. 'Same again?'

Roger tipped his head back and finished his drink. 'I don't mind if I do, squire.'

Graham let the packets of crisps drop from between his clenched teeth as he sat back at the table. Pushing a pint towards Roger he said, 'Now, where were we? Oh, yes, we were talking about Mary.'

'Why do you keep on about her? Sounds to me like she's happy with the situation. You've buggered off. She's found a new bloke. Job done.'

'But she's my wife. I want her back.'

'Can't see how you can do it, mate. If you go back, like you said, the army coppers will nab you. How's that going to help?'

Graham scratched the side of his head. 'I was thinking more along the lines of what you said before. Move far away, start all over again.'

'What? And forget Mary?'

'No, you twat. I'll take her with me. What's the point otherwise?'

Roger frowned. 'Don't sound like something the Mary I knew in the old days would do. I think you're barking up the wrong tree.'

'Why? I love her.'

'But it's not vicky verky is it.'

'What's vicky verky got to do with anything? Oh, I see, vice versa. Anyway, you're wrong. I'm sure she does love me deep down inside. It's just her stupid boss. He's got her under his spell.'

'If you want my opinion,' Roger said. 'You should cut your losses. Just sod off somewhere and forget her.'

'I can't. We've had our ups and downs, like all married couples.'

'Hang on, mate, don't include me and Mavis, we've never had a cross word.' He laughed. 'The secret to a happy marriage is simple. Tell the missus what you want to do, then do as she says.'

Graham wiped his mouth with the back of his hand and grinned. 'What happened to, ''I wear the trousers in this house,'' crap?'

'Anything for a quiet life,' Roger said. 'That's my motto. I wouldn't change places with you for all the tea in China. Mark my words, if you keep on the way you're going, it'll end in tears.'

'Maybe. But they won't be mine. I'm going back to sort things out, once and for all.'

Roger frowned. 'Look, mate. I know I'm probably wasting my breath, but you gotta see sense. All you'll do is end up deeper in the shit. Let it go.'

'Bollocks. She loves me deep down. I've just got to get her to admit it. I'll have it out with that tosser of a boss of hers.'

'It sounds to me like it's gone too far. Do yourself a favour. Just walk away.'

Graham folded his arms on the table, leaned forward and rested his head on them.

Unsure how to react, Roger looked at his friend, got up and headed toward the Gents.

'I got another round in,' Graham said, as Roger returned.

'Thanks, mate. I thought you'd nodded off. You feel okay?' He touched his glass against Graham's. 'Cheers.'

'Cheers. I've been thinking about what Mavis said last night over dinner, you know, about two wrongs not making a right, But I don't know what to do for the best. As far as I'm concerned, it's pretty straight forward. She's my wife. I still love her in spite of what she's done. Maybe your idea of moving away would work.' Leaning closer to Roger, he added, 'Especially after the business in the barn. Not that I can change anything. What's done is done. I count myself lucky not to have ended up in the frame. I'd love to know what they did after I ran off.'

'You silly bugger. Let sleeping dogs lie.'

'Maybe you're right, maybe not. But I think I'll give it a shot.' He pulled a face. 'Hmm, didn't mean it to come out like that. What I meant was, I'll go and see her and ask her to come away with me. If the answer's no . . .'

'I think you should stay with Mavis and me until you get your head sorted. You seem to jump from one bleedin' disaster to another. Try thinking with this up here.' He tapped the side of his head. 'Forget your dick for once, it's got you into enough bother.'

'Huh, easy to say, but try living away from Mavis for months at a time, see how long you last. No, thanks for the offer, but I think I'll get my arse into gear in the morning.'

*

Roger stood on the footbridge spanning the railway line. The winter sun turned the rails below blood red.

Graham looked up from the platform and waved as he chose a carriage.

Roger returned the gesture. 'Hope you know what you're doing, you silly sod.'

Chapter 44

December 1986

Banknotes, of different colours and value, were stacked on the bar counter. Mark Payne handed Samuel a wad of pesetas. 'There's your share. Not bad for our first week's trading. I know we're extra busy as it's Christmas, and I know the next few months will fall off slightly, but we should more than make up for it in the summer.'

'Thanks.' Samuel counted the notes. 'Are you and Isabel planning on taking your shares each week?'

'No. Once a month, it helps with the cash flow. Pedro helped me sort it out with her. He's a good sport, very helpful. That's why his drinks were on the house the other night, okay?'

'I thought you were buying them.'

'I was, out of the till. I always pay for services rendered.'

Samuel looked at the money in his hand. 'Do you?'

'Meaning?' Mark moved closer, his face only inches away from Samuel's. 'Aren't you happy with your cut? I can always find another idiot to take your place.'

'I didn't mean anything.' Samuel forced a smile. 'It's very generous. More than I thought. Thanks.'

'Good. I like to keep a happy ship. Now, back to work, it'll soon be the mid-day rush. I'll be on the terrace. Bring me a pint, and some nuts.'

Mark shielded his eyes. Teenage girls playing beach volley ball held his attention for a while. Turning his head, he watched middle aged Spanish couples walking along the edge of the sea, talking and gesturing with their hands They shook their heads in disapproval at scantily dressed visitors, prostrated on towels, paying homage to the sun with their pale bodies.

The peace was shattered by a woman's scream.

Mark stood up.

At the edge of the water, a mother was holding a young boy to her chest and screaming.

Mark ran across the road, jumped onto the beach, ran towards her. The people around him seemed to be moving in slow motion as he raced towards the sea. He could see blood running through her fingers as she clasped the boy's foot.

Snatching the boy from her, he examined at the child's foot. The sun glinted on a shard of glass embedded in his sole. The woman's outburst in Spanish was lost on Mark. He handed the boy back to her. 'I know you don't understand,' he said. 'But hold him still while I get this out.' He mimed his intended action.

The woman held out the child's leg. Mark took hold of the piece of broken bottle and pulled. The boy's scream caused the woman to clutch him to her body once more. Blood soaked into her dress.

Mark pointed towards his bar. 'Come with me. Get bandage. Get help.'

She looked from her son to Mark, then back at her boy again. The torrent of Spanish washed over Mark. 'I haven't got a clue what you're saying but we need to get him to hospital, pronto.'

Grabbing the boy, he held the wounded foot in a vice-like grip and ran. The woman chased after him.

'Pedro! Good man! This boy needs help. It's his foot, it needs stitches. Oh, and talk to his mother, she's going bananas.'

Pino frowned. 'Bananas?'

'Just tell her everything will be fine. Tell her I'll get my man to take you all to the hospital, where ever that is. Okay?'

'Yes. I understand. I will show how to discover hospital.'

'Samuel! Get your arse out here. Bring me the first aid box. And get the car.'

Mark sat the mother down. 'Pedro, tell her to keep her son's foot in the air. We've got to stop the bleeding. Sam, get some warm water, we need to wash this wound. Hurry!'

Mark helped the woman and her son into the rear of the car. Pino sat in the front alongside Samuel in the driver's seat. Taking his wallet from his trouser pocket Mark thrust four, one thousand peseta notes into the woman's hand. 'Tell her to buy the boy something, Pedro.'

'Si, Señor Mark, but is Pino, no Pedro.'

'Sorry, Pedro. I'll get the hang of it.' Leaning into the car he said, 'Sam. Follow his instructions and go like a bat out of hell. The sooner this kid's foot is seen to, the better. When you're done at the hospital, run her and the boy home. I'll help Isabel with the bar while you're gone.' He slammed the door and banged the flat of his hand onto the roof. 'Off you go. See you later.'

As the car disappeared from view, Mark opened the till.

Isabel frowned as he took four thousand pesetas from the drawer.

*

'*Buenas tardes.*'

Samuel turned his attention away from the stock list. Isabel turned away from talking to Pino and returned the woman's greeting. Mark looked up from his English newspaper. The woman brought her son to Mark's table. The boy's foot was bandaged up to his ankle, but the once pristine bandage was now very grubby. The child was carrying a book in one hand and a rainbow-coloured lollipop in the other. On the book's cover, a green dragon blew red and yellow flames from his nostrils.

The woman's white teeth flashed a smile.

Mark stood up. She kissed him on both cheeks. He looked embarrassed.

The boy put the book and lollipop onto the table, threw his arms around Mark's legs and squeezed. '*Gracias Señor. Gracias por ayudarme.*'

Mark ran his fingers through the boy's hair. 'Pedro! Over here, pronto. And tell Isabel to fetch drinks, whatever these two want, and a pint for me. Oh, and one for yourself.'

'Right Pedro, what are they saying?' Mark frowned.

'They say my name is Pino.'

'Sorry. Okay, *Pino*, what's this all about?'

Pino spoke briefly to the woman. 'She say she bring Daniel, her son, to thank you for your loveliness. His *herida*, excuse please, I not have the word.' Pino pointed to the boy's foot.

'Foot? Wound?'

'*Si*, wound. The wound is good. The hospital say you do a good thing. Francisco is happy.'

Pino bent down and whispered in the boy's ear. The boy held out the book.

'What's he want, Pedro? I don't understand a word either of them are saying.'

'He asks the book to be read. He bring it to you. He buy with the pesetas you give.'

'Okay.' Mark sat the boy on a chair and opened the book. 'If I had a son, I'd like him to be just like you.' The smile on his face quickly retreated to be replaced with a look of consternation. 'I can't read this rubbish, it's all in Spanish.'

The boy looked up at Mark. His brown eyes as appealing as a puppy dog.

Isabel brought a tray of drinks and set them down. Some of Mark's drink shot from the glass with the impact. He glared at her.

Pino pointed to a page. 'Try to do this. Daniel would like very much for you to read the story. Is pictures, some words.'

Mark took a gulp of his drink. 'Why don't you do it. You speak the lingo.'

'Do not make him cry. Is children book, you try.'

Mark licked his lips, laid the open book across his knees and ran a finger along the text. '*El–niño–amaba el–dragón azul.*' He took a sip of beer. '*Todos los días–iba a visitar la cueva del dragón.*'

'Bravo, Señor Mark, bravo.' Pino clapped.

Daniel's face radiated pleasure.

His mother bared her teeth in a huge smile. '*Gracias, Señor.*'

Samuel Beckworth emerged from the cooking area behind the bar. 'What's going on? I could hear all the clapping.'

'Nothing. I've been reading Daniel's book. It's all gibberish to me, but he liked it.'

Samuel pointed to the road alongside the beach. 'Seems like your audience is getting bigger. Look. The police have turned up.'

'Get some drinks then. Got to keep them sweet. And fetch another limonada for Daniel.'

Behind the bar Isabel busied herself polishing glasses.

The two police officers exchanged greetings with Pino before wandering through the tables towards the bar. Soon they were deep in conversation with Isabel. They turned and looked over their shoulders as she pointed at Mark. He waved to her.

Turning his attention back to Daniel's book, Mark attempted to make sense of the next part of the story.

A hand gripping his shoulder stopped his efforts. He tried to stand but the policeman's hand held him firmly in his chair. 'What's your game?' he said. 'Can't you see you're interrupting? Get off me!'

The ensuing stream of Spanish was as incomprehensible to Mark as the book had been.

'What's he saying, Pedro? Tell him to piss off, he's annoying me.'

'He say Isabel say you take money from her. She call them. They take you away, you must tell their questions.'

'Take money? From her? This is my fucking bar.'

'Bar belongs to Isabel, and maybe your amigo. The money is not for you.'

'Of course it is. I own this place. Sam only works here. Tell him, Sam.'

'He's right, Pino. I used Mark's money to buy my share. We're partners.'

Shaking himself free of the policeman's grip, Mark swung a fist. The officer clutched his jaw as he staggered back. He spat blood.

His companion raced across. He charged into Mark, knocking him to the ground. The man with blood dribbling from the side of his mouth kicked Mark in the ribs. Putting a finger into his mouth he explored the cavity where a tooth had been. Again he swung his foot into Mark.

The second policeman pulled Mark to his feet and forced his arms around his back. The sound of handcuffs clicking into place was followed by a boy crying.

'There! See what you've done, you bastards!' he said, inclining his head towards Daniel. 'Look at the poor kid. This is all a mistake. You'll be sorry. I'll make sure of that.' He tried to move toward Daniel but was yanked back.

Daniel gripped Mark's trousers. '*¡No! ¡Déjalo en paz!*'

Pino took hold of the boy. 'Is okay, Señor Mark. I look after him. You go.'

Mark fought all the way. Tables were pushed aside, chairs knocked over as he was dragged to the patrol car. 'Someone will be sorry when I get back! Tell the Spanish whore she's for it!'

Waiting for the car to start, Mark glared through the car window, watching Pino and Francisco comforting Daniel. Isabel was nowhere to be seen.

The two officers in the front engaged in an animated conversation. One of them opened the glove compartment and pulled out two sheets of paper. He jabbed at one, turned and pointed at Mark. Showing the other photo-copy to his companion he indicated the bar and said something. The second officer got out of the vehicle.

Samuel guessed he was in trouble and vaulted over the bar as the officer approached. A police baton, thrust between his legs as he ran, dropped him to the floor. Hands pinioned behind his back he was jerked to his feet and propelled to the car.

'What the fuck are these two playing at?' Mark said, as Samuel was bundled in beside him. 'Don't tell me you've had your hand in the till. This is a fucking nightmare.'

'I think it's worse than you think,' Samuel said. 'Pino said they told him we're both wanted back in the UK. The Police Nacional are involved, not just this local bunch.'

'Shit! I bet my sodding brother's been nicked and dropped me in it. I'll have the bastard when we get to England.'

The man next to to the driver turned and prodded Mark with his baton. '*Silencio! ¡No se permite hablar!* Stop talking!'

'Fuck off,' Mark retorted, and was rewarded by a blow to the head.

'You wanker! Wait until I get these cuffs off. Then we'll see who's the best man.' He turned to Samuel. 'You're my witness. This is police brutality and I'm not having it. I'll sue the arse off these two.'

Samuel struggled to make himself more comfortable. 'This bloody hurts, having your arms shoved around your back.' He paused. 'I can understand the bit about being wanted back home but why did Pino say Isabel accused you of taking money?'

'I only took what was mine, the stupid bitch. Now look at us, trussed up like a pair of kippers and probably about to be sent back home.'

'Can they do that?'

'They can try. I need to get hold of Twyford and start the ball rolling. There are people who can block our extradition if the law go down that route.'

'I knew you'd get us out of this.' Samuel smiled at his reflection in the car window. 'They picked on the wrong men this time.'

Chapter 45

December 1986

Leaving the train station behind, Graham headed towards the sea-front. Frost lurked in the shadows. Graham pulled his coat collar up. *This was a stupid idea. I should have stayed with Mavis and Roger.*

Standing in a bus shelter he cupped his hands around a cigarette. Mission completed; he hoisted his kitbag onto his shoulder. 'Now what? I can hardly walk around all day. Too bloody cold for a start.'

Acting on impulse he turned and headed for town and the café which had provided him with sanctuary a week ago.

*

Leaking from the extractor fan, the tantalising smell of fried bacon hung in the air. Graham's nostrils twitched; his gastric juices churned. He wiped dribble from the corner of his mouth with the back of his hand.

Lowering his kitbag, he pushed the café door open.

'Morning, Charlie,' Graham greeted the man wiping a table near the door. 'How's business?'

'I didn't expect to see you again.' Charles sniffed. 'How's your brother?'

'Brother? Oh, yes, sorry, it was all a storm in a teacup. Waste of time. He had it back under control before I got there.'

'Okay, what are you up to now? As you can see, I haven't managed to find a replacement.' He wiped his brow. 'Do you want your job back by any chance?'

Graham unbuttoned his overcoat. 'That would be great. Any chance of a bite to eat first? I haven't had anything since breakfast.'

'Help yourself.' Charles wiped his hands with the cleaning cloth. 'But I'm not cooking it. Come through to the back, there's something I need to tell you.'

'Thanks. And I'm sorry about dashing off and leaving you in the shit.'

Charles closed the door of the storeroom. 'You moving back in?'

Graham dropped his kitbag onto the makeshift bed. 'Any reason why I wouldn't want to? You don't sound too sure.'

'You had visitors. They only missed you by a couple of hours.'

'Visitors? Who?'

'Police. Military police. They said you've gone AWOL. Have you?'

Graham looked towards the door. 'Would it change things if I have?'

'Might do. Depends on why, I suppose. Do you want to tell me?'

Graham sighed. 'I got caught shagging my officer's wife.'

'Is that all?' Charles laughed. 'Is that why you and your wife had a bust up?'

'Yes. Although she's as bad. She's . . . forget it, it doesn't matter. Will they be back, do you think?'

'Possibly. I told them I didn't know what they were talking about. Didn't see the sense in getting involved. Said I'd never seen anyone matching the description. Besides, I couldn't have helped them if I'd wanted to, I didn't know where you'd gone. And I had enough to worry about finding a new cook and cleaner.'

Graham swallowed and looked down at his feet. 'Sorry to cause you any trouble. But in a way I'm glad the redcaps came after me. I had a suspicion someone might drop me in it. Now you know the trouble I'm in, does it affect my job?'

'With Christmas coming up, I don't have a lot of choice. Let's say the job's only temporary. I need permanent staff, and I don't think you're the answer.'

'Okay. I understand.'

'Let's have an agreement. I'll carry on advertising at the Labour Exchange while you sort out your problems. Seems to me we need each other at the moment.'

'Thanks, sounds like a good solution.' Graham patted his stomach. 'If it's all the same to you I'd like to start cooking. Do you fancy anything?'

'No thanks. I've had lunch. Get in the kitchen and cook yourself
something. After that you're back on the payroll.'
Graham smiled.

*

A robin, sitting on a fence post, greeted Graham as he walked
along the country lane, its cheerful song ringing out in the cold
early morning air. Jewels set in cobwebs sparkled amongst the
hedgerows. Further along, a FOR SALE BY AUCTION board on the
bend of the lane looked incongruous in this Christmas card
setting.

He quickened his step. 'I remember seeing that before. Didn't
realize it was this far though.'

Rusting farm machinery mounted guard on both sides of the
entrance. Large gates, adorned with patches of lichen, lay at
curious angles to the ground, the wood unable to support itself
once the large hinges had deserted their duty.

The doors to the barn were closed. A seed drill had cut shallow
furrows across the yard, dragged to block the entrance of the
building. High above, pigeons left white calling cards beneath
holes in the black corrugated metal walls.

Graham pulled the machine aside. Despite the wheels, it fought
him all the way. He removed his overcoat and tossed it over his
adversary. Sweat on his brow belied the temperature. A grey and
red jumper joined his coat. The armpits of his shirt developed wet
patches. Digging his heels into the ground he leaned back. 'Come
on you bastard, move.' Grudgingly, the obstacle inched away
from the barn doors.

Lifting his jumper and coat off the rusting metal he pulled them
back on, took a knife from his pocket and cut the dirty rope tying
the doors together. 'Roger was right, this is a wicked blade.'

Waiting for his eyes to become accustomed to the gloom, he
buttoned his overcoat. Shafts of light penetrated the gloom,
spotlights for a scene acted out weeks before. The actors had

gone, the stage pops remained. Graham walked forward, glancing at the floor, stepping around the potholes.

The Ford Escort had acquired a coating of dust and pigeon droppings. Graham used a handkerchief to wipe the windows. 'I guessed they would hide you here. Let's hope you start. I could do without walking back to the bus.'

Using his spare set of keys, he opened the driver's door. Inside it was obvious an excellent valet job had been carried out. Parking tickets, crisp packets, drink cans, all gone.

The engine started at the second attempt. Slowly, he reversed from the barn.

*

Tea urn switched on, both toasters plugged in, the merest hint of smoke accumulating above the grill plate, Graham was ready for the day ahead. Charles put his head around the door. 'Do me an egg and bacon sandwich.' He looked at his watch. 'Is that the time?' he said, shaking his wrist. 'Either this is wrong or my alarm clock is.'

Graham pointed into the café. 'The clock in there is right. I check it against the radio every morning.'

'Thanks. I wasn't late after all. Or did you get started early?'

'I couldn't sleep. Been doing a bit of cleaning. Hope I didn't disturb you upstairs.' Bacon rashers on the griddle spat at him. 'Charlie, I've got something to ask. I've parked my car around the back, is it okay?'

'As long as the dustcart and delivery men can get down the alley, I don't see it's a problem. But if you've got a car, why didn't you sleep in it instead of those benches on the seafront?'

Graham cracked two eggs onto the griddle to join the bacon rashers. 'Only just got it back from the garage, had to have a lot of work done to get it through its MOT. Cost me an arm and a leg.'

'I know what you mean. I sometimes think I should shut this place and open a car workshop, must be more money in it, the prices they charge.'

Graham grinned. 'If you do, let me know. I could lift car bonnets, shake my head and tell the customer, "It looks expensive to fix, but leave it to us, I'm sure we can do something." Or something like that.'

'Sounds like bitter experience to me,' Charles said. 'Is it?'

Graham used a stainless-steel slice to turn the bacon over. A mixture of fat and water hissed at him as he pressed it against the hot metal. 'Yes, but I didn't fall for it. I'm nobody's fool.' He jabbed at the rashers, sending them skidding across the griddle.

'Careful,' Charlie said. 'I want it between two slices of buttered bread, not off the floor.'

Chapter 46

December 1986

Mark Payne glared at the foul-smelling bucket in the corner. Flies gathering in a black cloud added to his bad temper. He lashed out at the cell wall with his foot then hopped around hugging his toes. 'Shit! I forgot these bloody flip-flops!' Dropping onto what was provided as a bed he spat on his hands and rubbed. He gritted his teeth. Blood seeped from beneath his toe nails turning his saliva pink. *All for the sake of a few lousy pesetas. Half the money was mine anyway. Bloody woman. I'll give her bloody pesetas when I get out of here. I'll shove them where the sun don't shine! It's my business if I want to treat Daniel, not hers. I really like him. If he was my son, he'd have anything he wanted.*

In the adjacent cell, Samuel sat disconsolately staring at the tiled floor. A cockroach ventured out and scurried toward the opposite wall. He watched as the insect passed under the door. *If it was only that easy. If Twyford messes up and we get sent back, we're really in the shit.*

The sound of footsteps passing his cell was interrupted by a crunch as the cockroach was turned to mash.

Samuel sighed. 'That's the end of that poor bugger. He'd have been safer in here with me.'

The footsteps continued, followed by keys in the door of Mark's cell. Samuel pressed his ear to the wall.

'You 'ave a visitor, Señor. Come.'

'Visitor? I don't know anyone. Who is it?' Mark screwed his eyes shut as he put his foot to the floor.

The police officer jangled the keys. 'You not come? I lock the door.'

'No, don't be hasty. Anything to get out of this shitty place for a while.' He stopped in the passageway. 'What about him?' Mark jerked a thumb towards Samuel's cell. 'Is he coming?'

'No.'

Mark shrugged his shoulders and followed his jailer.

The room was little better than the cell he had just left, albeit there was no stinking bucket. A table and four chairs provided scant furnishings. Mark stopped twiddling his thumbs as the door opened.

'Pedro! Daniel! And Francisco. What are you doing here?' Ignoring the two police officers he leapt up from the table and picked Daniel up. The boy shrieked with laughter as Mark swung him around.

'I bring them, Señor Mark. Francisco very sad. She not like police take you and Señor Sam. She say Daniel cry all night.'

'Thanks, Pedro.'

Francisco pushed a bag across the table. The police officers moved closer.

'What's this?' Mark delved inside. 'Cigars? And an English book?'

'She buy with money you give Daniel.' Pino smiled.

'Tell her, thank you. It was kind of her, but the money was for Daniel.'

'She has money for him. He has new book. He bring it for you to read.'

The police officers spoke to Francisco, opened the door and stepped outside. She grasped Daniel's hand and followed them toward the door.

'Where are they going, Pedro? Is visiting time over?'

'No. Police not happy. They say go now.'

'Miserable bastards.' Mark moved swiftly. Standing between Daniel and the door he bent down. 'Sorry, Daniel. I'll read to you another day.' He ran his fingers through the boy's hair. 'I hope to see more of you and your mother when this is over.' Daniel looked bemused.

Mark took hold of Pinto's arm. 'Can you make a phone call to England? I've written a message and the number. I was hoping to bribe one these idiots, but I'd rather trust you.'

Pinto took the sheets of toilet paper and read them. 'Yes, I can do this.' He stuffed the note into his trouser pocket as one of the officers came back. 'Good luck, Señor Mark.'

Chapter 47

December 1986

'Hello, my love,' Joseph said. 'What have you been up to? You look all out of breath.'

'Do I? Must be the bath I've just had. When I was a child, my mum always told me off for having my baths too hot. Anyway, don't stand out there in the cold, come on in.'

Closing the door, Joseph laughed. 'Pity I wasn't there in those days. I'd loved to have smacked your rosy red bum.'

'I bet you would. Get your coat off while I put the kettle on. I got you cakes from the corner shop. Real cream.'

'You know the way to a man's heart.'

'Do I? Is it cream cakes, or rosy red bums?'

'Both. Now, to business. Are you happy about Hughes sending PC Jefferson to Spain? Do you think I should try to get things changed? After all, it was my plan to have him help you while I take my break.'

'I would have preferred it, but I'm certain I can cope for a few days. Is he sending Jefferson on his own to escort two prisoners back?'

'Of course not. I'm going too.'

'Are you? How did that come about?'

'Make the tea and let me at those cakes. Then I'll tell you.'

'These are good.' Joseph wiped cream off his chin. 'But I think a fork would have helped.'

'You know where they are, help yourself. Before you do, what's this about Spain?'

'Not much to tell. Hughes called me in, told me what he had decided, then asked for my opinion. Waste of time, he'd already made up his mind. Who was I to argue? I used the opportunity to my own ends and offered to be the second man.' Joseph bit into a second doughnut. His tongue flicked out, seeking grains of sugar nestling on his lips. 'I told Hughes I'd count it as my holiday entitlement, but he wouldn't hear of it.'

'Very clever. I can see what you're up to, don't deny it, I can read you like a book.' She shook her head. 'Let me get you a fork, I can't bear watching you get into such a mess.'

'Any chance of another cup while you're out there?'

Mary gulped the last of the wine from her glass. 'Yes, I'll boil the kettle again. Won't be a minute.'

'Thanks. And you're right. I was planning to go to Spain at my own expense. When Hughes told me about the change of plans regarding PC Jefferson, I reeled him in. Now he's funding my trip and I've still got next years holiday allowance. Remind me to order some pesetas when we're in town tomorrow.' He put his plate down and pulled her close. 'Right, enough about my plans, let's discuss what you're going to do while I'm gone.'

'Fine, but aren't you jumping the gun? It takes time to arrange for extradition.'

'Usually, yes. I didn't tell Hughes but I spoke to someone in the Met. He's arranging for the papers to be rushed through. National security interests, all that sort of bullshit.'

'You really don't care what you do, do you?'

'No. Payne's a clever sod, he'll wriggle his way out of this, given half a chance.' He licked jam and cream off his fork. 'That's why I'm going out there to make sure he doesn't. I know there's at least one of the Great Train robbers still walking around out there, I'm not letting our two do the same.'

'Good for you. But I wish you were taking me, not Jefferson. Think of all the gorgeous sun and Sangria.'

'There won't be time for drinking and sunbathing. This is work. I won't be gone any longer than it takes to get those scumbags on the plane back to England. It will do Jefferson good to get involved in the arrests, he's put a lot of effort into helping us. He's a good man.'

'Are you staying tonight?'

'I thought perhaps I would, if it's okay with you. Let's snuggle up, watch telly, then make an early night of it shall we? I'm going to miss you.'

Mary sighed. 'And I'll miss you too. Are you sure you can't wangle me a place on the team? There must be something I can do.'

'There is, put the telly on, we may be in time to catch the news.'
Joseph dodged the flying cushion.

*

The illuminated sign indicated seat belts could be undone.

'That was bumpy,' PC Alan Jefferson said. 'Nearly spilled my
coffee.'

Joseph smiled as his travelling companion pushed his face
against the small window.

'What can you see?' Joseph asked. 'Apart from the wing.'

'Snow topped mountains, roads, clusters of houses in the
valleys. It's impressive. This is the first time I've seen the Alps
from above, most of our holidays in Europe were in our car.' Alan
turned away from the window to look at Joseph. 'Mum never
drove again after the accident.'

'Was that when your father died? You said before, he was killed
about eight years before you joined the force. Must have been a
terrible thing for you, and for your mother.'

'Mum's never forgiven herself, although it wasn't her fault. She
had only just taken over the driving from dad when a car came
round a corner on our side of the road. Dad was in the front with
her, I was in the back. It was over in seconds. Mum was only
driving because they shared it when we did those long trips, but
the accident couldn't have been avoided, whoever was at the
wheel.'

'Were you and your mother hurt?'

'Mum suffered cuts from broken glass, nothing serious. I
banged my head on the back of mum's seat, which is why my
nose looks crooked. It was lucky I was sitting where I was. If I'd
been behind dad, who knows?'

'Has it put you off driving?'

Alan sighed. 'No, not really. I admit my first driving lessons
were nerve racking, but I passed second time. Now all I have to do
is save up for a car.'

'You could have solved that problem with what you found in the
lock-up. The DI was satisfied with the amount of money I logged
in. You missed your opportunity.'

'But I kept my integrity, which matters to me.'

'Fine. But if you want to get anywhere in life, you'll need more than a halo.'

'Maybe, but I can sleep at night. My conscience is clear.'

Joseph pushed his lap-tray back into position and swung the retaining latch into position.

'Are you okay, sir?' Jefferson asked.

'What? Yes, sorry, I was miles away. Thinking about getting those two back to stand trial. How do you think you'll handle it, knowing one of them is probably linked to Kimberley's death?'

'Don't worry, sir. I won't let emotion interfere with duty. I'll be okay. I admit I will be good to see them both behind bars. This is the first time I've had any real connection to a victim, apart from empathy of course.'

'I think DCI Hughes picked the right man for the job. We'll get along fine together, I'm sure. Let's hope the Spanish police handle their side of things efficiently.'

'Excuse me saying this, sir, but you don't sound convinced. Why?'

'Experience. Also, I've spoken to friends of mine in the Met about criminals hiding in Spain. This may not be as straight forward as you expect. I'm going to shut my eyes for a while, we'll be landing soon.'

*

DCI Hughes put the phone down. Screwing up a sheet of paper he hurled it towards the electric fan heater whirring away in the corner of his office. 'No extradition? The Spanish police will be informed? Why? Who blocked the applications? This is serious, I've got two officers on a flight to Spain.' He doodled on his notepad. 'I knew Payne had connections, but I never realized they went so high. And what was all that about increased pensions for senior officers? I'm not ready to retire. Special financial packages based on performance? Never heard of such a thing.'

Leaving his desk, he headed for the coffee machine in the hall.

*

Alan handed his passport to the man behind the check-in desk, filled in the details below those of Joseph and stood back. His overcoat, scarf and pullover lay draped over his suitcase. Perspiration dampened his shirt. Above his head a ceiling fan creaked as it moved the warm air around. Flies hitched a ride on its blades before flying off to follow enticing smells from the buffet laid out in the hotel dining area.

'I didn't think it would be like this, sir,' Alan said, mopping his forehead. 'It's worse than a Turkish bath. Must be hotter in here than it is outside.'

'Don't let it get you down. You'll get used to it. Besides it's only for a few days. As soon as we get things arranged, we'll be heading back to the delights of a British winter. I suggest we make the most of our time in the sunshine. Let's find the bar and have a nice cold beer, suit you?'

'Bit awkward to answer, sir. Are we on duty?'

'We're being paid if that's what you mean. But I'll decide when we're actually on duty. Relax, most of our time will be spent waiting. If you thought red-tape was an English thing, you're in for a surprise. And as for getting things done in a hurry, forget it, they call the afternoons out here siesta time, time to take a nap. God only knows how long this will take.'

'Can we go to our rooms for a quick wash before we have a drink, sir? I'm feeling sticky.'

'Good idea. One other thing, drop the ''sir'' while we're out here, it isn't necessary. You call me Joe, and I'll call you Alan, okay?'

'If it's what you want, sir. I'll try to remember.'

'Let me give you an incentive, every time you call me sir, it's your turn to buy the drinks.'

'Not bad,' Joseph said, licking his lips. 'Bit gassy, but welcome enough. What are you thinking? Sorry you agreed to this trip?'

'No, just wondering how long it is to dinner. I think the flight gave me an appetite.'

'You must be reading my mind.' Joseph moved away from the bar. 'Let's go and see what this place has to offer. We'll visit the local police tomorrow and get the extradition rolling.'

Chapter 48

December 1986

Dead moths and flies lay amongst the dust on the window ledge. Out of respect, the hotel staff did nothing to disturb them or their final resting place. Sunlight streamed through the window behind the breakfast buffet, warming their desiccated corpses.

'Is that it?' Alan looked at the plates of rolls and croissants, individual packets of cereal, jugs of milk and fresh orange juice.

'What did you expect? Bacon and eggs?' Joseph used tongs to pile a plate with rolls, packs of butter and jam. Picking up a second plate he used it to carry two croissants, along with more butter and jam. 'This'll do for starters,' he said. 'The cereals can wait until I've finished these. Where's the coffee?'

Dejectedly, Alan pointed to the end of the long table. 'It's probably it at the end, sir, sorry, Joe. In those Thermos flasks.' He shook his head. 'I think I'll just have coffee. But if we see a burger place on the way to the police station, I'll grab one. I never enjoyed continental breakfasts when I was a kid, still don't. Mum always gives me a good breakfast to start the day.'

*

Joseph handed his letter of authority to the Oficial de Policía sitting behind his desk. The police officer opened a drawer and compared it to the one received yesterday from his superiors. 'Is no good, Señor. These men are free.' He pushed his letter towards Joseph.

Alan looked over Joseph's shoulder. 'Is it true? The extradition's have been cancelled? Both of them?'

'It must be a mistake. We've flown all the way out here only to be told we can't execute our warrant? What the hell's going on?' Joseph read the second letter again. He jabbed a finger against a paragraph. 'He's right. They've been told to release their prisoners.'

'Si, Señor.' Producing a fax, he pointed. 'My boss in Madrid say is accident. He say the British men go free.'

Alan stood with his mouth open. 'After deliberately killing someone with a car?'

'Where are they? Are they still here?' Joseph glanced towards the door at the rear of the police station.

'No. They go. I can do nothing.' The man used both hands to express his frustration. 'Steve is British like you, but Isabel say he is good man.'

Joseph's face masked his feelings. 'Do you know where they are?'

'One of them has bar. Steve was owner. Now this man is Isabel's partner. Is Stevie's Wonder Bar. Many British drink there.'

Joseph exhaled deeply. His knuckles whitened as his hands formed fists. Shaking his head he turned to Alan. 'They've beaten us. Without extradition papers we can't arrest them. Who the bloody hell's behind this? Hughes warned me Payne had friends who could make things difficult, but I never imagined they had this sort of power.'

'We can't let it go like this,' Alan said. 'Kimberley deserves justice. And his other victims of course. There must be something we can do, surely.'

Joseph reached over the desk and shook the officers' hand. 'Gracias, Señor. Thank you for your help. Sorry this has all been a waste of time. We will be leaving as soon as I can book our flights.'

The man responded by scribbling a number on his notepad. Tearing the page out he passed it to Joseph. 'If you speak with Señor Payne, call me. The mountains are silencio.' He slowly closed one eye as he held Joseph's attention.

*

Turning away from the police station Joseph and Alan turned down a side street. The shops on either side framed a view of the beach and sea. One of them attracted Joseph's attention. 'They look the part,' he said, pointing at replica weapons displayed in the window. 'If they were real, there'd be enough to equip a small army.'

'Why would anyone want a copy of a Japanese sword? Or a flintlock pistol?' Alan shook his head.

'A lot of Brits do. You can't get them this cheap back home. That's why shops like this do so well. People hang these things on their walls.'

The conversation about weapons continued for a while as they headed towards the sea. Minutes later they jumped down onto the sand. Holidaymakers used towels to stake their claims for space on the beach. A man of African appearance walked amongst them, one of his arms adorned with gold chains he was offering for sale.

Joseph kicked at the sand. 'It still hasn't sunk in. How on earth did those two slimey bastards get away? We almost had them.'

Alan stared out to sea. 'Beats me, sir. But I must say I'm surprised how well you've taken it. I've heard rumours back at the station, people say –'

'Never listen to rumours. And you owe me a drink.'

'Why?'

'You just called me, sir. Come on, the beach bar will do. Buy the beers and then we'll sit and mull things over. Consider all our options.'

'God, that was welcome. It didn't touch the sides. Stay there, I'll get us another.' Joseph stood, shook sand off his trousers and headed for the coconut palm thatch shading the bar.

'Thanks.' Alan took the frosted bottle. 'Are you really giving up?'

'As I've told you before, you've got a lot to learn. I told the Spanish guy what I wanted him to believe, nothing more. You can't trust anyone. He may be reporting back to Payne, who knows? Payne has money, lots of it.' He looked up and down the beach. 'I brought a stack of pesetas hidden in my suitcase to grease a few palms, but it appears someone beat me to it.'

'Perhaps you're right. What did he mean about the mountains being silencio? Silent? Seems a strange thing to say.' Tipping his head back he gulped at his drink.

'I think I understand. I've heard how some of the police out here operate,'Joseph said. 'Anyway, I don't know about you, but I've had enough of sitting here. This heat and sand brings back memories of friends I've lost.' He held up a hand to ward off the inevitable questions. 'Don't ask.'

'Fair enough. What do you want to do?'

'Find a café and have lunch. I think better on a full stomach.'

*

'Shall we go back to the hotel?' Joseph said, pushing his plate aside. 'We need to talk and I've got airline tickets to organise.'

'So you're giving up?'

'Am I? If you'd let me finish I was about to add the words, four of them.'

'Four tickets? What *are* you up to? We can't do anything with things the way they are. Our hands are tied.'

'Pardon? Did I hear you say there was nothing we can do?' Putting a finger in his ear he wiggled it. 'Must be something wrong with my hearing.'

*

Joseph sprawled on the bed. Alan sat in a chair beside the solitary window in the hotel room. Bottles of beer languished in the washbasin. Ice cubes from the mini-bar kept the drinks at an acceptable temperature.

'I think it's the sun, I've got a blinding headache,' Joseph said, putting a hand to his forehead. 'But getting the tickets was a lot easier than I expected. They'd just had cancellations the woman said, some sort of stomach bug in one of the hotels. The flights are booked for tomorrow so we don't have much time. I couldn't get four together, it's two lots of two. I'll sit with Payne, you take Beckworth.' Joseph sat up and leaned against the wall behind the bed.

'I don't have a problem so far, but how do you plan to get them onto the plane? They're not likely to go of their own free will.'

'Which is why I asked you into my room. I need to know how far you're prepared to go. It won't be easy, and it's not legal.' Joseph stared at his companion. 'Officially they're not wanted back home. Which means we have a decision to make. Either we go along with this extradition decision shit and leave the scumbags to spend their leisure in the sun, or we take them back to stand trial. Even that depends on getting the CPS to proceed with the charges. I know you don't think too highly of me, for reasons which I fully understand, so if you want no part of it, no problem.'

Alan tapped his teeth with his fingernails. 'As we're not on duty, strictly speaking, can I tell you how I feel with no comeback when we get back home?'

'Go ahead.'

'I know I apologised for my outburst in hospital, but I still lay the responsibility for Kimberley's death at your doorstep. I understand you acted for what you saw as legitimate reasons, but you were wrong. I don't think I'll ever come to terms with the suffering you've caused.'

'Don't you think I'm suffering too, you self righteous prick? Do you think I can get her out of my mind? I'd give my right arm to be able to turn back the clock and make a different decision, but it's not possible. I have to live with what I've done.'

'You deserve it. I don't have any sympathy for you.'

'This is getting us nowhere. We need to put our personal differences to one side. I want to nail Payne and Beckworth and see justice done. I may be able to accomplish it on my own, but you could certainly help. Will you?'

Alan bent forward, lacing his fingers behind his head.

Joseph waited.

'I don't know,' Alan said. 'I want to get the bastards as much as you do, but it's got to be within the law. What you're suggesting sounds like kidnapping.'

'Fine. Leave it to me. You keep your delicate little hands clean. But I have to start planning. With or without you, I intend to take those two back.'

'I need more time to think. This should have been straight forward. We've got arrest warrants to escort our prisoners back to the UK.'

'And we would have, but someone tossed a spanner in the works. I'll leave you to work out what you want to do about it.

I'm off to the chemists, I need something for this headache. Can I get you anything?'

'No. No, thanks. See you when you get back. I'll be in my room.'

*

Joseph knocked on the hotel door.

'It's open,' Alan called. 'Come in.'

'How are you feeling? Have you decided what to do?'

'Yes, but it's churning me up inside. I keep seeing Kimberley's body.' He turned his head away. 'But I still can't go along with what you said. I'm a trained police officer and I mean to keep to what the public expect of me.'

'Fair enough. I won't force you to act against your principles. It looks like clever lawyers have won the day once again, and Kimberley's killers are free to enjoy the rest of their lives.'

The anguish in Alan's face told Joseph his words had struck a chord.

Chapter 49

December 1986

Graham sipped his drink then held the cocktail glass up. 'Cheers, Sandra, you haven't lost your touch.'

'Thanks, it's my own concoction. Rum mainly. Becoming popular with my regulars. I must be doing something right.'

'Has Mary been in lately?'

'Yes. She was in the other day, with Joseph.'

'Oh. Were they on duty?'

Sandra glanced around the bar then lowered her voice. 'They said they were, but I think it's to do with the new owner.'

'New owner? What happened to –'

'Oh, he's gone. Shows how long since you've been in here. I don't see much of this one, he pretty much leaves me to run this place.'

'Which explains the poster outside, about a disco. When is it? I've forgotten already.'

'Next Friday. Perhaps I should add more fruit juice to your next drink and leave out the rum.' She laughed.

'Getting back to Mary, how was she?' Graham frowned. 'I think she takes her job too seriously. She's always doing extra hours. I'm sure it's that Fargough wally who's the attraction.'

'No, I don't agree. She's just enjoying her career. There's plenty of women would love to change places with her.'

'I suppose they would.' Pointing back to the entrance, he said, 'Are you expecting many to come to this disco?'

'Of course. A lot of the regulars say they're looking forward to it. Although the two-for-one offer on first drinks could be the attraction. If it goes well, I might consider having a music-night once a week. You know, folk, jazz, that sort of thing.'

'What's the DJ like? Is he any good?'

'I certainly hope so. I haven't been to any of his gigs, but he comes highly recommended.'

Graham put down his empty glass. 'Another of those, please, Sandra, and then I must be off. Can't have more than two, I'm driving. I'll look in again on Friday, see if the DJ's playing my sort of music.' Bending down, he pushed the sheathed knife deeper into the top of his army boot, the presence of the weapon against his leg a constant reminder of the jealousy fuelling his actions.

*

'Thank God the heater's working again, certainly need it in this weather.' Graham fiddled with the controls of the fan. Warm air bathed the interior of his car with a vague electrical smell. He flicked the windscreen washers on. Rubber blades swished dirt and water aside, allowing him full view of the block of flats through twin arcs of clear glass framed by detritus. 'I wonder if she's home? Only one way to find out, I suppose.'

Graham rang the doorbell for the third time. 'Come on, my bloody key don't work. I'm freezing my nuts off out here.' The door shuddered as he kicked it. Taking off his gloves he rubbed his hands together vigorously. 'More overtime, is it? Okay, you win this time, but there's always another day.'

*

Graham put his cup into the sink in the café cooking area. Pulling on his overcoat he let himself out onto the pavement. Globes of orange from the street lighting hung in the air, enveloped by a sea mist. The silence of early morning greeted him. He walked around to the rear of the café to his car.

Graham pulled into the kerb. The mist had not penetrated this far from the seafront. Turning the radio up to overcome the noise of the heater, he listened to the weather forecast followed by the news. As he watched, the door of Mary's flat opened. She turned, flicked off the hall light and closed the door. Pulling a scarf up to cover her mouth, she thrust both hands into her coat pockets.

Graham jumped out of the car. 'Mary! Wait!' He ran across the road. 'I want to talk to you.'

She stopped. 'Graham? What are you doing back here? I thought you were miles away.'

'I was. I stayed with a friend for a while. Why did you put the army onto me?'

'Let go, you're hurting me. As to calling the army, I didn't.
Joseph did. What did you expect?'

'I might have known it was that sod. I knew you wouldn't let me
down. You still want us to get back together, I know you do. Be
honest with me.'

Mary pulled free. 'Get off! Leave me alone. For Christ's sake,
go and get on with the rest of your life.'

'How about if I was to hand myself over to the army, face the
charges and take my punishment. I'd be free to start all over
again. We could do anything. You could get a transfer to another
part of the country. I'll take you anywhere. You choose. Please.'
Graham sank to one knee. 'Please, sweetheart. I'll make it up to
you, I promise.'

'It's too late. Do yourself a favour. Hand yourself in before they
catch up with you. I need to move on, maybe with Joseph, maybe
not. Who knows what the future will bring?'

He fumbled with the leg of his trousers, seeking the knife.

The sound of a motorcycle, magnified by the buildings,
approached. Graham waited for it to pass. It braked hard. The
rider turned his machine around and rode back. Sitting astride the
bike, both feet on the road, the man raised his visor. 'Mary?
What's going on? Have you got a problem?'

Mary looked down at Graham, then back to the rider.

'It's okay, Dave,' she said, quietly.

'Are you sure? I can give you a lift if you like. I've just dropped
Madge off. She's working the early shift this week. You can use
her helmet.'

'What's blocking your ears? She told you everything is okay.
Why don't you sod off?' Graham got to his feet.

'I think I'll take you up on your offer,' Mary said, stepping
towards the bike. 'If you're going near the police station, I'd
appreciate it.'

Graham took hold of her arm. 'Wait, sweetheart, we haven't
finished talking yet.'

'You mean *you* haven't. I've said all I'm saying. Goodbye.' She
accepted the helmet and struggled to pull it over her hair.
Swinging a leg over the pillion seat she grasped Dave around the
waist as the bike pulled away. Graham raised two fingers. 'Bitch!'

Chapter 50

December 1986

Joseph dropped the beer bottle into the wastepaper basket. It chinked against others. 'Will you go out for more supplies, or shall I? I got those at the supermercado. It's only a couple of minutes walk, next to the chemist.'

PC Alan Jefferson shook his head. 'Let's wait. I need to think this out, and beer's not helping.'

'We've talked this round and round. As I see it, there's only one way to deal with this problem. *My* way. I do sympathise with you, but sometimes principles are excess baggage. Ask yourself this, if we go back empty-handed, will you be able to live with the knowledge we could have nailed them?'

'No.'

'So?'

'I'll think about helping you. If the legal system won't get justice for Kimberley, then they're letting her down. I joined up because I thought the law was impartial. From what you've been telling me, I'm beginning to think it's not.'

'Don't get too jaundiced. Ninety-nine times in a hundred it is. But in this life, you have to realize a lot of people with money consider themselves exempt from the rules of society. And Payne's definitely one of them.'

Alan stared through the window, chewing his lip. 'Are you sure we can't get the cancellation of the warrants reversed? Isn't there anyone you could call?'

'I could try. But someone's got a lot of influence with whoever pulls the strings. They could be using money, blackmail, who knows? Even if I contacted friends, how do I know they haven't been got at? Face facts, we either do it my way or forget the whole damn thing and get on the plane.'

'Okay, you win. I don't like it but what other choice is there? I owe it to Kimberley.'

'At last.' Joseph put a hand onto Alan's shoulder. 'Some statues of Lady Justice wear blindfolds. I think it's because they don't want to see what we sometimes have to do. Now, let me tell you how I see it and if you've got any suggestions, speak up.'

'I will, but I'm sure you've got all bases covered. Just tell me what I have to do.'

'First, we go to the bar our Spanish colleagues mentioned. Spy out the land, so to speak. Good intelligence backed with reconnoitring can make all the difference to an operation. Then we can come up with a plan.'

'But Payne's bound to see us. Won't he run?'

'Where to? Home? I wish he would, but that's asking too much. No, he knows the score. He'll enjoy seeing us, knowing we can't touch him without extradition papers. Let's prove him wrong.'

'How?'

'Leave it to me. Tonight, we'll just walk past the bar to see if they're both there. Tomorrow, we'll call in for an English breakfast. How's that for a plan?'

'A plan? The flight's tomorrow and the best you can come up with is to have breakfast? I must be missing something.'

'Trust me. I know what I'm doing. Do you think I haven't done this sort of thing before? Not as a police officer, I grant you, but if you do as I ask, we can get justice for Kimberley.'

'Which is what I want more than anything in this world. I just wish could be done within the law.'

'Spare me the sermon. Come on, let's check out Stevie's Wonder Bar.'

*

Revellers wearing Christmas hats, clip on reindeer antlers or tinsel garlands, thronged Stevie's Wonder Bar. Fuelled by cheap wine and beer, bawdy drinking songs added to the cacophony of voices competing to make conversation heard.

Alan grinned. 'Sounds like fun.'

At the rear of a car parked outside the bar, Joseph ran a hand over a dent in the bodywork. 'This looks like the one in the photo,' he said. 'That's a bonus. I thought they may have abandoned it. Cross over the road, we may be able to see better from there, although I'm not too worried, if the car's here, so are they.'

'Can you see either of them?' Alan said, bobbing his head from side to side. 'I can't. There's too many people jigging about.' He grinned. 'The song's spot on, girls out here really do want to have fun.'

'Bit rowdier than I expected, I must admit. I don't want to chance going in, Payne may see us before we see him.'

'I thought you weren't worried?'

'When I'm ready to act, I meant. Timing is everything,' Joseph said. 'Let's walk past, come back and try again. Then I think we'll eat at *The Cheeky Leprechaun* before having an early night. Got a busy day ahead of us tomorrow.'

'I wish I knew what you're planning,' Alan said as they resumed walking. 'How can I help, when I don't know what's going on?'

Joseph tapped the side of his nose. 'All in good time. I don't want to complicate matters. I dare say I'll be thinking on my feet, plans often go astray. Don't worry, you'll get your chance to help Kimberley. You just have to trust me.'

'You haven't left me with much choice.'

'Okay. This is what I want you to do. Tomorrow morning, six o'clock, meet me in the foyer. We'll have breakfast at Paynes' place before we escort them to the airport.'

'How are we going to do that? Taxi?'

'No. We'll use their car.'

'You make it sound easy. I don't think I'll get much sleep tonight so why don't we go now?'

'Think about it. If we grab them, the flight's not until tomorrow afternoon, what do you plan to do with them? Walk around all night? Take them back to our rooms? Do you really fancy sharing a bed with Payne or Beckworth?'

Alan kicked a discarded beer bottle. 'Sorry. It was a stupid idea. I just want to get this over with. It goes against all I believe in, and if it wasn't for Kimberley I wouldn't get involved.'

'And if I could manage them both, I wouldn't ask you to. If things go to plan, all you have to do is act as an escort for Beckworth. When we get back home, I'll take full responsibility. As a constable you are acting under my instructions, no blame will fall on your shoulders, I promise.' He patted his stomach. 'Right, now let's go and eat.'

'Not for me, thanks. I don't think I could force anything down. I'll come with you though, perhaps have a coffee or something.'

'Okay, if it's what you want. Me, I'm making the most of tonight.'

*

The pavement and road glistened as the street cleaners' vehicle sprayed water across the marble tiled thoroughfare.

'All looks different without the sunshine,' Alan said, shifting his flight bag from one hand to the other. 'Why so early?'

'The fewer people there are around when we snatch Payne and Beckworth the better. Another couple of hours and this place will start to come alive. Come on, let's get this over.' Joseph increased his stride.

Fransisco and Maria scuttled around, laying tables, checking condiments. Joseph and Alan chose a table. Maria handed them a menu and waited for them to point at pictures of eggs, bacon, sausages, toast, hash browns and chips. Many combinations, same end product.

Orders placed, Joseph sat back and surveyed the road alongside the bar. Maria returned with their coffees. Alan sipped his cautiously.

The sound of a car pulling up competed with unseen but animated conversation coming from the kitchen.

'That's them!' Joseph said. 'I was hoping to eat before they arrived.'

Alan's coffee spilled as he pushed his chair back and got to his feet. 'What are we going to do? You still haven't told me your plan.'

'Leave it to me, go to the men's room before they see you. I'll take care of it, just be ready to do as I say.'

He watched until the toilet door shut before scooping up a newspaper and holding it up in front of him.

Payne and Beckworth greeted Francisco and Maria as they entered the rear of the bar.

Maria emerged carrying two plates.

Joseph nodded his thanks and unwrapped the utensils. Brown sauce soon smothered Francisco's creation. Toast, dipped into the yolk of one of the eggs, crunched as he attacked the oversize breakfast.

Payne emerged from behind the bar. The lighter stopped in mid-air; his cigar dropped from his mouth. 'You! What the hell are you doing here?' He smirked. 'Doesn't matter, you can't touch me here and you know it.'

Beckworth turned on his heel, rushed to the kitchen and returned carrying a large knife, the blade wet from slicing tomatoes. 'Leave him to me, Mark. I'll fillet him.'

Alan opened the door, took in the situation and crept up behind Beckworth.

Joseph reached into his flight bag and produced a gun. 'Sit down Payne,' he said. 'I haven't finished my breakfast.'

Alan threw his arms around Beckworth before driving a knee into his kidneys. Beckworth grunted and sagged in Alan's embrace. The knife clattered on the marble tiles. Alan kicked it away.

'Bring him over. Your food's getting cold.' Joseph pointed at the plate.

'How can you think of your stomach at a time like this? What are we going to do with these two?'

'Invite them to join us of course. My treat. Go and order a couple of meals and get some coffee for our guests. When the breakfasts are cooked, lock the girl and the chef in the loo. Don't want them calling the police, do we?' He winked. 'I hate being interrupted when I'm eating.'

Alan headed for the kitchen area.

'Beckworth, stop shitting yourself.' Joseph motioned towards a chair. 'Just sit down and behave.'

'What the hell are you up to, you stupid bastard!' Payne snarled. 'Coming in here waving a toy gun?'

'It's no toy. Want me to prove it?' He released the safety catch. 'Belonged to my father, he kept it as a souvenir of the assault on Salerno during the war.'

'You haven't got the guts,' Payne mocked, gripping the side of his chair. 'You've been watching too much television.'

'Okay. You've called my bluff so –'

'Don't, sir!' Alan stopped in his tracks as he returned carrying trays with the meals and coffee. 'You can't kill him in cold blood.'

'Why? He's responsible for Kimberley, albeit indirectly. I thought you'd be glad to see him dead.'

'I would, but it's not up to us. He has to stand trial.'

'That's not going to happen. You can't take me back, son. You haven't got the authority.'

'Wrong.' Joseph brandished the Beretta. 'This gives me all the authority I need.'

'And if you get us back, then what? My friends in high places will crucify you. Kidnapping is a serious offence, as a copper you should know that.'

Joseph pushed the safety catch back in place and lowered the gun. He grinned. 'I do, but I scared the crap out of you, didn't I? Listen, we didn't even know you were here, pure coincidence bumping into you two. Let's forget our differences and enjoy our meals, shall we? I'm starving.'

Payne banged a fist on the table. 'Eat with you? Fuck off. I'd rather starve. Come on Sam, leave these two losers to hold hands. I've told you before, they can't touch us.'

'I don't blame you, Payne.' Joseph held up both hands. 'You've got us by the short and curlies.' He picked up his mug and sipped his drink. 'Here's to you, you clever bastard. Alan, go and free those two from the loo and pay for these meals.'

Payne and Beckworth involuntarily followed the direction of Joseph's pointing finger. Joseph took advantage of the distraction, dived a hand into his pocket and held a small bottle labelled *Jarabe de Ipecacuana* over one of the drinks.

He held the mug towards Payne. 'Let bygones be bygones. it's a bit early for a beer, coffee will have to do. Let's have a toast to crime. After all, we both owe our livings to it.'

Mark sneered. 'Yes, but I make real money, you just scrape a living.'

'Touché. If you ever come back to the UK maybe I'll consider working for you. I'm never going to get rich serving Queen and country.'

Alan winked at Joseph as he rejoined them. 'I told the pair of them it was a joke, but I don't think they understood.' He looked at Payne. 'Oh, and did you know your phone's not working? I tried to check our flights.'

'Nothing new, it often happens,' Payne said. 'You could be useful to me, knowing what you do.' He chinked his mug against Joseph's then downed the contents. His arrogance vanished as he pulled a face. 'What the fuck? Urghh, this coffee tastes like shit.'

Joseph took a mouthful. 'Bit cold, I give you that, but it's fine.'

Payne got to his feet, spitting and rubbing a hand across his mouth.

'Are you okay?' Beckworth said.

'Francisco needs lessons in how to make coffee,' Payne snarled. 'What's he trying to do? Ruin me?' He cleared his throat and spat again.

'Let me make some fresh,' Beckworth said, heading for the kitchen. 'And I'll fetch toast and marmalade.'

'Shame,' Joseph said. 'If you don't want your breakfast, I'll have it.'

Payne put a hand to his stomach and left the table. When he was beyond earshot Alan said, 'What's going on? Where did you get a gun? I thought we were taking these two back to the UK. Instead, you're offering to work for Payne.'

'Did you fix the phone,' Joseph said, prodding a fried tomato with his fork.

'Yes. I gave the wire a yank, and it snapped. I don't think much of Spanish electrics from what I've seen.'

'Well done. As to what's going on, be patient.' He tapped the side of his nose. 'Everything is going to plan.'

'What about the gun? I didn't know you carried one.'

'I don't, it's a reproduction. Bought it in the shop we stopped to look at, remember?'

'You had me fooled. And Payne.'

'That was the idea. Just act as if the gun is real. This isn't over yet, we need –'

He was cut short by violent retching coming from the toilets.

'Here we go,' Joseph said. 'Keep an eye on Beckworth, keep him away while I deal with Payne.'

'How do you know it's Payne? I didn't see him go in there.'

'I told you, my plan is working. Now do as I say, keep Beckworth occupied.'

Payne was on his knees throwing up on the floor.

Joseph batted the air, the tainted air in the toilet facilities attracted every fly from miles around. 'Something you ate?' He grinned.

Payne arched his back, reached down deep inside and threw up again.

Joseph pulled a handkerchief from his pocket. 'You're making a real mess in here. Here, let me clean you up.' He stepped around the stinking vomit and wiped Payne's mouth. 'There, that's better.' Grabbing Payne by the hair Joseph jerked his head back and forced the handkerchief into his mouth. 'Let's stop you making it worse in here.'

Payne's body contorted as he sought to free himself from Joseph's grip and the contents of his stomach. The vomit would not be denied, but the handkerchief prevented it seeing the light of day. Joseph stood, legs braced apart, as his victim choked on his own puke. Payne slumped forward into the vile smelling pool he had created. Joseph used two fingers to check fo life signs. Satisfied, he removed the handkerchief, dropped it down the toilet and attempted to flush it away.

Back in the fresh air he called across to Alan. 'He's had a heart attack, I think. I've made sure he's comfortable, there's nothing more we can do. We need an ambulance.'

Alan increased his grip on Beckworth's arm. 'How are we going to call one? There's no phone.'

'Get in the car,' Joseph said. 'We can call from the Irish pub.'

'You won't get away with this, you stupid bastard!' Beckworth yelled. 'Mark's got friends. They'll come down on you like a ton of bricks.'

Isabel came down from the apartment over the bar. She joined Maria and Francisco as they peered over the bar counter. Questions were answered with a shake of heads.

Grabbing his other arm, Joseph helped Alan propel Beckworth towards the car.

Joseph wrenched open the rear door of the vehicle. 'Move your arse, Beckworth, or die here, your choice. If you want my advice, don't chance your luck.'

During the struggle Beckworth's head tried unsuccessfully to remodel the design of the vehicle.

'Get in, I said.' Joseph brought the compact weapon down on fingers curled around the door frame.

'Bollocks,' Beckworth retorted. 'You're a dead man.'

'And you're not far from joining me.'

Joseph held the gun to Beckworth's head. 'Put the cuffs on him,' he said. 'First stop, the Irish bar, then I'll drive to the airport.' He turned in his seat to face Beckworth. 'Any funny business and you won't live to regret it.' Turning his attention to Alan, he said, 'Are you okay?'

'Yes. Just get on with it.'

'Okay, let's get this show on the road.'

Joseph started the car and pulled away from Stevie's Wonder Bar.

Minutes later he stopped, leaned back and handed Alan the gun. 'Keep an eye on our friend. I'll phone to get help for Payne.' Jumping from the vehicle he ran inside the Irish bar.

'We're not open.'

At the sound of the Irish brogue, Joseph produced his warrant card. 'I know this is Spain, and this doesn't impress you, but it's an emergency and I need to use your phone. Okay?'

'You only had to ask. No need to flash that.'

'Thanks. It's only a local call, not the UK.'

'Help yourself. It's behind the bar. You can buy me a drink next time you're in.'

'Si, Señor, dead. Can you help?' Joseph glanced back at the car. 'The toilets at Stevie's Wonder Bar. Gracias. Yes, he'll love the view from the mountains. *Adiós. Gracias.*'

'All sorted?' Alan asked as Joseph clambered back in. 'Are they sending an ambulance?'

'It's all taken care of. Now let's get this piece of filth to the airport.'

The sound of the tyre bursting echoed back from the trees on either side of the road. The car left the tarmac and rumbled over ground churned up by vehicles during the winter and baked solid by summer sun. 'Shit!' Joseph thumped the steering wheel with both fists. 'That's all we need. We can't miss our flight, not with him in tow.'

'Have we got a spare?' Alan asked.

'How do I know? This isn't my car.' He turned to face Beckworth. 'Is there one?'

'Yes.'

'Good. Okay you two, out we get. We need to change the wheel ASAP. Alan, you do the necessary. I'll make sure our friend here behaves.'

While Alan jacked the car up and loosened the nuts, Joseph stood behind Beckworth with the gun jammed into his back.

Beckworth suddenly turned and lashed out at Joseph, causing the gun to fall to the ground. Joseph swung a punch. Beckworth parried the blow and landed one of his own. Joseph staggered back, recovered his balance and launched another attack. His fist smashed into Beckworth's face and Alan winced as he heard bone break. Beckworth clapped a hand to his mouth. Blood leaked through his fingers. He tried to speak.

'Save yourself the effort,' Joseph said. 'Looks like you've bitten your tongue.'

'And you've broken his jaw by the look of it.' Alan shook his head.

'Possibly. Get the wheel fixed, time's running out.'

'Aren't you going to do something to help him?'

'Such as what? No, he'll just have to wait until we get him back home, then he can go to hospital.'

*

Holidaymakers, many imitating the colour of lobsters, thronged the departure lounge. Luggage was dragged like a fractious child. Tempers were tested by the heat inside the building.

'Okay, listen to me,' Joseph said. 'Either you behave and book yourself onto this flight, or I'll take you for a ride in your car and chuck you out miles from anywhere. What's it to be? Are you going to be sensible?'

Beckworth held the side of his face and nodded.

'Good. I'll come with you to the desk. If they ask about Payne, I'm going to tell them we've had a car accident and he's in hospital.'

Alan moved the two bags along the floor of the Departure lounge with his feet as the check-in queue shuffled forward. Joseph kept a tight grip on Beckworth's arm.

At the counter the attendant smiled as she handed Alan his flight pass.

Joseph gave Beckworth his ticket and nudged him forward.

The young woman, dressed in the uniform of the air-line, winced as she saw the pain on Beckworth's face. She checked his passport and ticket, returned both along with a boarding pass and beckoned Joseph forward.

'That went smoother than I expected,' Joseph said. 'She didn't even ask about Payne.'

'Perhaps they're used to people missing their flights.' Alan reached forward and pulled the in-flight magazine from the back of the chair in front of him. 'Too much sun or booze.'

'Or both.' Joseph watched through the small window as the air-field flashed past, then rested his head back as the plane clawed its way into the clear blue sky.

Chapter 51

December 1986

Detective Chief Inspector Hughes ran a finger down the typed list of expenses Joseph had submitted and shook his head.

'Perhaps we could claim the money back for Payne's flight,' Joseph suggested.

'I was about to ask you about him. You say you called the local police when he suffered a heart attack.'

Joseph shifted his weight from one foot to the other. 'As I'd had dealings with the local police, I thought they would deal with the matter quicker than I could.'

'It's all very strange, Fargough. The Spanish police have no knowledge of Payne after he was released from custody. How do you explain it?'

'Someone messed up the paperwork?'

Highes sighed. 'This all sounds very suspicious to me. Beckworth corroborates your story up until the time you left the Bar, but he then states you assaulted him.'

'Me, sir? No. He's lying. We had a bit of an accident on the way to the airport and he hit his head. I'm sure you've read PC Jefferson's report.'

'I have. And it matches your own, word for word.'

'Proves what I said, sir. The lad shows promise.'

Hughes dismissed Joseph with a flick of his hand and a shake of his head.

*

'Beckworth will go down for life,' Joseph said. 'Pity they did away with the death penalty.'

'You got away with it?' Mary looked surprised. 'Hughes isn't going to look any further into what happened to Payne?'

'Not much point, is there? He's dead. Saves the taxpayer the cost of his trial and incarceration. Besides, what do you mean about me getting away with it? Got away with what?'

'Come off it, Joe. You connive to get sent to Spain to bring Payne and his sidekick back to this country and what happens?

One ends up with a broken jaw and the other one disappears from the face of this earth.'

'I don't see anything wrong. Kimberley wasn't his only victim. Don't shed any tears for scum like him.'

'I wouldn't dream of it. It's you I worry about. All this gung-ho, pistols-at-dawn sort of stuff is going to land you in hot water sooner or later. And me too, by association.'

'Don't worry, I'll make sure you're never implicated in anything not strictly *Kosher*. But let's face it, getting the job done is my duty. Whatever it takes.' Joseph winked. 'Let's change the subject, shall we? How do you fancy the disco at Hornigold's on Friday? We could have a few drinks, let our hair down, should be fun.'

'Why not? I missed you when you were away. A good night out sounds great to me.'

'It's a date. Now, back to my favourite pastime, filling in useless paperwork that will gather dust until the end of time.'

Mary nodded towards the office door. 'I'll fetch some coffee.'

'Great idea.'

'Are you going to tell me what really happened?' Mary pushed a mug across the desk. 'Payne's heart attack came out of the blue, didn't it?'

'Let's just say it was a *stroke* of luck for me and Jefferson. Getting Payne and Beckworth onto a flight home was never going to be easy. Friends of his had pulled strings. Payne knew we couldn't touch him.'

'I was speaking to Jefferson in the canteen. He said Payne was violently sick before he had his heart attack. Do you think that had anything to do with it?' She tapped a spoon against the side of her mug.

'Possibly, but only a post-mortem would establish cause of death. I phoned the police chief and he promised to take care of everything.' Joseph put his hands in the air. 'I know what you're going to say, and the answer is no. I don't know how the body disappeared, or why the local police deny any knowledge of Payne after he left custody. Further more I don't give a toss.'

'The same police who weren't happy about releasing Payne? They were who you phoned?'

'Yes.'

'That does it. I'm going to resign. I helped you cover up one murder and now you're implicated in another. I can't take it any more.' She held out a hand, fingers splayed. 'Look, my hands are shaking. I have to have a drink every night to get any sleep. I should have thrown in the towel when Payne's brother was shot. I'm not cut out for your type of policing.'

Joseph pushed his chair back from the desk and stood up. Reaching across the desk he placed a hand on Mary's shoulder. 'Pull yourself together, love. You need a break. I'll have a word with Hughes, get you some leave. Failing that, I'll bring your holiday entitlement forward. We'll go away somewhere, leave all this garbage behind while we enjoy ourselves.'

Mary wiped tears from her eyes. 'But I'm still going to resign. I mean it. This job's got the better of me. I need to change my life around.'

'Fair enough. I tell you what, why don't we both do it? We could find a pub somewhere and run it together.'

'Do you mean it? Would you really throw all this away?' She pointed around the office in a circular motion. 'And start a new life?'

'Why not? Paperwork's never been my forte. Besides, Hughes has hinted more than once I may be in the firing line. Perhaps I should jump before I'm pushed? At least that way I get to keep most of my pension. Added to my military one, I should get by.'

'And the pub?' She motioned raising a drink to her lips.

'Oh, I don't know, the thought of a place in the country just appeals to me. We could do meals and –'

Mary laughed. 'I knew food had to come into the equation! You get to play *Mine Host* and I get stuck in the kitchen, is that how you see it?'

Joseph walked around the desk and pulled her close. 'No. I see us as a team. We'll both be behind the bar and we'll get ourselves a chef. How's that sound?'

'A bit of a surprise, but I'm all for it. There's just one fly in the ointment, my husband. Or had you forgotten him?'

'Is he still around? I thought the Army would have got hold of him by now.'

'He was, but he seems to have moved on. Now and again, I call into the café where he worked, but he's not been there. The chap who runs it is doing the cooking, and pretty much everything else. I haven't been in the last few days but I'd be surprised if he's turned up again.'

'Where does that leave us?'

'We'll cohabit, and to hell with him. There's not a lot he can do about it, especially with his track record.'

'Exactly what I've been saying all along. But you should give this some more thought, my love. Throwing away your career isn't a thing to take lightly, leave it a month or two, then see how you feel about retiring. I promise whatever you decide I'll be right beside you.'

'Aren't you worried about me drinking?'She pulled away from him. 'All that temptation? Be like putting a poacher in charge of a salmon river.'

'Don't be daft. Once you're away from all the stress you won't need it. Besides, you can keep an eye on me with the food and I'll do the same with you and the wine. Now, let's get stuck into all this bumf.' He patted the manilla folder. 'All this just because I brought Beckworth back for trial. I must be mad.'

'Never mind, at least we've got tonight to look forward to. We may even get to have a boogie at Hornigold's.'

Chapter 52

December 1986

Joseph tapped his feet and nodded in time to the beat as *Frankie goes to Hollywood* belted from the the speakers dotted around Hornigold's. 'I like his taste in music,' he said, leaning into Mary's ear. 'But he should turn in down, it's hard to hear yourself think.'

'Don't be such a sourpuss. Come on, let's dance.' She put her cocktail down and got to her feet.

'Not yet. I need a few more of these before I join you on the floor.'

Mary sat. 'Okay, but you did promise.'

'I know . . . and I will, but I feel out of place amongst all these youngsters. Give me time to get a few drinks down me, then I'll show you.'

'If we can find a space. I've never seen so many people in here, Sandra and the new girl look rushed off their feet.'

'Remind me not to have music if we get a pub.' Joseph shook his head. 'This isn't what I want for my retirement.'

Culture Club drowned out Mary's response. Realizing the futility of repeating herself, she smiled. Getting to her feet she entered the mass of swaying bodies. Joseph raised his glass. 'Go for it,' he mouthed.

Graham rubbed his eyes. Smoke, curling from an abandoned cigarette on a nearby table, insisted on drifting towards him. Reaching across, he picked it up and dropped it into a glass of Piña Colada. *That's sorted that out.* He drained his drink and wobbled towards the bar.

'Another of your specials, Sandra.'

His hand struggled to retrieve his wallet, fingers bending against material as they sought to enter a pocket.

'Are you sure?' Sandra frowned. 'Wouldn't you prefer a coffee?'

'No. Give me another. I can handle my drink.'

'Okay. But watch yourself, Mary's here, with her boss.'

'Is she? I haven't seen her.'

Sandra pointed. 'There. There she is, dancing on her own.'

'Thanks. Forget the drink. I'll come back later. It's time to dance with my wife.'

Graham approached from behind, put his arms around her and put his lips close to her ear. 'Hello, love. Didn't expect to find you here. How are you, sweetheart?'

Mary twisted free from his embrace. 'Graham! Where the hell have you come from?'

'Is that all you've got to say? Not, I've been worried about you, are you okay?'

'Why would I care? We're finished. I'm moving on, you should do the same.'

'Come over to my table. We can talk about our future.'

'You're not listening, are you? Joe's here, if he sees you, there'll be trouble.'

'Bollocks. I'm not scared of him. Come and have a drink.'

'No.' She turned and threaded her way through the dancers.

'Bitch.'

'That was quick, had enough? Shall we go?' Joseph swirled the last of his drink around the glass.

'If you want to, but you said you'd dance with me. Have you changed your mind?'

'No. I'll stay if it's what you want. I'll get more drinks, wait for the next song I know, and then we'll dance.' Holding the empty glasses above his shoulders, he headed for the bar.

'Graham's here, did you know?' Joseph set the glasses down.

Mary swallowed. 'Yes, he spoke to me while I was dancing.'

'You didn't tell me. What did he want? Perhaps I should have a word with him, tell him to stay away from you.'

'No, leave it. I can handle him any day of the week.'

'Maybe, but how can he believe he can turn the clock back after all he's done to you.'

'Don't worry, I know what I want out of life and it isn't him.' She picked up his hand and kissed the back of it. 'Pay no attention to him, we came to celebrate your return from Spain, don't let him spoil it.'

Graham picked at his teeth with the stick of the cocktail umbrella. *Bitch. She's never going to change. Why him, not me?* He dropped a hand to the side of his lower leg to check for the secreted knife. Satisfied the weapon was in place, he raised his glass, fished out the cherry and popped it into his mouth. 'Time for . . . another drink,' he said. Gravity had other ideas and he sank back onto his seat. The dancers appeared to fade and snap back into focus in time to the beat of the music. He closed his eyes. Flashes penetrated his eyelids as beams of coloured light filtered through occasional gaps between people on the dance floor. Using both hands, he pushed against the table top and willed his legs to move.

Despite the odds, he made it to the bar, got served and made it back with most of his drink. Slumping forward he rested his head on his arms. *Bloody music. Bloody noise. No wonder she isn't listening to me. I need to get her to come outside.* His drink ran across the table and dripped to the floor as he knocked the glass over.

'Come outside,' Graham slurred. The table shifted under his weight as he leaned onto it. 'We need to talk.'

Mary batted the air, much as she would to ward off an angry wasp. 'No, I'm not interested in anything you've got to say. Go away.'

Reaching out he grasped her arm and pulled. 'I said we need to talk.'

'And she told you to go away.' The menace in Joseph's voice cut through the wall of sound. 'If I were in your shoes I'd listen.'

'Bollocks. Keep out of this. She's my wife. I got rights.'

'Yes, you have, and they include treatment free at the point of delivery. The hospital's not far, either go away or spend the rest of the evening at A&E. Your choice.'

'If that's a threat, I think –'

Joseph pushed his chair back. 'Sod off, before I do something you'll regret.'

Graham turned and stumbled into the crowd.

'Thanks Joe. Do you think we should leave?'

'No, I'm not ready. I haven't finished my drink and we haven't had the dance I promised you. Wait for a slow record and we'll give it a try.'

'Okay, if you're sure, thanks,' Mary said, raising her glass. 'Apart from running into him, I'm glad we came.'

'It's not bad in here and Sandra's drinks take the edge off of it, at least it blocks out thoughts of the report I've got to finish for Hughes.'

Phyllis Nelson urged every one to "*Move closer.*" On the dance floor, arms reached around waists.

Mary toyed with her drink. 'Are you still waiting for a song you like? Or shall I dance on my own again?'

'Come on,' Joseph said. 'This is your chance. I think I can shuffle around to this one.'

'Great! At last. And it only took a Nelson in a pirate themed pub to get you on your feet.'

'Smart arse.' Joseph grinned.

Inside a cubicle in the Gents, Graham bent down and removed a knife from the sheaf attached to his leg. He tried to brush his trouser leg back into place, toppled forward and struck his head against the door. 'Shit! That hurt.'

The second attempt to conceal the knife up the sleeve of his jacket succeeded. He slid the lock of the door open and lurched toward the mirror over the sink. Running the cold tap, he filled cupped hands and plunged his face into them. The roller-towel mopped up most of the errant water from his shirt and jacket. Stepping back into the bar area he he looked around for Joseph. *Tell me to sod off would you? Well sod you. It's time you went down. With you out of the way, she'll be glad to come back to me.*

Joseph nuzzled Mary's neck and whispered the words of the song into her ear. "*Move your body real close until –*"

'This . . . my dance.' Graham pulled at Joseph's jacket. 'Let go,' he mumbled. The dancers nearest the confrontation moved away.

Joseph released his hold on Mary, turned and grabbed Graham. 'She told you to leave. Why don't you and I discuss this outside?'

'Suits me.'

Mary edged between the testosterone fuelled men, two stags facing off in the time-honoured way. Only one would leave the field with pride intact.

'Stop it you two, this isn't going to settle anything. Joe, sit down, please. Graham, I'll have one dance if you promise to go back to where you're staying afterwards. Do you hear me?'

'Yes.' He took hold of her hands and leaned forward to kiss her. She moved her head to one side. Joseph moved to intervene.

'Leave it, Joe,' she said. 'I can look after myself. Sit down, I won't be long. He's too drunk to dance if you ask me.'

Joseph glared, but turned and headed back to their table.

The DJ continued the slow tempo by following Phyllis Nelson with, "*I want to know what love is.*"

'I could tell him,' Graham said, his grin more lopsided than his stance.

'I don't think so,' she replied. 'He said *love*, not *lust*. And let go, you're hurting me.'

'Sorry, didn't mean to.' He released his embrace and tried to persuade his feet to obey his brain.

Mary turned, waved to Joseph and headed towards him. Graham grabbed her. 'One more. Just one more. Please, I love you. Dance with me, please.' He lost his balance and fell against her.

Joseph pushed indignant couples aside as he headed for Mary.

Graham saw him coming, fumbled with the sleeve of his coat and managed to pull the knife free.

'No, Graham! Don't!' Mary reached for the weapon. 'Give it to me.'

Joseph rushed forward, both fists raised. Graham held the knife at chest height and lunged toward him. The antagonists morphed into early cinematic attempts to portray motion as strobe lighting broke the visual action into sections of jerky movement. Joseph grabbed his rival's wrist and forced the hand holding the knife down. Graham swung a punch into Joseph's kidneys. The left-handed blow had just enough weight behind it to cause Joseph to exhale sharply and release his grip. Seizing his chance Graham stabbed again. The knife pierced clothing and forced its way into flesh. Joseph's face screwed up in pain. Pulling the blade free, Graham struck again. Mary moved to block the move and the weapon slid between her lower ribs. She slumped to the floor, blood seeping through her fingers.

'You stupid bastard!' Joseph took hold of the lapels of Graham's jacket and thrust his forehead into his opponent's face. Nearby spectators winced as the sound of breaking bone took advantage of the silence between records to make itself heard. Graham dropped the knife and put both hands to his face. He gulped for air as blood coursed down his throat.

Joseph slammed a fist into his mid-riff, making the job of breathing increasingly difficult. Graham lost consciousness and fell to the floor.

'Phone for an ambulance! She's been stabbed!' Joseph yelled as he lashed out with a foot at the recumbent figure of Graham. Two of the dancers attempted to drag him away as he stamped on Graham's head.

Tearing himself free from their grasp, he dropped to his knees and felt for Mary's pulse. 'Hold on, my love. I've sent for an ambulance, you'll be okay.' She didn't respond. He pulled a handkerchief from his pocket and clamped it over the wound and watched it change from white to red in the blink of an eye. 'Sandra, bring me some cloths, clean ones! She's losing a lot of blood.' He put a hand on his shirt. 'Shit! And so am I.'

Her reply was lost in a vortex inside his head. Green blobs of light invaded the darkness that was his vision. He put out his hands as he felt himself topple over.

The dance floor cleared, leaving the participants of a moment of madness laying bathed in the lights from the DJ's console. A tragedy worthy of Shakespeare. The eternal triangle of love.

*

Detective Chief Inspector Hughes stood clutching a bag of grapes and a selection of magazines. He sighed audibly as he waited for the receptionist to deal with an elderly man enquiring after his wife. After the third time of explaining how to find the ward in a voice loud enough to be heard in the car park, the man thanked the woman and shuffled towards one of the corridors.

Hughes stepped up to the desk. 'Good morning,' he said, 'Two police officers were admitted last night, can they have visitors?'

'Names, please.'

'DC Fargough and WDC Wells. They were brought here following an incident in a nightclub.'

The receptionist checked the chart on her desk and shook her head. 'Sorry, they are not allowed visitors. She is in intensive care, and he is in the recovery ward following surgery. I'm afraid you've had a wasted journey. Try phoning tomorrow, perhaps it may be possible then.'

'How about Mr Graham Wells? Can I talk to him? There are questions that need –'

She lowered her voice. 'He died. I'm sorry.'

The hospital restaurant was busy. Hughes sat idling stirring a cup of tea. *There's no way you can avoid prosecution, Fargough. I can pull a few strings, but not when it comes to a charge of murder.* He pulled a Danish pastry apart and popped a piece in his mouth. *I've warned you in the past, now your pigeons have all come home to roost.*

In a side ward, a nurse frowned at the display on the bedside monitor, adjusted Mary's saline drip and rushed to search for the duty doctor.

End

Printed in Great Britain
by Amazon

84188997R00159